TARA W...   ...ks as a
copyw...   ...r.

The
Stranmillis

fodder
tara west

THE
BLACKSTAFF
PRESS

BELFAST

First published in 2002 by Blackstaff Press Limited
Wildflower Way, Apollo Road
Belfast BT12 6TA
With the assistance of
The Arts Council of Northern Ireland

Tara West has asserted her right under the Copyright, Designs and
Patents Act 1988 to be identified as the author of this work.

Typeset by Techniset Typesetters, Newton-le-Willows, Merseyside

Printed in Ireland by ColourBooks Limited

A CIP catalogue record for this book is available from the British Library

ISBN 085640-729-1

www.blackstaffpress.com

Thanks

To Mummy and Dave for your love, support and patience. To everyone at Blackstaff, for your belief and help. To Stanley, Peter and Bill for giving me the chance to write. To Billzo for reading this thing and Fiona for letting me witter on about it. To Siobhan for helping out in the initial stages and to Dr Tracy Cruikshanks for advice. Finally, to all my mates, the brilliant storytellers.

Try this. Lie on your kitchen floor in the middle of the night and toss a raw hamburger towards the ceiling like a frisbee. I swear to God, four dogs will appear from nowhere and jump to catch it. It's true. I discovered that the night I got my first punishment beating.

It was a Saturday night and the ten-week anniversary of my mother's disappearance. Not that I was counting or anything. I was heading out to The Collective, the cafe in central Belfast that drew my brother Oisín and his friends like scum towards the plughole. He lurked about there, in between the medical research and sporadic prostitution that sponsored his Buckfast habit. Nobody called him Oisín. He was nicknamed Prince when he was at school and even I called him that. No offence to anybody called Oisín but it's a real wank of a name.

I was home alone with a tower of cling filmed turkey ham sandwiches that Bonehead's ma had made for me. Bonehead was my best mate and had been since we were kids. He'd just spent a few months in a young offenders centre for stealing a lorry full of pigs and he was always good for a lift. His ma was Big Julie and nobody fucked with her, except for the occasional woman, since Bonehead's da got put away for the possession of a rocket launcher and she discovered lesbianism. With her sturdy build, broad back, waistless waist, tight blue drainpipes and long shaggy blonde hair, she was just like Ozzy Osbourne, except she wasn't exclusive to bats. She ate the head off everybody.

I could still see where she'd pressed her thick fingertips into the bread before slicing it, like what she really wanted to do was throw it on her kitchen floor and Riverdance on it. Everything about her was rough and fast and heavy-handed. She was a packer up at Weirtown Meats, the meat processing factory on the outskirts of Weirtown in north Belfast where we lived.

The factory had just been made main supplier to a big supermarket chain, which was supposed to be good news for the people of the estate. Mountains of orders = loads of reliable overtime. Loads of reliable overtime = loads of dough. Loads of dough = bigger house in a nicer area. Bigger house in a nicer area = escape from all the loyalist loopers in the estate. Who also worked in the factory, would get loads of overtime, earn loads of dough, buy bigger houses in nice areas alongside the people who were trying to get away from them. There is no easy way out, you know. Anyway, a factory full of loyalist loopers isn't so bad when it also supplies cheap CDs, foreign fegs and Christmas presents to order.

Big Julie had taken it upon herself to see that I was well fed since mum went. She sent Bonehead down with meat parcels every other day. The shelves in our poky brown kitchen were strained like hammocks under the weight of contraband from the factory – all kinds of canned, foil-fresh and vacuum-packed mystery meats. What got me most was the twin pack of catering size luncheon 'meat' sausages she told me to keep in the freezer. Twin one with five loaves of bread and you'd still be feeding the Jews.

I stared at the sandwich tower for a couple of seconds and then I sprinted upstairs, two at a time, to my room. I still hid things there even though I was living in the house on my own. Prince had moved out five years before, when he was seventeen, after a major bust-up with mum and was living in a shared house near Queen's University. I was sixteen and already had a toilet and kitchen and fridge all to myself. But I still slept in the boxroom on my old-fashioned camp bed, instead of moving into mum's room, spreading myself all over her double bed, wallowing in volumes of porn and having the odd orgy. I still kept my few crackly-paged mags down the back of my bedside unit.

Mum's old Martin 12-string lay on my bed, still in its soft case. I unzipped it and felt around for the quarter bottle of Kulov I'd nicked from Prince's house earlier that day. And he thought I carried that guitar around for pose value. I rummaged through the piles of paperbacks and magazines at the bottom of my bookcase for the litre bottle of white lemonade I'd nicked from Tesco. I only ever nicked groceries from Tesco, even though it was a mile and half from our house. I didn't nick from the Stop'n'Shop down the road. The doddery oul fella that owned it had a hump, every tie he wore had an ancient stain on it and he was a complete fust fest. I couldn't nick from him.

I kneeled on the bed, kind of precarious if you're not used to camp beds but I had it sussed, then I opened the window and poured most of the lemonade down into the winter-dry jungle below. I topped the bottle up with the vodka and leaned back, my elbows sinking into the stained quilt as I tipped up the bottle to drink. I didn't know what was in white lemonade and I didn't know what was in vodka but I could guarantee both were better for you than Weirtown's Finest Tip Top Tasty Turkey Ham. I couldn't eat Julie's sandwiches. I couldn't eat anything she sent down for me. I would just hold onto them, the way I held onto a lunch box with the only packed lunch mum ever made me still inside it.

She took the head staggers one time and bought me and Prince coloured plastic lunch boxes, determined not to let us eat the muck they served in the school canteen. But at lunchtime, I just stood at my locker, holding onto the plastic box, fighting against my hard dry throat. The lunch box stayed in my locker until I left school at the end of third year, and then I brought it home and kept it behind my books. I'm glad I couldn't eat the packed lunch because she didn't make any more after that. A crappy old sandwich made of hard plain bread and a nameless meat product is much more than that, if somebody else makes it for you.

I had a nice buzz on by the time I came out of my room. The narrow stairs swam around nicely as I slid my shoulder down the well-worn route above the banister. My cheeks were hot and blotched as I stood in front of the mirror in the kitchen, soaping my hair up into the usual six-inch spikes. I pulled my record bag (also nicked from Prince) carefully over my head and fixed the strap across my chest, bag under my right hand. It looked innocent enough. Nobody would ever suspect it held ammunition for the first wave of my campaign – one pork sausage wrapped in a yellowing sheet of the *Evening News* (deaths page), three hamburgers (thawing), twenty Consulate (refreshingly minty), one lighter (Stop'n'Shop brand), one giant luncheon meat sausage (still frozen) and one cow's tongue (fresh from the butcher that afternoon).

My mother was a vegetarian. She let me and Prince eat meat when we were growing up like, she wasn't a complete nut or anything. She didn't force her vegetarianism on anybody. She never forced anything on anybody and made a big point of it. Me though, I think people are scavengers – people can digest most things.

I formed my opinions early, following an episode with green velvet soup. Buckshot was one of mum's on-off boyfriends and he brought the soup round to our house, no doubt thinking it would score him points because he was a boner in the factory. Buckshot's brother got the soup from the hotel where he worked and even though it was probably on the turn, I ate it. I really liked it, although it made Prince sick. Mum wouldn't let us have anything else he brought round after that so I tried eating anything that looked like green velvet. The fact that I wasn't exactly sure what velvet was didn't really matter.

I later spent many fascinating lunch hours entertaining primary school classmates with my ability to consume anything they cared to present. Baps filled with Heinz Sandwich Spread, worms, earwigs, coal, cat food, grass – mostly the unprocessed green type. Sometimes they really pushed the boat out and brought me hot water bottles or unwanted toys but I had to admit defeat on those. I did try though. It was when I got to secondary school that things got out of hand.

I got an A in my 11-plus and could've gone to the local grammar but mum said streamed education was both a cause and symptom of capitalism and instead sent me to the comprehensive at the bottom of the estate, Weir High. I swear to God, that's what it was called. It took in kids from all the Proddie estates in the area, and when most of my friends went off to the grammar, I found myself floundering in an undiluted syrup of thugs. My year had more convicted criminals than a reoffenders reunion.

I was one of the smallest, I soaped my hair into spikes as often as I could get away with it, I came from a fucked-up oddball family and, as if that wasn't enough, I had a stupid name. A stupid Fenian name, even though I was a Prod. Well, as far as the fatherless son of a female Ulster republican atheist anarchist can be a Prod.

My mother was a punk in the late seventies. She ran away to London (for a weekend) and bought a pair of fishnet tights in Sex. She thought she had the right to do her own thing. She thought she had the right to give me and my brother devastatingly Irish names, even though she came from a Protestant family and lived right in the middle of Weirtown, an estate built in the sixties and known for its violent loyalism. She thought she had the right to ignore politics and religion and still live there. She also thought she had the right to keep my father's identity a secret. And Prince's too. Because she said it meant we both had a clean slate.

She thought it would be a great idea to call me Cuchulain because it showed an appreciation of Ulster's heroic past. I was actually called Setanta for the first few weeks, which was Cuchulain's name as a boy, because she thought it suggested future greatness. But Prince got me mixed up with the baby Jesus and told the whole street I was the baby Santa. So Setanta got knocked on the head.

The real problem though, was that my ma had absolutely no appreciation of my future. The kids who tortured me at Weir High were too fucken stupid to know that when Cuchulain was around, we were all bloody pagans. It didn't matter that Cuchulain was an Ulsterman who fought to keep the men of Ireland out of the North. A few loyalists who'd taken the time to actually read a book had caught on that Cuchulain would make a brilliant mascot but they were fighting a losing battle against the traditional Proddie suspicion of anything Irish. Except Guinness, like. My name was spelt suspiciously like tiocfaidh ár lá because anything spelt in Irish looked like tiocfaidh ár lá. Bord Fáilte, Aer Lingus and Bus Éireann – they all spelt death for me. To make matters worse, we had a typically Catholic surname – Fitzpatrick. So even if we weren't Catholics now, we sure as hell must have been at some point. Fucked-up oddball Fenian family.

I remember one time it was snowy and mum gave me money for the bus so I wouldn't have to walk home from school. The bus was packed with a writhing cloud of black and green school uniforms, fitting, jerking, jeering, tossing and twisting on almost every seat and all along the aisle. They soaked the atmosphere with rampant hormones and overpowering BO and steamed up the windows with noise and sticky heat. We'd only gone about two hundred yards up the estate when Wilson McCullough, one of my usual torturers, squawked, 'That fucken Irish is gettin' everywhere! Fucken Fenian bastards! Look at that there! Look! Look!' His voice was high and low and all over the show, like his balls had just dropped mid-sentence. He pointed at the street we passed. Weir North Cul-de-Sac.

Cul-de-fucken-Sac.

I was dead.

They trailed me onto the floor of the bus but I squirmed under the seats and sniper-crawled up through the passengers' legs towards the front. Every now and again somebody landed a well-aimed boot in my kidneys or on the ear, but I eventually made it to the front, bloody, dizzy, damp and dirty. There was nothing the bus driver or any of the passengers could do and I didn't blame them for not helping. My torturers kicked me off at my stop. Which was kind of them. I lay on my back in the slushy snow, staring up into the soft dull sky as the light flakes swirled down on me. Then I got up and went home.

When they discovered my incredible eating powers, you can imagine what I had to swallow. Actually, you probably can't. I've never been so sick so often in all my life, and believe me, I have a strong stomach. Hamster shit, dog shit, human shit, horse shit, roadkill, phlegm, piss, all manner of bodily fluids. I had a go at drinking disinfectant, simply because I knew I'd be hospitalised and get a week or so off school. But at the end of third year I was at the end of my tether. Literally.

You know the looped cord you tug to draw the curtains in classrooms? My torturers tried to lynch me with it. I was leaning back on the hind legs of my chair and one of them, Glen Donaghy, sat behind me. It was geography. Precipitation. I remember useless stuff like that. Donaghy looped the cord around my neck and kicked away the legs of my chair. It was the funniest thing the geography teacher ever saw. That's when I left.

If it hadn't been for the torture, I think I would have been good at school. I had a brilliant memory for words and facts and could memorise stuff as soon as I saw it. But even that had consequences. In a first year spelling test, I was the only one who could spell both precocious and unconscious. Right, wrong and prophetic, all at the same time. I had the nerve to say Rangers's weekend performance was stupendous. Bonehead stood across the room mouthing fuck up fuck up fuck up! Me – window – darkness – stitches. I had a better vocabulary than most of the teachers but I still had a lot to learn.

Mum said she would educate me at home and Prince was really annoyed. He was just jealous. I was stoned out of my bollocks for months. She sent me to the library every morning to read the papers, thumb through books and listen to classical and jazz cassettes until lunchtime. On my way back I had to bring buns from the bakery, tobacco and papers from the Stop'n'Shop and we'd sit and listen to

Radio 4, eat the buns and skin up. Our last meal together was chip butties and a pot of mushroom tea in September and I hadn't done any drugs or chip butties since she left. I hadn't really done much of anything.

I headed out to the barrack-like bus shelter across the green from our house. I kept the bottle of vodka and lemonade inside my zipped up studded leather jacket, the one with the anarchy sign on the back. It was also poached from Prince and was miles too big, but it was November, for God's sake. Weirtown was about twenty minutes on the bus from central Belfast and while the city centre was bursting with new apartments, satellite estates like Weirtown were shrinking. Anybody with any money or any sense wanted out.

The Housing Executive was in the process of levelling most of the estate, replacing vacated houses and flats with expanses of green. Kind of ironic for thoroughly Protestant territory, I thought. We lived in a maisonette, a sort of terrace of houses with a layer of flats above. The house used to belong to my granny and Prince and me grew up there with mum and granny until granny's clogged arteries had their own wee bombscare and decided not to let any more traffic through. Then the house belonged to mum. A tragic freebie.

It was in the middle of a block, and the block was part of a huge square of maisonettes that was being demolished. They'd already knocked down the block behind us and the blocks to either side. Ours was the only occupied house left. The Housing Executive wanted to buy it back so they could knock it down but mum refused every offer they made. I think they were praying she would just pop her clogs because they knew what she was like, but her clogs were tied on tight.

Cockroaches might have withstood ice ages and catastrophes but they don't have anything like the resilience of my mother's liver. I think her home brew had medicinal qualities. Anything that tasted that bad had to be good. I liked the house like that though. I liked the lack of neighbours. I could play the Pogues tape Prince made me really loud and nobody ever came to the door to ask what the fucken Fenian racket was.

Even the vodka couldn't keep me warm as I waited in the bus shelter. I still hadn't made it out of the estate and already my spikes were beginning to topple from the vibrations of my chattering teeth. I ducked to look in every car that passed in case Bonehead was about but there was no sign of him. I hugged the bottle inside my jacket and balanced my chin on the lid, keeping an eye out for the tracksuit-sporting, skinny-necked, Corsa-driving spider-men who raced round the estate every night. I was usually pretty good at dodging spit but sometimes they caught me out.

My granny said the best thing you could do was keep your head below the parapet because people like that were 'connected' – they scuttled about at the bottom of the paramilitary pecking order. Every estate had its ruling class of hoods and in Weirtown, it was the Protestant People's Army. The estate served as their training ground, the place where the young served apprenticeships in bullying, and if they survived that, moved on to full-time terrorism. People put up with them because after all, these were the people who would protect them from the Republican Menace. And get them cheap Celine Dion and Garth Brooks CDs, of course.

'Alright, wee love?' Josie Baps said. 'On you go. Prince's up the stairs.'

Josie Baps always let me into The Collective for free, even though it was against the egalitarian ethos of the place. She was one of the volunteers who helped run it and she liked to mother me. She sat at the spindly, teak-top table at the door, her huge braless shelf of a chest brimming over the cash box. She took my hand and rubber-stamped it with the kind of precision that betrayed a secret wish to work in a post office.

She had dyed black, curly hair, thick orange make-up slathered over worn out skin and she always wore black leggings sucked into 14-hole Doc Martins. She had a different embroidered velvet top for every day of the week, kept a constant roly clamped between her stubby fingers and she could have been anywhere between 35 and 50. She liked to mother everybody. Except Prince. She liked to fuck him.

Prince was taking care of Belfast's sexual revolution all by himself. He was a slut. He was ridiculously good looking and the long scar he'd got across his left cheek last April was so perfect it looked like movie make-up. Even with my six-inch spikes I still couldn't match his slim 6'2". His features were sort of girly, with pale green eyes and extra long eyelashes. His short spiked hair changed colour constantly, one week black, the next white, the next pink, the next green. His goatee was a sharp black upturned triangle from his bottom lip to the tip of his chin and below his nose was a long thin moustache that stretched slightly beyond the width of his mouth. If I ever managed to sprout facial hair, that's exactly what I wouldn't have. He was a real live handsome devil. He looked like a rock star, but he played guitar like a chimp plucking out its own fleas.

But anybody can sound like a rock star if they just learn a couple of chords and progressions, plug in the guitar and apply liberal amounts of distortion, and that's what he did. His band – that's him on guitar, his crusty mate Dave on bass and never the same person twice on drums – only ever played at The Collective because nowhere else would have them. Their 'music' filtered down from the top floor, loud enough to make my sinuses pulsate as I headed for the stairs.

The Collective occupied an old red brick warehouse in Hill Street in Belfast's Cathedral Quarter, a knot of narrow cobbled streets behind St Anne's Cathedral. The area backed onto the Art College and aspired to be Dublin's Temple Bar, with small contemporary restaurants and galleries nestling alongside grubby old bars, new gay bars, cafes, artists' studios, a tattoo parlour, sex shops, an arts centre and a shop selling hash pipes, garden fertiliser and bondage gear.

The bottom floor of The Collective was a shop that sold books and pamphlets on how to cook vegetarian, organic or spiritually enlightened food. The middle floor was the cafe where they sold vegetarian, organic and spiritually enlightened food – including Josie's baps – and the top floor was where the bands played. It wasn't licensed so people stood around in the dark with their blue plastic bags, avoiding Josie's alcohol-free, allegedly healthy cocktails, all the colour and consistency of blood. Since Prince told her we'd temporarily misplaced our mum, she kept giving me drinks called Vitamin Jection and Auntie Oxidant and standing over me while I drank them.

I pushed my way up the congested stairs, hauling my boots off the sticky cement steps and tripping over legs and feet. On the top floor, I side-stepped into a warm wave of darkness and painful noise and moved through tight clumps of people, variously inhaling leather, Lynx, sweat, peaches, piss, hair, patchouli oil, blow and – not so strange if you've been to similar places – wet dog. I mopped my dripping nose on my hand and squinted past the slam-dancers trying to cheerfully annihilate each other in front of the band.

I couldn't see Wilson McCullough anywhere. But he'd turn up. He worked as a security guard in Pick Donal's Burgers in Belfast and finished his Friday shift at lunchtime. He drank his wages on Friday night and recently he'd started coming here on Saturday night with a carry-out and a pocket full of drugs to sell. I took out my fegs and sparked up.

Tonight Prince had called the band Awayn Fuck. The week before they'd been Asharra Shite. Prince was creative in his own wee way like. He was good at art at school but one night when mum came home from the life-drawing class she taught at the community centre, she fell asleep on the settee and dropped her joint on Prince's portfolio. Whoof. The one GCSE he would have got, he didn't get.

The Collective's naked bulbs highlighted his sprays of spittle as he crashed and popped into the mic. He'd perfected his pose in front of the mirror – legs slightly bent and planted far apart, the guitar slung as low as playably possible in front of his thighs. Since they'd got Sky TV in their house, MTV had become the love of his life. Well, second to himself, of course. I told him his preference for the performing puppets of American capitalism was an affront to punk and it would be better if he just killed himself. He promised when he was rich and famous he'd buy me Buckfast Abbey so I could move in and live like a king. I kicked him but he caught me in a headlock and managed to fart on my neck.

He roared one of our more stupid songs into the mic. Mum taught us both to play guitar but I was the one that stuck at it, mainly because mum didn't like me watching TV and because Prince was always too busy hooring and touring about the town. When we wrote our songs, they were a lot slower, some were even kind of good, but when

Prince performed them he tripled the speed, cranked up the volume and just roared them all in one note, so each song was pretty much indiscernible from the next. The song he was singing was called 'In Another Life' and was all minor chords, throbbing guitar, slave-driven bassline and yet more demonically roared vocals. One of the local fanzines said it had a love across the barricades theme, and you never know, it might have had. The words went 'I must have learned to line dance, in another life. I find it really easy, Garth, won't you be my wife'.

Imagine it. Young line dancers shunned by their respective communities and driven to hitch and stomp in secret, on the edge of the night. And rightfully so. New government bodies encouraged people to explore and love all kinds of dance, music, sport and culture. Everything from line dancing to salsa, ice hockey to circus skills was sponsored by European peace money and celebrated with aggressive enthusiasm. And strange as it is, line dancing does have the ability to unite a divided people. You might faint at the sound of 'The Soldier's Song' or have a fit when you hear 'The Sash' but I bet you'll sing along to 'Achy Breaky Heart'.

Dave swayed around slowly on bass, every so often knocking over and then expertly catching his mic. He was about 6'4" and looked like an exotic poisonous frog, in an oversized woolly jumper with horizontal rainbow stripes, red dreads palm-treeing away from a wide face, and huge eyes that were so far apart they seemed to operate independently. He was the oldest member of the band but his distant unchallenged expression made him look not just younger but childlike.

He was another helper at The Collective, making porridgey soups and organic bread and biscuits for the cafe when he wasn't painting and decorating, washing windows, building sheds, shearing sheep or knitting. He was very handy, Dave was. He'd developed a way of heating a sandwich toaster through bicycle power and had almost perfected a pedal-powered amp. The only problem was, he puffed and panted so much, anything we tried to play sounded like the soundtrack to a porn movie.

As for drums, I could only guess at who was playing, and I was seriously fucked off when I guessed right. He was a good drummer like, I gave him that. Incredible energy, unexpected arrangements and the brilliant spontaneity of a Tourette's syndrome sufferer. His drum kit was colossal, of mythical stadium rock proportions. It left hardly any room on the stage for Prince and Dave and even though I couldn't even see the drummer behind it, I knew it was him. Mountains and skyscrapers and towers of drums, a stormy landscape of high hats, cymbals and percussion, a heaving, teaming semi-circular sea of gleaming silver and black, whacked and thrashed like it was caught in a whirlwind, and a huge big fucken gong at the back. It all looked brand new too.

I just knew it was Kloot, a spidey scrote from Weirtown, small but built like a door, with a shaved head and glasses porthole thick. His real commitments lay with a loyalist flute band but he 'bumped into' Prince just before the marching season started and offered to join Prince's band once it was all over. When the summer street violence came to an end, he would need somebody or something else to take his aggression out on and

Prince wasn't going to argue when he picked on drums.

I was about to head out for a whizz when I spotted McCullough standing on the top floor landing, feet astride a blue plastic bag. I stepped back into the room where the band played. As usual, he'd made an effort to fit in, wearing a black hooded top and black combats instead of his usual Tommy gear. It probably would have worked except for the curtained hair which he'd slicked down over his forehead like Herman Munster in a headwind. He was only a wee bit bigger than me but he was heavier, blobby and unfit. He felt around in his back pocket for cigarettes and lit himself a Lambert & Butler.

A wave of shouts and scuffles rose from below and he hooked his hand under the handle of his blue plastic bag and stepped back as a team of peelers jogged efficiently up the stairs to a chorus of ingenious obscenities. They pushed past McCullough, then past me, then into the room where the band played. The music disintegrated. Prince stopped first, followed by Dave, when he eventually woke up, but Kloot played on. He thrashed his way round the monster kit, completely oblivious to the five peelers who'd started dismantling it around him. Short squeals of feedback and muffled bumps and thuds sounded from the PA system as the cops moved around, lifting and unscrewing equipment.

Kloot finally drifted to a stop and I heard his high-pitched whine – 'Whaddya doin? Whaddya doin?' – as Josie Baps scurried from cop to cop, trying to find out who was in charge. Dave balanced on the edge of the stage, staring around in mild surprise, but Prince set down his guitar, stepped off the stage and cheerily looped his arms round a couple of girls at the side of the room. The bastard had planned it. Kloot's drum kit was nicked and Prince had squealed on him. Not as green as he's Fenian looking, my brother.

I glanced back out to the hall but McCullough was gone. I dodged through the tide of people coming in and squirmed my way down the stairs, almost surfing the crowd. Two cops stood by Josie's vacated table at the bottom of the stairs, watching me without expression. I scooted by them and out into the cold damp street. It had started to rain. Two police landrovers took up most of the narrow road and a few cops lingered around by the vehicles, exchanging easy chat.

McCullough was way ahead of me, walking casually along Hill Street's shiny wet cobbles. I slipped past the landrovers, head down, then I broke into a run, Prince's record bag bouncing off my hip. I followed McCullough into Gordon Street, the long, dark, narrow road where the circus school, gay bar and another new restaurant were. Later on drag queens and punks would scrum for taxis with middle-class clowns who dropped chopsticks all over the road but for now the place was empty.

McCullough slowed to take a can out of his plastic bag and I ducked in close by a wall. He cracked open the can and continued in the direction of Dunbar Street, drinking as he walked. I followed, gaining with every step. He didn't know I was there. He didn't know I had flipped open my record bag. He didn't know it was me who tossed two raw burgers way up over his head so they rained down in front of him like flat and freaky pink hail. He looked up, then he knelt down to have a closer look.

'What da fuck ...' he said. 'Fucken burgers! What da fuck ...'

He didn't know I had grasped the giant luncheon meat sausage, now defrosting but still a brick, or that I'd started to run. He didn't know I used both hands to hold it out by my right hip. I think he started to get the idea as my boots thudded up the cobblestones behind him. I swung the sausage and it hit the back of his skull with a good solid thwonk and sent him sprawling chin-first onto the slippery stones.

I gripped his hooded top and every muscle strained in my shoulders and back as I dragged his semi-conscious body to the side of the road and leaned it against the side of a pissy-smelling gate. It wasn't my intention to kill him or anything. Jesus Christ, what kind of person do you think I am? All I wanted to do was set fire to his dick.

I lifted his light wrist and pressed for a pulse. I was SAS man Andy McNab. I just hadn't figured on my heart increasing to twice its normal size and thundering along like a lorry doing sixty over speed ramps. My fingers shook as I unbuttoned his fly, rummaged round in my bag and pulled out the pork sausage wrapped in the sheet of newspaper. I tucked the paper inside the front of his trousers and arranged the sausage so it looked like his wee pink willy was hanging out the fly. Then I felt around in the bag for my lighter. I stood up and tilted the opened bag to the streetlight. No lighter. Not even any fegs. Just one cow's tongue and another softened burger nestling at the bottom of the shiny polyester lining, stained with gunge and grease.

Josie said we should really tell the cops that mum was missing and the cops said it was unlikely she was kidnapped or murdered or anything like that. They said there were no suspicious circumstances surrounding her disappearance. The fact that her clothes were gone, along with a holdall and her passport, led them to believe she had left of her own accord. They also said the fact that it wasn't the first time and that she'd always came back before meant she'd probably come back this time too. I said she never took her clothes, holdall and passport before. They said did I want them to let social services know I was there on my own. I said no, I was sure I'd survive.

She disappeared for three days when she turned forty,

for four days when her best friend died of breast cancer and for five days when her mother died. When her short stories failed to win competitions, she took off for an average of two days. The 1998 World Cup final was a long weekend and when U2 played at Slane Castle she went AWOL for a week. When she got into rave, she disappeared for more than three weeks.

That was when Prince and her had their big fight. When she eventually came home, we were all a lot thinner but it was summer and there was no school so nobody really noticed our weight loss. We ate everything we had, even things that were long out of date, but it didn't bother me. Mum was never a very organised housekeeper. I got a taste for stale Cup-a-Soup followed by age-old rice topped off with tinned stewing steak from Weirtown Meats that must have been lying round our house for a hundred years. Prince asked Big Julie if there was any chance she could get him a job in the factory, just till mum came back. There was. And she could.

Billy Dick was a supervisor in the factory. He was another one of mum's old boyfriends and he took Prince under his wing. Which would have been fine except Billy was a member of the Protestant People's Party, the political wing of the Protestant People's Army. Billy asked Prince what his career plans were. He gave him a free subscription to the PPA's monthly magazine and a lift to work every day. He 'let' Prince sit with him and his PPA comrades in the canteen and spent days lovingly teaching him how to use the factory's packing machine.

Prince used to cry into his tea before he went and cry into the frying pan when he came home. I said I'd get a paper round or help the milkman so he wouldn't have to go but he said he'd hang on till Sunday because she'd probably come home by then. Sunday would come and she wouldn't appear and he would have to go back on Monday. He was only in the place a few weeks but by the time she came home all the fun had been sucked out of his normally cheeky face and his energy was gone. His eyebrows were slanted at a constant twenty to four, he was far paler than usual and his long slim limbs were light and lifeless.

They had a stand-off over the frying pan on the Sunday morning she came home, offering us soda bread for breakfast. He just stood there, staring and shaking, probably trying to decide whether the soda bread or the frying pan would make a better weapon. Then he attacked the living room and gave the stereo a good kicking so she couldn't play the white label recordings she'd picked up on her rave tour. And then he left.

Mum slept for a few days and then she sold her white labels and bought eight bags of food in Tesco instead of the usual three, which I thought was brilliant. Although I always hated rave.

could hear footsteps clipping along the cobbles in the next street.

I sat back, McCullough's knees still trapped under my ass, and watched as Marilyn Monroe turned into Gordon Street. She drifted up towards me, her peep-toe shoes clicking along the cobbles. Her white, flared dress billowed and waved and her yellow hair bounced. She was tall, with the muscley build of a swimmer, but she walked lightly. I was still sitting on McCullough's legs as she passed but I couldn't move. She stopped beside me and hitched up her dress.

'My card,' she said in a soft, breathy voice, pulling a tiny white card out of the frilly white suspender belt that gripped her meaty thighs.

I took it and she carried on, heading for Dunbar Street. I pulled my fegs out of my back pocket and lit one. My hand suddenly hit itself off my head, Wile E. Coyote style. My fegs were in my back pocket the whole time. Where I usually kept them when I wasn't carrying a fucken handbag.

I dropped the cigarette and knelt beside him to light the newspaper. It caught easily. The rough edges writhed red and grey and flicked up into small flames. I could smell the sausage. Barbecuey. Quite nice.

'McCullough,' I said, rattling his shoulder. 'McCullough.' Rattle. 'McCullough.'

'Mm-muh ... mm-whuh?'

'Your dick's on fire.'

He looked down at his crotch and screamed, scrabbling to his feet and beating at his dick. It flew off and rolled along the road to settle between two cobblestones. You know the really long note Whitney Houston holds on the word 'I' in 'I Will Always Love You'? McCullough let out a similar sound, and then looked as though he was going to faint. He took off towards Dunbar Street, his trousers sliding down to his ankles as he ran, bawling and howling like a toddler afraid to use the big toilet. He bent to look at himself one second, then star-jumped about in imagined agony the next. And I ran too, back to Hill Street, then turned sharply when I saw the peelers still outside The Collective. I jogged backwards, yelling, 'Black bastards!' Then I headed towards Waring Street at the edge of the Cathedral Quarter, laughing my tits off.

I calmed down a bit when I turned into Waring Street, vague and soft in the drizzly streetlights. Ornate nineteenth-century buildings sat crumbling and neglected on one side, while their neighbours across the road got makeovers and were turned into new restaurants and bars. Inside, trendy thirty-somethings admired their new money in the mirrored walls, but outside grey dereliction still nodded back to the seventies.

Mum said the contrast was unconscious but deliberate. People needed to remind themselves how much they deserved their success. She said the biggest problem for the new Northern Ireland wasn't continued sectarianism or the growing gangsterism or even the embarrassingly bad spelling of a loyalist outfit called the Bayroot Hoods. These days, it was guilt.

Prince said she had far too much bloody time on her hands.

I slowed and breathed deep as I passed the steamy windows of the new bar on the corner of Waring Street and Bridge Street, where the bus left for Weirtown. My lungs rattled from too many smokes, which was why I'd given up the rolies and gone back to the Consulate I liked as a kid. The thumping in my chest finally eased off and I wheezed noisily but happily.

The rain felt good on my sticky skin and I didn't care that the damp air was turning my spikes into sudsy curls. The bus wasn't due for another twenty-five minutes and I patted my back pocket for my cigarettes and lighter as I stood in the bus shelter. They weren't there. I opened the record bag and felt around but they weren't there either. Just my unused ammo and my prized cow's tongue.

I'd lost them again. Fuck it, they cost nearly a fiver and I'd only smoked a few. I had a card from Marilyn Monroe though. I took it out of my pocket and looked at it. It was a while-u-wait-in-the-shopping-centre business card that said

EVERYONE STAND FOR THE QUEEN

MO CROWE'S DRAG-A-GRAMS

CALL NOW FOR A QUOTE

Mo Crowe sounded familiar. I supposed it was a stage name or something and was supposed to sound familiar. Fucken subliminal marketing tactics. Bastards. I'd use the card for a roach. At least I still had my *pièce de résistance*. I'd freeze it and keep it for the second wave.

The last bus to Weirtown is a bollocks. It's full of people who have problems. For example, if your girlfriend kisses you goodnight before you board the bus, it means you aren't getting any. If you sit at the back eating a McDonalds, or even a Pick Donals, it means you're pissed and/or you have no friends. Either way, you've probably wet yourself. If you sit behind the driver and distract him with stupid questions the whole way home, it means you have no social skills, you need stronger glasses to read the 'Please do not distract the driver' sign or you never learned to read at all. If you stay on past the last stop, it means you have no home to go to. If nobody sits anywhere near you, it means you smell. Or you're talking to yourself. Or your spikes are very long. If you fall asleep against the window, you're all three.

I woke up as the bus took a violent rollercoaster bend as it swung into Weirtown. My head boinked off the window and I peered out at the dark streets. The lights inside the bus made it difficult to see out but I knew where I was out of habit. I looked at my reflection as I straightened up. My hair looked like a mop that had been left to harden after cleaning up black paint.

Mine was the last stop in the estate and there were two people left on the bus when I got off. You'd be hard-pushed to miss our house from the road, cast adrift in demolition and devastation. The lights were on and I dragged my heavy boots towards them across the green. I could hear music as I approached. It was loud and I recognised it. I forced my legs to go quicker. I knew that song. Only one person I knew ever liked that song.

I ran up the path and pushed open the door. I didn't even notice that it had been forced. I looked about the living room while the song blasted from the stereo, all fizz and crackly vinyl. Two men got up from the settee. One was in his early twenties, thin and skittish, with a short, gelled-down fringe, black bomber jacket and Levis. The other was older and heavier, late thirties, wearing similar clothes, but the leather jacket he'd upgraded to only skimmed the edges of his paunch.

'Fixed your record player,' the older one said, nodding at the stereo in the corner. He pulled at the waistband of his jeans to ease the pressure on his gut and skimmed his fingers over his greying crewcut. 'Haven't heard that record in years,' he said. 'I like music while I work.'

I began reversing. 'You've got the wrong house.'

McCullough appeared at the door into the kitchen. His chin had a smudge of road rash and he was puffing on one of my fegs.

'How the fuck do you smoke these?' he said, frowning at the cigarette and studying the pack of Consulate as he turned it over in his hand. 'Mental cigarettes? What the fuck's mental cigarettes?' He still wore the charred trousers and he tweaked at his crotch as he dropped the cigarette on the carpet and tossed the pack across to me. 'Here. Y'might need one.'

I turned for the door and heard the stampede behind me. One of them caught my hair and tore out a fistful as I tried to pull away. I would like to say I was booted to a pulp to some really moving music. Like the way 'Ride of the Valkyries' is used in *Apocalypse Now*. Or maybe 'Canon in D' by Pachelbel, sneakily re-invented for just about every TV movie about dying kids. Or maybe something funny and poignant, like 'Teenage Kicks'. But oh no. None of that was good enough for me.

The song 'Iko-Iko' is a happy, clappy, Caribbean style number by a singer called Natasha, which was out around '81 or '82. It's worth tracking down just to fully appreciate the banality of my swan song. It only lasts two and a half minutes. One minute was gone by the time I realised why they were there, and when the song ended, I was lying on the floor in the kitchen, where I'd crawled trying to get away. They tried to break my arms between their fake Timberland boots and the dusty, empty hearth in the living room, but my arms were made of the same stuff as my mum's liver and refused to give in. My nose was full of something and my eyes watered so much I could hardly see past my tight blinking lids. I think I still had all my teeth but my face and tongue were fiery numb so I couldn't tell.

I curled up on the kitchen floor, still wearing Prince's record bag, as they threw in a few more tired kicks. I was starting to go. I felt McCullough hunker down beside me, then he nudged me over onto my back. I looked up at the younger guy in the bomber jacket. He had such a hard on he could barely straighten up. I started to cry.

'Aw, poor Cookie,' McCullough said. 'Stupid wee dickhead.'

'Wugh,' I said.

He inspected my mashed face with approval. 'My da, y'see. Friends in high places.' He laughed down his nose with a snort. 'You are mental, arncha Cookie?'

'Wugh.' I slid my hand inside Prince's record bag and tucked my fingers under the slippery tongue.

'Got somethin' to say, dickhead?' He tilted his ear to my face.

I dragged the tongue out of the bag and slammed it into his mouth. He sprang away like he'd been stung, wiping at his lips with both hands to get all traces of the smelly, greasy flesh off his skin.

He stopped and looked down at me. He laughed. I saw his trendy trainer coming.

Some man I didn't know was pulling me up, shuffling his arm round behind my shoulders. 'Boo,' he said.

I started to cry again.

There was a black blanket of blood on the floor. It

seeped under the curling squares of patterned lino.

I pushed my dead hand into the stained record bag and pulled out the last burger. I tried to hit him with it but I couldn't control my arm. The burger hovered under the yellow fluorescent light winking and humming above us. And that's when the dogs appeared. Big ugly mongrels, baying, rumbling with bitter determination. They all leapt to catch it.

'Dog Frisbee,' I told the man. The money in my meter ran out.

Big Julie didn't speak to me the whole way home. I was in the Mater Hospital on the Crumlin Road for less than a week but it was long enough to become Ward Shitting Champion. It was a mixed ward and I was the youngest, and the healthiest, even though I was in such bad shape. Still, my guts worked just fine and seeing as the main topic of conversation always came round to the old folks' last and/or next dump, I became extremely popular due to my uncanny ability to excrete waste at a fairly average rate.

The ward had its own TV and it sat beside my bed, which would have been great if I'd been allowed to go anywhere near it. The senile militia outnumbered me seven to one and they just wanted to watch news, news and more news. In complete silence. I wasn't even allowed to squeak the springs of my bed when the news was on, although they slapped me on the back in congratulations when my beating got two seconds coverage. The reporter called me a 'boy' though, which sort of pissed me off. I think I would have preferred 'youth'.

I couldn't stand the news. Even if I heard it on the radio in a shop, I'd get really frustrated. I just didn't want to hear it – because the local news always drew me in and had me taking sides. And the worst of it was, I always took the Prod side. I hated myself for it. I didn't want to be a Prod. Prods were really embarrassing. Any time a Prod from here appeared on TV, they were either waving a bible or doing a stupid walk. It wasn't that reasonable Prods didn't exist. It was that they kept their heads below that bloody parapet my granny went on about, so you only ever heard about extremists. I didn't want to belong to a community of embarrassing nutters but I just couldn't shake it off. Newspapers were much better. You could pick and choose the news in a newspaper.

Mum said TV was an 'anathema to creativity' but I liked it. We had an old black and white portable with cracked yellow casing and half a fish slice for an aerial. It overheated and died after about an hour and even kicking it didn't help, as the cracked casing proved. Bonehead had Sky TV, which was my original motive for being his mate. Then when he didn't try to make me eat shit and I didn't throw his glasses onto the road, we just sort of hit it off. He wasn't the greatest conversationalist but that's a good quality in a TV mate. Whenever the news came on, we'd flick over to Jerry Springer for some screaming, shouting, scrapping and some good old-fashioned entertainment. Ah for fuck's sake, we might as well have just watched the news.

Julie picked me up from the hospital in her Ford Fiesta and I sat in the passenger seat while Bonehead sat in the back, his spindly legs so long his knees hovered between me and Julie like two stonewashed skulls. He was shorter than me at school but he'd grown dangerously tall and thin since I left. His long skinny neck jiggled his head around like a balloon on a stick, his shaved head was criss-crossed with old scars and his dim half-grin revealed a gap where he'd lost a front tooth in a stolen Ford Puma. He didn't crash it or anything. The driver caught him before he got away, dragged him out onto the road and kneed him in the face. He'd had his glasses fixed since then but they were always taped somewhere.

Bonehead loved Fords and hated Catholics, and that was about the height of him. Fords because they were built to last and Catholics because, well, have you got a map? You'll need one to find the sense in this. Something about land and ancestors and him being the new generation. It was like somebody else was operating his mouth. I told him my da was the Pope but he just said I should try and keep it to myself. He had dreams of becoming a hard man so I told him he'd have to start making positive moves if he wanted to achieve his goal. Move number one would be to stop being so generous about me and the Pope. Number two would be to use headphones when he wanted to listen to death metal.

Your musical preference says as much about you as your name in Belfast. And in Belfast, names can leave you upside down in a wheelie bin (third year, courtesy of Lindsey Scott). Nobody's going to kill you for your musical preference but right now, the accepted listening for your up-and-coming young paramilitary is hard house and trance. And maybe a dose of overproduced R 'n' B but only when *she* wants it. Listen to anything that's less than 9 billion bpm and the spides think *you're* a freak. But the freakier your taste in music, the less interested you are in traditional politics and the whole fight thing. Slipknot fans are the most well-adjusted members of society.

Big Julie drove past the demolition crew behind our house. 'Where we goin?' I asked.

She didn't answer. She drove on and stopped outside their house a few streets away. She turned to Bonehead and poked her fingers into the hip pocket of her tight jeans. 'Away and get us twenny Berks, Robert.'

'Fuck off,' he said. 'We're in the fucken car. Drive to the shop.'

'Do what you're fucken told!' She forced the money onto his chest.

'Ma ...'

'I'm lettin' yuh have the car, aren't ah?' Grey eyes fierce.

'Nice one,' he said, nudging me. 'Where y'wanna go for fegs? Portrush?'

'Cookie's comin' w'me,' Julie said. She pressed the release on my seat belt, leaned across and opened the door on my side.

'But ...'

'Geddout!'

I hauled myself out, she got out her side and Bonehead scrambled like a spider into the front seat. He revved the bollocks out of the car and Julie banged the roof. 'Go easy, y'wee bastard!'

Bonehead raked down the street with the careless abandon enjoyed only by those who've been banned from driving before they've even passed their test.

She nodded at the house. 'In.'

I followed her up the garden path, shadowed on each side by a towering, dense row of pine trees. She opened the door and let me in.

Their house always fascinated me. Those trees hid a fucken semi-detached palace. She had really good taste and was obsessively clean. The house always smelt as if the tumble-dryer had just turned itself off before you walked in. It was always tidy and they always had the latest styles from MFI. She redecorated constantly and threw herself into DIY, fitting a modern new kitchen herself, all gleaming white cupboards with brass handles and plastic marble worktops. The house even had a conservatory on the back, the tiniest conservatory you've ever seen, only big enough to hold two narrow wicker chairs and a miniature wicker and glass table. And that's where we sat.

She opened a window and pulled an unopened pack of twenty Berkeley out of her shirt pocket. She handed me one, lit us both up and sat back, her muscular bulk shrinking the chair to kiddie size.

I rattled my fingertips on the arm of my chair and looked at her. Then out at what was left of the back yard. Then back at her. God, it was quiet. 'Saw yer mate Billy Dick on the news,' I said. 'See the factory's in trouble again.'

Billy Dick acted as spokesman whenever anything happened involving the local people, whether it was employment, pedestrian crossings or murder. He was a thoroughly upstanding and law-abiding citizen, who just happened to have gone to prison ten years earlier when a Catholic taxi driver was murdered in the estate. Concealing evidence was the most they could get him for. A shady past was an NVQ for the new breed of loyalist politician. A prison sentence was a field trip in the training. He was in his forties, with bright orange hair swept across a shiny nut and I loved it when they interviewed him in a crosswind. I swear they did that on purpose. He'd been on the local news, talking about a director at the factory who was being investigated for fraud.

After the weather, the factory was the most popular topic of conversation in Weirtown. Discrimination, compensation, robberies, strikes, pay-offs, investors, new jobs, new robberies and hilarious industrial accidents. I'd been raised on it. It employed hundreds so I suppose getting a mention on TV, even collectively, was important to a lot of people. Personally speaking, I preferred the rumours. Lost digits, chicken cysts and missing dogs. That was class.

I looked at Julie but she still said nothing. I rattled my fingers again and nodded. 'Capitalism corrupts.'

She leaned forward and slapped me twice round the head – the side without the bandage – flicking my straggly hair across my face. I tried to back away but the chair was jammed up against the conservatory's double glazing and all I could do was wrap my elbow over my head and pull a knee up in front of me. She was nearly Prince's height and probably five stone heavier than me.

She dragged her hand down over her face and leaned forward, hands hanging loosely between parted legs. She twisted her mouth to puff smoke towards the window.

'Can I go home now?' I asked. Pinpricks of sweat had broken out on my face and neck. I was going to puke and I didn't know why. I looked round for somewhere to put it but there was nowhere – no bin, nothing. Everywhere gleamed sparkly clean.

'Do y'not know who Wilson McCullough's da is?' she said.

'You just hit me.'

'*Tommy* McCullough is a commander in the PPA. What the hell were you playin' at?' She ran a thumbnail over her lips. 'You have to get out.'

I stood up but she took hold of my hand. 'I mean the estate, y'twat, not my house. Sit down.'

I sat slowly but looked back into the kitchen. If I ran, I might make it to the sink. If I sat quietly, maybe it would stay down.

'What did Prince say?' she asked.

'He called me a twat as well.'

'Did he say about movin' up to Belfast with him?'

'I'm not goin'.'

'I'm not advisin' yuh, Cookie.' The wicker creaked as she leaned forward. 'I'm tellin' yuh. You have to get out of the estate.'

'I'm not leavin' our house.'

'Christ, Cookie!' She shook her fists in the air like a bad actor. 'You can't live here any more!'

I dropped my cigarette and then rushed to pick it up off the spotless floor. 'Sorry.'

She sighed. 'I'm in an awkward position here.'

'These chairs look really comfortable too.'

'You're not half as smart as you think you are.'

'There is no answer to that.'

'I'll take you up to Prince's house.'

'Look, you know them,' I said. 'You can put a word in for me, can't yuh?' It was coming up. No no no not here. I sucked in another breath and glanced back at the kitchen. I was really sweating now.

'I don't have a say in what they do, Cookie,' she said. 'I'm just protectin' me own, love. They told *me* to tell you, understand? I can't help ye. Will y'just go? Please?'

I slapped my hand over my mouth and my head began to buzz, like my brain was a huge bluebottle that wanted out through any cranial orifice. I stood up and leaned my hand on the double glazing but I was making greasy marks, so I lifted it off again.

'Cookie?'

I looked around in desperation. The house was spotless. Really, really lovely. I pulled my T-shirt out at the neck and puked up inside it.

'I think my ma fancies you,' Bonehead said.
    'Shite or sugar, what's the best?' I asked.
    'Not talkin' from experience, sugar. I'm serious but.
Givin' yuh a big hug an' all when y'left our house the
other day? What does that tell yuh?'
    We sat in my kitchen, listening to the rattling engines
and scraping diggers behind the house. I was planning the
second wave of my campaign. Glen Donaghy had a
scooter. Sugar in his petrol tank or shite in his helmet? It
was a difficult one.
    'Swear to God, Cookie, I think she's into you. This could
be your big chance.'
    'Chance to what?'
    'Get your end in.'
    'Oh Jesus.'

'No, swear to God.'

'Look, I am not the man to convert your mother back to heterosexuality. And I've already got my end in somewhere else, thanks.'

'Aye, right,' he said. 'You're the only person I know who goes to the hole in the wall and makes a fucken deposit.'

He sat on the table next to the mouldy turkey ham sandwich tower. I sat on the draining board and bounced my heels off the cupboard door below. 'I know where there's a rat's nest. What could I do with a rat's nest?'

'Who is it?'

'The rat?'

'Whoever it is you're pokin'. Who is it?'

'Who *was* it.'

'You chuck her?'

'No.'

'She chuck you?'

'No.'

'You're a fucken liar.' He pushed his glasses up his nose and crossed his arms.

I kicked my heels rhythmically. Buh-dump, buh-dump, buh-dump-bump-bump. The door detached itself and clattered to the floor. 'Oops.'

'Nice one,' Bonehead said. He inched his arse off the table and stood up. 'I have to head on. I've a wee job to do.'

'What did I tell you about workin'?'

'It's a wee drivin' job. I like drivin'.'

'You're gettin' sucked into the machine, Bonehead. You're condemnin' yourself to a life of slavery.'

'What the fuck are you talkin' about?'

'Work is for wankers. You want somebody to tell you when to eat, when to sit down, when to talk, when to go home, you want that until you're too old to figure out when you want to do it yourself and then you'll need somebody else to dress you and take you to the toilet and wipe your arse for yuh? You want that?'

'What in the name of Christ are you talkin' about?'

'Work. It's a trap, mate.'

'A trap w'money and cars and holidays and drink and new clothes. Oh aye, and soap, mate. Yeah, soap, that's what work does for yuh.'

'Whah?'

'Nothin'. Anyway, it's not that kind of job.'

'What kind of job is it?'

'They want me to get a car for them.'

'Who's they?'

He looked round the kitchen. 'Hammy an' ... all.'

I stopped swinging my feet. Bonehead dug his nails behind the thick black plastic edging that ran round the table, scraping out the gunge and looking at it without thinking. Hammy was one of the men who drank with Tommy McCullough in the Weirtown Arms.

'What the fuck are you doin'?' I asked.

'Standin' here.'

'No, y'tit. What the fuck are you doin' with *them*?'

'They're my mates.'

'No, I'm your mate.'

'Well, I'm fucken here, aren't ah?'

I glanced back at the demolition crew, slid off the draining board and leaned the cupboard door back up against the unit. 'Remember in old war movies, they always cut the motorbike Nazi's head off with a wire across the road?'

Bonehead loped across the kitchen in two steps and swung open the cupboards one by one, to find lots of mismatched plates and cups and a lot more foil-packed meat.

'Where d'y'keep the sugar?' he said.

'Haven't got any.'

'Well, y'know what that means.'

I get my lack of height, over-large dark eyes and small features from my mother. Nice in a woman. More than useless in a man. Or even a youth. She looked like a pretty wee girl. I just looked like a girl.

I'm not oedipal or anything but she was good-looking. And even though she pierced her nose and dyed her hair every stupid colour and wore clothes that other women sniggered at, the men in the estate flirted with her as she pushed me about the shops in the buggy. I know she had Prince stick things in his pockets in the Stop'n'Shop while she flirted with the fusty old man who owned it. My buggy was packed full of stuff too, down my back and under my legs.

Her popularity with the men made her unpopular with

the women and there was this one time a woman from the estate came to our door and dragged mum into the garden by the hair. Granny called the cops and eventually they were able to break it up but that woman never gave up. She actually tried to bomb mum with rotten cabbages once, down the shops when I was about seven. I swear to God.

The shops were in a square like the maisonettes – flats were built on top, but this time their front doors faced inwards on the square. There was a post office, a chemist, a butcher, a bakery, a launderette, a chippie, a bank, a hardware shop and of course, the Stop'n'Shop. The front doors of the flats opened onto a suspended balcony walkway, which ran right round the square and looked down over the shoppers.

The woman, Jean, lived above the bakery with a fella called Ian who used to materialise at mum's side every time she went to the shops. He would strike up a conversation and she would chat away because she was good at that. Good at small talk. She made people feel like she was interested in what they had to say. Even women, when they talked to her. But nobody ever got past that flirtatious small talk.

Mum was Jean's burning passion. She must have been saving those cabbages for weeks. I mean, it was a veritable cloudburst of rotten veg. We had to run for cover, all the shoppers, all the civilians, had to run, as Jean launched those cabbages into the square in total silence. Whhhhhhhhhhhhhhhsh-bshh! Whhhhhhhhhhhhhhhsh-bshh! Whhhhhhhhhhhhhhhsh-bshh! Mum laughed and laughed as we sheltered below the balcony. She couldn't breathe she laughed so much. She doubled over and clutched at Prince and my shoulders and we just stood there, wordlessly watching the old folks run.

Prince was quiet for days after that.

Glen Donaghy's problem was that he had two hands and only one arsehole. When he sat on that wee scooter, his thighs split over the seat like a mattress flung over the bedpost and his head was so well insulated with blubber he could hardly get a helmet to fit. His round features were scrunched up behind the visor and he was forever pulling the helmet off and leaving it hanging on the brake lever, his face red and sweaty like he'd just been born. He worked in a double-glazing factory in the same industrial estate as Weirtown Meats and he went to the bank every Friday lunchtime to lift his wages. He was only seventeen but his weight and height made him look a lot older. My lack of weight and height, plus my girly features, meant I looked a lot younger. And of course, like a girl.

Bonehead came with me to Dunnes to find a dress. I favoured the Sunday school teacher look, pearls included, but Bonehead thought I would suit something younger and trendier. I had the figure for it. We flicked through the sale rails and chose a short creamy coloured skirt with stud buttons down the front and a tight pink and red striped jumper. I paid for them with the last of my money but we had to steal the red tights and bra. Bonehead guessed 36B and was quite accurate, once we stuffed the cups with my old school tie, a tie Bonehead kept for court appearances and some socks – his, of course. Mine were a bit crusty and interfered with the line.

I got the superglue from the hardware shop and there was still some of mum's make-up lying round the house so I experimented all day Thursday. I also spent a few days eating a lot. And isn't it just the way that when you really need to have a dump, you can't? I sat on the bog on Friday morning, heavy orange make-up covering my bruises and accentuating my eyes, hair pulled into a tiny knob of a pony-tail below a baseball cap, skirt hitched up round my waist, tights spanning the gap between my para boots, pushing and pushing and pushing, but to no avail. It got closer and closer to lunchtime and I was beginning to panic. I was running out of time every way you looked at it. They'd smashed all the windows in the house and I knew they wouldn't drop many more hints.

Bonehead called round to see how the preparations were going.

'I'm on the bog!' I shouted when I heard his familiar bump-biddy-bump-bump on the door. 'Come on in!' I didn't even bother locking the doors any more. If anybody wanted to steal anything, they were welcome. If they wanted our stuff, they had to be really desperate. And if they wanted to come and kill me, at least I'd die doing something I enjoyed.

He appeared at the bathroom door as I sat on the pot.

'You're disgustin',' he said. 'Would you not even close the door?'

'I can't shit, Bonehead.'

'Here,' he said, throwing me a small brown and pink box. 'We had them in the house. I brought them just in case.'

I gobbled down a few. 'How long till they work?'

He shrugged. 'Pity you're doin' this the day. I'm goin' up the town. There's this Ford Puma that parks in the multi-storey in Chichester Street. You wanna see it. Black. Gorgeous. You should come.'

'Maybe next time.' He knew I wasn't into that but he always invited me.

He stepped forward and held out his hand. 'Seeya then. Good luck.'

'Thanks, mate. You too.' We shook hands in his biker style grasp, fingers up, over and round.

He left and on I went, the effort making me sweat and see stars. Finally I squeezed out one pathetic Malteser of a poo. I was exhausted. Thank God I would never have to go through childbirth. I scooped it out of the bog and carefully wrapped it in a Wrigley's Juicy Fruit paper. It was makeshift though. I had actually put aside a plastic box for this amazing shit I was going to produce.

I recommend a skirt and make-up to everybody. I was somebody else entirely. I was Andrea McNab. I still had para boots on but I walked differently. I slouched at first but then I positively bounced, well, as much as my injuries would allow. I totally loved it. Until I reached the shops and Mrs McAteer, an old woman who spent her days at the Stop'n'Shop and always smelt of piss, said, 'Ach hello, Lizzie. Hi y'keepin'? D'y'think it'll rain? Sure it always does, doesn't it? It does, doesn't it?'

Christ Al-fucken-mighty. She thought I was my ma. OK, so Mrs McAteer was a complete looper and everybody was surprised she'd managed to live this long but still. Christ. Still.

A sharp pain shot right through my stomach. Shit. Literally. Bonehead's laxatives were finally doing their work. I smiled at her and sped by, clutching my stomach, all my confidence gone. I skulked by the bank but Donaghy hadn't shown up yet. Shit oh shit oh shit. It had to be long after one o'clock. My stomach gurgled and cramps rippled all round my guts. I wanted to cover my bum with my hand but I was already starting to get odd looks.

I clutched the tube of superglue in my left hand and held the Wrigley's paper delicately in my right. Three times I stalked past the bank, head down, staring at my scuffed boots, sphincter clenched tight against the watery onslaught. Finally he rode up to the car park outside the square, like a tubby toddler astride a hamster. He took his feet off the pedals and held them out to the side to balance as he ran the scooter up onto the pavement. He got off and tugged at the helmet. And tugged. And tugged. Finally his fat head popped out and he looked round in relief. I stared in the window of the butcher's as he hooked the helmet onto the brake lever and headed into the square.

I didn't want to, I didn't want to, I didn't want to, but I couldn't stop myself. I walked past him as he headed for the bank. And he ignored me. I was really disappointed. I thought I was quite pretty.

I had to hurry. I was going to shit myself. I quickly emptied the poo into his helmet and tossed away the gum wrapper, then I squeezed a big blob of glue in after it and spread the rest along the handgrips, looking round the whole time. I hoped anybody who noticed would think I was admiring the scooter, but the people using the car park were too busy avoiding each other's eyes, inching back and forward in spaces created for a 1960's traffic flow.

'There's the rain comin' now, so it is.' Mrs McAteer's voice came from behind me.

My stomach bubbled and my arse muscles gripped like a thriller. I turned and smiled tightly.

'Y'keepin' alright then?' Mrs McAteer moved closer and clouded me in a whiff of piss. Mum always had time for her even though she was a family short of a picnic. The smell, plus the feeling that I was going to shit myself any second, made me feel light-headed and lost. Sweat made my make-up slick.

'I have to go,' I said, my voice unnaturally high.

'What about Buckshot?' she said. 'You and him was great, weren't yiz? His mammy passed away there. Seen his brother at the funeral but I never seen Buckshot. Did he never come back, Lizzie?'

'Ahm, no.'

'See the factory's payin' more people off? I like their sausage rolls. The Stop'n'Shop has an offer on. Two for one. Do your boys for lunches, so it would.'

Donaghy came lumbering out of the bank, tucking his money into the back pocket of his jeans. I felt sick and didn't know which end it was going to come out of first. I looked at Mrs McAteer in desperation. 'Cheerio then.'

'Nice t'see ye again, Lizzie,' she said. 'I think it's goin' to rain. Sure it always does, doesn't it? It does, doesn't it?'

Donaghy approached, looking at us in wrinkly-lipped disgust. He looped his hand under the helmet, flung it back and then jammed it tight down onto his head. He swung his leg across the scooter and turned the key. Whiiiiiiing, he revved it. Whiiing whiiiiing whiiiing.

Mrs McAteer took a step towards him and touched his elbow. 'What about yer mammy? Hi's she keepin'?'

'Fack aff,' he said, gripping the handlebars and leaning down over them, as if his bulk could ever be streamlined. He tilted his wrist to accelerate and away he went, bumping down onto the road, head down, elbows out, a speed demon, all of fifteen miles an hour.

'Awful nice fella,' Mrs McAteer said.

'Shit head.'

'You always look lovely, Lizzie. Hi do you stay so young? What's your secret? I'm goin' to bottle it and sell it, so I am.'

My stomach cramped again and I looked round in panic, seriously sweating now. I wasn't going to make it home. 'Bye then. All the best.'

'Bye bye, love. Watch that rain – catch ye out, so it will.'

I speed-limped through the shops, head still down, and hobbled up to the house in less than a minute. The fact that the hall was on fire didn't even stop me. I leapt the smouldering hall table and telephone – which had been cut off a month before anyway – and charged up to the bathroom.

There was shit on my tights. I sat on the toilet and let it all go. It was explosive. So much shit, so little time. I had to put the hall fire out.

Buckshot was the drummer. Pete Fleming played guitar. Paranoid Stuartie played bass and Mum sang. It was 1979 and I think she was 'great' with all of them, on and off. She had a very healthy appetite and didn't restrict herself to band members, or punks either. She had one yellowy polaroid of the band and she brought it out every summer, as the Twelfth of July bonfire was constructed on the stretch of green between our house and the shops.

In the photograph, mum and the band members are standing in front of the bonfire, washed pink in the evening light as the monster fire gains momentum behind them. They look like a half-hearted Boomtown Rats tribute band with their neck scarves, badges, striped tops and taily hair. Mum was going through her Deborah Harry phase. Her black hair is peroxide blonde, long and flicked out, her small lips are smudged glossy red and her high wooden heels look dangerous. She's laughing and waving a tin of Tennents with a half-dressed brunette on the side of it.

Paranoid Stuartie is on mum's left, bug-eyed and uncomfortable. He has a straggly, shoulder-length mullet he probably thought detracted from his prematurely balding dome. Pete, his face tanned and his hair bleached blonde too, is a smug Hugh Grant lookalike. He stands on mum's right, his arm round her waist and his lips next to her ear. At their feet, splayed out on the grass and apocalyptically off his face, is Buckshot, otherwise known as Samuel Buchanan. He's dark and thickly-built with a shaved head and a tattoo on his neck. Everybody said he was a mad bastard, but she said there was no harm in him.

The photograph was tucked away in granny's old handbag in the landing cupboard but I didn't like to look at it because it made me a bit sad. They looked pretty happy like. They had a manager and everything and played loads of gigs all over Belfast, in bars, Orange halls and gaelic football clubs, the original cross-community venture. But it all just fizzled out. Paranoid Stuartie got a job in Crazy Prices, which later became Tesco, and Pete went to London to become a session guitarist and played with some of the biggest bands of the time. He came back to Belfast in the mid-nineties and launched his own radio station, Sound as a Pound FM. Mum pretended she didn't know him.

Buckshot got a job in the factory and got involved with the PPA. He ended up with one of those faces you know has been pressed against a cold pavement all night. Later he disappeared altogether. Mum told me he probably left the country for his own safety. When he was drunk he used to list everybody he knew in the PPA and come up with a new and more inventive profanity for every one of them. The thing was, he also tended to get very loud. I think Mum was too busy choking on her own vomit at the time to really worry about it though. She almost killed herself, and nearly lost us to social services, except granny was there to look after us. And her.

Her near-death experience prompted a week-long disappearance, followed by a lengthy earth mother phase when she went veggie, wore tie-dye and flirted with wicca, but old punks never die. Her 'phases' meant she had a brilliant record collection and I had explored folk, trad, prog rock, African tribal, blues, reggae, ska and punk before I started school – where I learned to play the recorder.

The house was too damp to burn with enthusiasm. I'd
run out of coal three weeks before and with no fire of its
own and no neighbours to nuzzle against, the place had
gone dank and wintry cold. I stripped as I sat on the bog
and chucked the skirt, jumper, bra and shitty tights out the
bathroom window. I slipped my feet back into my boots,
ran downstairs, stamped out the smoking hall table and
then ran back upstairs to hit the toilet again. I did that a
few more times and when I was sure the fire was definitely
out and my guts finally emptied, I tumbled onto my camp
bed, pulled the quilt over me and grinned.

The hall had been petrol bombed. And even with time
to prepare, they still couldn't get it right. Probably got
some kid to do it, a saucer-eyed apprentice who thought

he was Jack Shit because the hoods knew him by name. It was probably the same kid who'd smashed my windows. Now that was something else, it really was. It was the night I got back from hospital. I was dozing off in bed when the whole house erupted, like every wall had come to life. Waves of overwhelming noise from every side, relentless crashes and smashes and sprays and thuds as bricks hit walls, ornaments flew and glass splatted. It just went on and on. At first I couldn't figure out what it was but then I caught on and just stared into the dark, heart thumping, breath caught in my throat, arms over my ears, waiting for it to end, waiting for me to end.

It did stop, eventually. Silence followed, and the purest stillness. Curtains swirled out softly from the windows and the lack of noise pressed against my ears like it wanted into my head. I listened to it for hours – a numb hush and then a distant whistling. Then the sun came up and I slept.

Prince came down the next day and helped me clear up the glass and board up the windows but he went home in a serious huff when I wouldn't leave with him. He tried to drag me out and we nearly ended up fighting, which we just didn't do. We play-fought and mucked around but we never really tried to kill each other, the way some brothers do. But then we were only half-brothers and maybe that made a difference. I knew he'd be back.

The nurse from the hospital leaned down over me. Her white uniform was tiny and low-cut, pulled in tight at the waist with a wide red belt and her long tumbling fair hair fell down over her shoulders. She shook her head and tossed her hair away from her neck as she came closer. Her top button popped open and she looked down in surprise at her smooth round glistening chicken fillets surrounded by roast potatoes and veg on a huge silver platter with gravy ...

'Jesus, Cookie, some tent on ye!'

I scrambled awake and blinked at Prince as he stood in the doorway of my room, his hair newly blue.

'One,' he said, 'the front door was open. Two, the hall is barbecued. Three, it's four o'clock and you're in bed. And four, are you wearin' make-up?' He came into the room, leaned a hand on the windowsill and hovered his arse over my bed. I drew my legs up just in time as he plonked himself down. The fabric stretched and the bed shook and strained unsteadily.

'And you're buck naked under there, arncha?' he said.

I backed up against my wall-headboard as he looked round the room. I'd brought the TV up and set it on top of my narrow chest of drawers. Plates and cups were scattered around the floor. Clothes were everywhere. I didn't bother picking anything up anymore. If it was on the floor, I knew where to find it.

He leaned over and lifted my matted hair away from my temple. Wilson's trainer had left a bubbly scorch mark and an uneven cut.

'Nike would pay for a photograph of that,' he said.

'Did you want somethin'?'

'Just visitin' the sick.'

'I'm not sick. Anyway, visitors bring presents.'

'I bring you the gift of ahm ... anticipation. We're havin'

a coupla mates round the night for Dave's birthday.'

'Nah.'

'Come on. It'll be a geg. Come up to our house. There's a bus in fifteen minutes. Come on.'

'Nah.'

'Why not?'

'Well, you won't let me come home again for a start.'

He leaned forward and scooped mum's guitar off the floor. He tucked it under his arm and shook the whole bed with a rapid burst of short, choppy downstrokes. He sang, making it up as he went along.

'You let me in, I sat in your room, you smelt like shit, while I sat in your room, come on come on come on you stupid fuck, I've got poteen mixed with clove rock, you know it you know it you know-hoooe-hoooooooe it. You stupid fuck.'

He looked at me, then he set the guitar down and leaned back, his shoulders thudding off the wall below the window, the back of his neck hitting the sill. 'This isn't very comfy,' he said. 'Move over.'

'Two of us can't lie on the camp bed.'

'Don't be so selfish. Move.' He squirmed up alongside me and the bed creaked and swayed ominously.

'Fuck's sake, Prince!'

'Move. Shift over.' He wriggled and wriggled.

'The bed's goin to break! Fuck yuh, Prince!'

The bed collapsed and we crashed to the floor, amid ripped fabric, torn wood and crusty tissues. We stared up at the violent puff of dust that drifted towards the ceiling.

'There. See?' he said, his green eyes close to mine. 'Now you have to live in my house.'

'I'll sleep in mum's bed, so I will.'

'Go on, y'freak. Sleep in mum's bed. Y'fucken freak!'

I tried to get my hands round his neck but he was always too quick for me. He tweaked me in the ribs and punched me lightly in the side but I was still tender and surprised myself by yelping. He eased off and I lay back.

He leaned down beside me on an elbow. 'I'm serious, mucker. Come to my house.'

'Can't.'

'Why not?'

'I have stuff to do here.'

He sat up and rubbed his hand through his blue hair, his back to me. I could smell the familiar damp of his green army jacket.

'Can I have that jacket?' I asked.

'You can have it if you come to my house.'

'Will you show me how to make me a Sunday dinner?'

'On Sunday?'

'Today.'

'By the time we get across town and then put a dinner on? Sure, that'd eat into valuable drinkin' time.'

'Aw.'

'I'll get you chicken and chips in the chinkie's, alright? Y'comin' then?'

'I would've, if you hadna woke me up.'

'Come on, get your clothes on. An' take the make-up off. You're like a drag queen on a dirty protest.' He took a pack of Bensons out of his pocket and lit up.

'Can I have one of them?' I asked, sitting up behind him.

He handed the fegs and lighter back over his shoulder.

'What's wrong you're on the Bensons then?' I asked,

lighting up. He was always trying to give up because he had pneumonia when he was nineteen and always took bad chest infections. Pneumonia and smoking were both serious disadvantages for a medical research volunteer but Prince just used Dave's name and national insurance number, which Dave gave him for Christmas the year before.

He sighed out smoke. 'Fuck me, Cookie, what could be wrong?'

I patted his shoulder. 'Don't worry, mate. I will go. I just can't. Yet.'

He glanced back at me. 'She's not comin' back, y'know.'

I said nothing.

'I swear to God, Cookie. Move on,' he said. 'She has. She had enough trainin' runs.'

'Aye, but she always came back before.'

He pivoted on his backside and swung his twenty-hole DMs round, his normally smiley eyes intense. 'I got a postcard.'

'Hurray, the postal system still works. What should I do, email the media?'

'Fuck up. It was from her.'

The bluebottle was back. 'What she say?'

'Nothin'.'

'There was nothin' on it?'

'Not really.'

'What the fuck does not really mean? Did she say somethin' or did she not?'

'You can see it. It's in the house.'

'Oh, right, that's what this is all about. Did you think I'd fall for that? Jesus, I'm surprised at you, Prince. Fuck away off. Go on, away an' fuck.'

He got up onto his knees, suddenly fierce. 'Well, fuck yuh, Cookie.' He stood up. 'Do whatever the fuck y'like, the two of yiz. Jesus Christ, I don't know. Fuck me ...' Mumble mutter swear mumble he went, stomping out to the landing.

I watched him go, then I got up and followed, the quilt wrapped round me. 'Houl on! Wait for me!'

The technical term for Belfast City Centre is completely fucken schizo. During the day, shoppers, students, shop and office workers buzz and dodge and fuss and flit, jamming the streets in chaos. Every Saturday, young punks, goths, skateboarders and drunk puking kids in baggy Nirvana sweatshirts hang about the grounds of the City Hall, more and more of them every week, from every background and every religion, coming up from behind the parapet for a peek. War torn? Us? Nah. We're modern, we're European, we're affluent, we've moved on, we're different now.

At night, the city centre is empty. Bereft. If you want a taste of Belfast at the worst of times, that's one of the places you'll still find it. No evidence of bombed buildings or bullet holes or anything like that. In the city centre, the bars close early, as if they're still in mourning. There's an odd atmosphere, a desperation seeping out of the walls and onto the streets. You feel it press on you and you walk quickly.

The heat is on the edge in Belfast. Walk five minutes from the heart of the city and everything changes, like you turned the knob on the cooker. Going south along the Dublin Road towards Shaftesbury Square, the bars flare up with laughter. The air bristles with cagey humour. But it's just the people and their stories. Belfast people are good at stories but they're raw as fuck, they really are.

Then there's the city's Hyacinth Bucket side. We know what we want to be and boy, do we try. That's where the line dancing, salsa, ice hockey and circus skills come in. And God loves a tryer, doesn't He? Or She, to enter into the spirit of millennial Belfast. Bring out your sexual preference, bring out your gods, bring out your artistic expression, bring out your fucken line dancing and we'll embrace it all because this is the new Belfast.

Hyacinth's bandwagon was getting more popular by the day. Me and Prince had to get off the bus in York Street near the Cathedral Quarter because the rush hour traffic had come to a standstill. I thought it was a bombscare but Prince told me otherwise. A street carnival was winding its way along Royal Avenue towards the City Hall.

The rain was flicking about haphazardly but the Christmas lights swinging about above the road made the parade almost cheery. The stilt-walkers' satin stick legs were whipped by the drizzly wind, kids with painted faces shivered as they tramped along in over-sized clown suits and blew the occasional whistle, and theatrical types in leotards, tights and huge papier-mâché masks zigzagged and twirled about the road, embarrassing everybody in their path. A line of tired Chinese carried their dragon by their sides like heavy shopping and a samba band rattled along grimly at the front. Ahead of them, walking backwards and ducking to take photographs, was Josie Baps.

I struggled to keep up with Prince as he strode alongside the parade, through homeward-bound shoppers and shop workers who glanced at the carnival with strained good humour. Prince approached Josie and touched her arm and she swung round and hugged him. I paced them, side-stepping through the crowd, as they walked backwards. He shouted in her ear and she stared at him for a second, then she shouted back in his. She dug in the pocket of her tassely velvet top and handed him something. He leaned in close, gave one of her baps a squeeze and left without looking back. He joined me and we out-paced the parade and headed towards the City Hall with its blinking Christmas lights.

'What did you just do there?' I asked, out of breath, as the parade grew distant behind us.

'Got an advance.'

'You dirty bastard.'

'You're gettin' chicken and chips in the chinkie's, arncha?'

We passed the City Hall and walked along Bedford Street against the flow of office workers heading for city centre bus stops. They looked at Prince curiously but he stared deep into the distance. He walked as though there was more gravity on his planet. Women looked at him because even with a weird walk, blue hair and a conspicuous scar, he was still far too bloody good-looking. Men looked at him in ridicule, disgust and envy, as they trudged towards the bus in suits from Next and Burtons. Nobody saw me. No, I stand corrected. A couple of spides in baseball caps and shiny sports gear spat on me as we approached the junction where Bedford Street became the Dublin Road.

'Tell your sister your ma was better!' I bawled.

Prince reached back and yanked me into the road between the cars before the spides could catch up. His pace was relentless and his reckless disregard for my life wore me out. I fell behind as we hoofed it along the Dublin Road.

'Come on,' he said, walking backwards. 'First the offy, then the chinkie's, then home.'

'Is Josie comin' the night?'

'Aye. Why?'

'Just wonderin'.'

'She wanted to ask you somethin'.' He turned and slowed to walk at my pace. 'Somethin' to do with her new job.'

'What's her new job then? Zookeeper?'

'Youth and community worker.'

'That's what I said.'

'She helped organise that parade back there. They're goin' to St George's Market to put on some display thing and then she's comin' up to our house. We've got a surprise lined up for Dave. It's goin' to do his head in.'

'What is?'

'It'll do your head in too.'

We called into the offy on Botanic Avenue where Prince bought three bottles of Buckfast, a half bottle of Kulov, and three litres of cider for me. We nipped into the Chinese for chicken and chips and headed round to Prince's house on India Street, one of the streets that ran off Botanic Avenue. I carried the chicken and chips like a hot water bottle inside my studded leather jacket.

Botanic was about as close to cosmopolitan as Belfast was going to get. In summer, restaurants set tables and chairs out in the street and everybody could flick on a pair of shades at a moment's notice. In winter, the windows of the cafes and bars were bright and steamy with laughter. Night or day, it was never deserted. It had an overwhelming student population, but families, hotels, bars, restaurants, businesses, beggars and down-and-outs all put up with one another in a kind of rolling time share arrangement.

The houses along India Street were packed with students and 'young professionals', all crammed into rented rooms. Prince and Dave shared a house with a Queen's student called Alex and a bloke called Damien or, as Prince and Dave called him, Satanic Hearses. He was from Cookstown and worked in the morgue at the City Hospital. He completely ignored me when I visited, which really pissed me off. He was tall and wiry and unnaturally oily and he kept his long, shiny black hair in a pony-tail. He spent his nights silently in his room, working out strategies for role-playing games with his other-worldly mates or writing poetry to read to his writing group.

Alex was an over-smart law student who was into rock

climbing and trekking and canoeing and was just too fit and energetic for her own good. She was fair-haired and freckly and had that sort of wide, chunky build that outdoor girls sometimes have. Friday night was her night for getting smashed in the Bot, a pick-up joint for students who couldn't wait to get a mortgage and disappear up their own arses, and other people's too, if the opportunity came up. She'd slap on the make-up before she went out and then she'd come back at half two in the morning, sad, tearful and alone, with her make-up forming a greasy orange tide mark round her chin. Prince told me the first time he saw it he laughed, but then she floored him with a drunken punch to the throat.

Alex and Satanic Hearses had rooms on the top floor, Dave and Prince had rooms on the first floor and they all shared the living room and kitchen. The carpets were so damp you couldn't walk around in your bare feet and the kitchen was a disaster area you ventured into at your own risk. The back yard was a stop-off point for the luckiest rats in the world. But Prince and his housemates had Sky TV so I thought it was bloody perfect.

It's hard to follow *Wonder Woman* when you're a litre and a half of cider down. It's hard to follow *Wonder Woman* at the best of times. I sat at the end of the settee, legs under me and a cushion over my lap, staring at the mute TV. The house had filled up with Dave and Prince's mates and they shouted along to some shouty oi somebody had brought on vinyl, falling over me as they stomped around the living room in monster DMs.

Prince was still in the bathroom. He spent forever in there. Dave didn't mind, he didn't wash much. He didn't like to waste the planet's resources. Even when he took a dump, he didn't flush. As for Satanic Hearses, I'm not sure if he actually had any bodily functions. It really pissed Alex off though. Whenever she wanted to go for a slash or put on a face, he would be in there.

She was very patient with Prince's friends and they were very patient with her. In fact, they were downright polite to each other, carefully moving out of each other's way and exchanging cheerful small talk when necessary. But she was losing patience with Prince. He'd been in there an hour and she wanted to get ready to go out. She hammered on the bathroom door.

'What the hell are you doing in there, y'big ponce?' she yelled. 'Come on, hurry up! I was meant to be away ten minutes ago!'

I heard him reply but I couldn't hear what he said.

'I'm going to find out what you do in there, you know!' she called back. 'I will not rest until I do! This is just not normal!' She clattered up the stairs to the top floor and I heard her door slam. The curiosity was killing her. She was dying to know why he spent so long in the bathroom. Nobody else really cared. Except Prince like. He cared.

Everybody on the screen smiled and *Wonder Woman* was over. I pushed myself up off the settee and flailed towards the stereo in that standing-up-for-the-first-time-since-the-drink-really-hit-you kind of way. I got a circus gasp and whooooa from the rest of the room and a giant skinhead called Mark caught me, set me upright and pushed me towards the kitchen, where there was another party going on.

The air was sluggish with smoke and rang with the screams and laughter of jumpy girls in short skirts and huge boots, who leaned against the cluttered worktops, smoking and smoking and smoking, waiting for the Prince of Ponce. A bunch of people in various states of crustiness stood in the middle of the room, gathered round Dave and his long and involved bong, made from an oil lamp, a bicycle frame and a recorder. You could actually play tunes as you sucked. Dave was my hero. He could play the theme from *Close Encounters*. Very fast. I tried playing 'Three Blind Mice' once and ended up on the floor, eyes wide with deadly paranoia, physically incapable of movement and Prince had to drag me out like a damp carpet.

I tripped across the room and pulled open the back door, desperate for air.

'Alright, mate?' Kloot said, as he jiggled nervously on the doorstep. 'Gonna invite me in or what?'

Last April, while Mum was off on an Ashtanga yoga weekend on Rathlin Island, Prince and Dave came down to entertain me while I got over glandular fever. It was a Sunday night and we still had a few neighbours at the time – two other families left in the block. We were just having a bit of a jam with mum's acoustic, nothing too intrusive. Prince had brought his Fender Squier Telecaster and amp, in case we felt like getting powered up, but they lay neglected on the floor.

I peaked too early, having greedily downed all the cider Prince brought within an hour and I was falling asleep on the settee when Prince decided to try the intro to Guns'n'Roses 'Sweet Child o' Mine', powered by Dave's pedal amp. I didn't even know they had the bike with them. They'd brought it on the bus and left it in the hall. When they linked it all up, I swear to God, it was like the worst case of horny cat you ever heard, so offensive even I protested.

It was almost 1 a.m. but on they went, Dave humped over the elderly Raleigh Triumph, puffing and pumping, sweating and grunting, Prince sitting on the amp in the middle of our small, smoke-fogged living room, ridiculously cool, feg in mouth, guitar balanced on a flexed thigh in the best-worst Slash fashion. And just these squealing, moaning, painful sounds, over and over and over, deafening one minute, dying the next. It took so much effort I could actually smell Dave. After half an hour, I was hypnotised. I was on another planet when the front door rapped.

Dave swivelled his eyes at Prince. 'Hnnh. Maybe we should eat the acid.'

'We did,' Prince said, watching something invisible crawl across the ceiling. 'Twenty minutes ago.'

Dave dragged himself off the bike, his eyes huge and distantly concerned, and opened the front door. Three masked men thundered in, a small bristly one at the front followed by two huge steroid munchers, all with baseball bats.

'Where the fuck do yiz think yiz *are*?' the leader screamed, looking round for something to smash. 'There's fucken decent people in this street tryin' to get some fucken *sleep*!'

Maybe it's because something like this scares the shite right out of you. And maybe it's because we're physically pre-programmed to require a shite-bubbling shock every so often. But when something like this happens, you get a horrible, distasteful, guilty buzz.

My arse froze to the edge of our elderly brown velour settee and I stared up at the masked men, motionless like a midnight bunny. I wondered how Dave and Prince were going to cope. I asked Prince about it later and I'll tell you pretty much like he told me.

All three hoods looked around frantically for something – anything – to break, but the room was bereft. Prince's arse disguised the amp, Dave's bike looked like it had been run over by a car, the 1980's stereo had boot prints in it and the settee looked like it had already taken a beating. Mum's acoustic lay in the garden where Prince had chucked it earlier when he got too drunk to fight with all twelve strings. The only other breakable was a small lamp on top of the stereo. Mum had made the base and woven the nauseous orange shade herself. Attached to the shade was a tinfoil star that Prince made as a Christmas present for her in primary two.

One of the bigger hoods spied the lamp and gave it a quick jab. Prince said it winked at him as it toppled off the stereo, tossing away its star like a base jumper's parachute. The hood nodded at his big mate in satisfaction but the lamp didn't break. He gave it a kick but it just rocked from side to side, mocking him. He went on jabbing with the bat and it went on dodging him and grinning and winking at Prince.

The leader suddenly pointed his bat in Prince's face. 'Was that you makin' that fucken racket?' His voice was Mickey Mouse high and he had the kind of bright intense eyes that by law should only belong to people who race motorbikes. He stared down at the tennis racquet Prince was holding. He followed the racquet's lead down to the rip in the space-time continuum Prince was sitting on. *'Well? Was it?'* he screamed, tilting his head like a Jack Russell.

'I am the light,' the lamp said to Prince.

'Was that you makin' that fucken racket?'

Prince stared into the leader's mad eyes. 'Kloot? Is that you in there?'

The leader squinted closely. 'Prince?'

'Prince?' the lamp piped up. 'What kind of name is *Prince?'*

'No.' Prince shook his head. 'Nobody knows about ...'

'Nobody knows about Prince?' Kloot glanced back at Dave. 'Nobody knows why we call you Prince?'

'No!' Prince struggled to ignore the lamp, which started dancing across the floor towards him, Eric Morecambe style.

'Nah, it's all right, mate.' Kloot straightened up and pulled off his mask to reveal his shaved head, busted tomato cheeks and a delighted grin. 'I'd be scundered too. Fucken Jesus Christ. Haven't seen you since school. I didn't know yuh w'the blonde hair. And the wee beard thing.'

'I didn't know you without your glasses on,' Prince said. 'And the balaclava like.'

'Well, have you ever seen a masked man with glasses on?'

'Hnnh,' Dave said. 'Is that why loyalist paramilitaries always miss?'

Kloot leaned into Dave's face. 'Fuck up, smelly.'

'Okey dokey.' Dave nodded.

'Jesus!' Kloot turned back to Prince. 'So what're doin'

w'yourself these days?'

'My light shines on,' the lamp said, hopping onto Prince's knee.

My brother sprang to his feet and brushed the lamp onto the floor. 'Fuck *off*, y'wee cunt!'

Oh yes, kids. Drugs are dangerous. Prince had to take liquids for weeks after Kloot smashed his left cheekbone with his baseball bat.

Of course he let him join the fucken band.

'You alright, mucker?' Prince said, patting my back as I bent double in his back yard, leaning one hand on the high pebble dash wall. Prince's hair was now green.

'Just had to geee-ugh-huuah-heegh!' Mashed up chicken, chips, gravy, cider and blobs of hardened fat splatted over the bursting black bags by the bin. Cider scorched the inside of my nose.

'Well, you will eat meat,' Josie Baps said from the top of the steps at the back door, arms folded against the damp chill of the yard. Behind her, squeals and laughter went on in the kitchen. Smoke drifted out all round her. 'You should have a cuppa tea w'fried food, not a cold drink. Tea'll stop the fat hardenin' up in your stomach.'

'Yeah, alright,' Prince snapped.

'D'y'wanna wee cuppa tea then?' Josie asked me.

'Nah, cider. I'm celebratin'.' I looked at Prince in disappointment. 'I just lost a litre an' a half a cider there.'

'Ah well, sure,' he said, handing me a piece of stringy pink bog roll. 'Drink the Buckie when y'run out. It's medicinal. What're y'celebratin'?'

I blew the cider out of my nose. 'Karma.'

'Who's she?'

'Don't know but she keeps comin' round.'

'Nice one.'

We went back inside and I found a space in the kitchen and drank the cider slowly. Josie sidled up on my right and settled her arm round my shoulders. 'Ach, look at your poor bruises,' she said, pressing my head into her huge baps. I thought about falling in a cold river.

Kloot sidled up on my left, tin of Steiger in hand. I swung the cider up and drank.

'Alright, Cookie?' he said in his chirpy, high-pitched voice. 'How's it goin'?'

I looked from him to Josie to Prince. Prince turned quickly and slapped his lips on some bird's face.

'Me and Kloot wanted to ask you a wee favour,' Josie said, withdrawing her arm and whipping out her Drum and Rizlas. 'Y'know I got a new job?'

'At the zoo.'

'Yeah. What? No, a youth and community worker.' She licked her roly paper, expertly tucking in the tobacco and smoothing down the edge – one of the few people so expert at skinning up they could do it standing in a headwind during an earthquake getting run over by a bus. 'We're organisin' another festival in time for Christmas.'

'Oh?'

'We've got a theme and everything. The New Sound of Ulster.'

I rattled an imaginary machine-gun into the air.

'Wise up, you,' she said. 'No, we've got the Chinese community involved and the Indian community and the

Different Drums of Ireland and the Belfast Breakers and DJs and rock bands and youth groups ...'

'Y'see, Cookie,' Kloot said, poking his glasses up his nose and wrapping his arms over his chest. 'I'm ah, I'm doin' this ... voluntary work in Weirtown.'

'Community service?'

He frowned. 'Yeah, well, I'm ah, I'm workin' w'like, y'know, like the youth clubs and after school clubs an' that sorta thing?'

'That sorta thing?'

'Gettin' them interested in music an' ah ... that sorta thing?'

'Flutes and drums an' that sorta thing?'

'Well, it is our ah, heritage, Cookie. But other stuff as well like. The wee girls are into dancin' an' all the wee fellas wanna be DJs. And then there's music they can do on the computer an' that. They're into all that. Josie thought it'd be good to get them involved in the festival, y'know?'

'Gives them an interest,' Josie said. 'So they don't get involved in, what would you call it, anti-social behaviour?'

'Aye,' Kloot added. 'It ...' He looked at Josie. 'What was that thing you said ... riches in the community?'

'Enriches the community,' Josie said, settling an arm round my shoulder again. 'What we were thinkin' was that maybe we could come up with a song for the festival?'

They looked at me expectantly.

'And?' I said.

Josie exhaled a gutful of smoke and hawked like she was choking on a chicken bone.

'Y'see, mate,' Kloot said. 'We sort of thought like, ah ... you bein', like, a kid an' all, and you bein' from ah ...

Weirtown and into music like, we thought maybe you'd get involved ... like?'

Josie sucked in an urgent breath to speak and let out another resounding hollow cough. She held up a hand, indicating for us to wait. She went blue, then red, then back to orange, and said, 'We thought you could write a song for the festival. There'll be kids from Weirtown and kids from Catholic estates and UTV'll be there and it'll get loads of media coverage and everything.'

'I'm very busy, y'know,' I said. 'I have stuff to do.'

'We thought you could write a song for peace,' Josie said. 'Just a wee one, like.'

'You,' I said to Prince, another litre and a half down. 'Fucker.'

'What?' he said innocently. He was jammed onto the settee along with four others who shouted and skanked along to the same oi record.

'*What*?' I mimicked. 'You volun-fucken-teered me.'

'There'll be TV cameras an' all. This could be your big break.'

'*Your* big break.'

'Lighten up, Cookie. Here, y'want to see this postcard?'

'God. Yeah.'

He sprang up off the settee and the girl next to him hooked her hand into his belt to tug him back down but he pulled away from her and fell over me. He giggled silently and pushed me away. He was a giggly, silly drunk. He would go all giggly and silly and later he'd go quiet and conk out and all the Buckfast he'd drunk would make him fall off cliffs and kerbs in his sleep. I'd be torn between getting him a blanket and setting him on fire.

I followed him upstairs, the blackened floral stair carpet swimming and swirling around below my feet. In his room, the abused bare floorboards were painted black and a double mattress lay on the floor, covered with quilts and clothes. Above the bed hung a purple lampshade with tassels and mirrors, more than likely a gift from Josie. Two full-length mirrors, both mounted on doors ripped from old wardrobes, leaned on one wall alongside his guitar and amp. Another wall was covered by an abstract mural, painted by Dave during his days at the Art College. He'd brought his tutor out to see it one time while Prince and some girl were still in bed. He said it was an installation called You're Not Supposed To Still Be Here, Y'Bastard. They had to do it another three times and Dave graduated with a first.

Prince's bedroom furniture was a small CD player and an unpacked rucksack by the bed, spilling over with clothes and CDs and magazines. He rifled through it as I collapsed on the mattress.

'Here.' He handed me the postcard.

I rolled onto my front and struggled to focus on the picture – a reproduction of William of Orange on his white steed, his luxurious long black hair falling down past his shoulders. I turned the card over. It was her handwriting, round and fat, primary school style. Prince's name and address were on the right and on the left was just one word. DICK. The writing swam. I tried to focus on the postmark.

'Amsterdam?' I looked up at Prince.

He nodded blankly.

'*Dick*?'

He nodded again.

'What the fuck does *dick* mean?' And why the hell did she send *you* a postcard? *You* and her didn't even speak.

He looked at me. 'Maybe I'm a dick?'

Josie bustled in and hugged Prince from behind. 'Alright, baby? What's this, a threesome?'

Cheers and whistles rose up from downstairs and Prince glanced back to the door. 'It's Dave's surprise!' He darted out the door and thudded downstairs.

'Happy birthday, Mr Daveeeeeeeey,' she sang in a deep breathy Marilyn Monroe voice, skimming her thick fingers under Dave's chin. 'Happy birthday ... tooooooo yoooooooooooooooooooh!' She threw her arms into a V above her head with a wide, lipsticked smile and curtsied, the pleats of her white dress spreading out and almost catching fire on Dave's roly.

The cheers were crazy. And yeah, it did do Dave's head in. He sat on a kitchen chair in the middle of the living room and stared, deeply in love and terrified at the same time. It was the same Marilyn who'd passed me in Gordon Street.

I tugged on Prince's T-shirt. 'Is that Mo Crowe? It is, isn't it?'

He didn't answer. He went on cheering and whistling.

'Jamember?' I said. 'Mo Crowe was the band's manager, jamember?'

Prince scrambled drunkenly towards Dave and made Marilyn sit on one of Dave's knees while he sat on the other. I turned round to face Mark and the bong. He held the recorder up to my face. I sucked and he covered the holes. Name that tune in ...

'Wave,' I said soundlessly.

Mark wriggled his fingers at me.

Shaftesbury Square, 1 a.m. Too dark. Too bright. Too many people, more to come, nowhere to go. Wide road. Walk. Flashes of taxi. Screams. Laughing. Whiney shouts and scary shouts. Girl runs. Girls run. Drink swear fight laugh. Taxi. He's eatin' gobble scoop gobble givvus a chip fuck off I'll kill ya y'gypsy cunt. Potato teeth. Stagger. Taxis. Taxi run you over. Legs don't work. Lamp-post. Laughing. Worried run.

Wake up. Pavement. Sore. Quiet. Peeler. 'Come on, son. What's your name? Where y'live?'

'It's alright officer, I know him.'

They both look down at me, stars behind.

Who the fuck? I know you.

'Boo.' He smiles. 'Up y'come.'

Arm behind my shoulder again I tired.

You know the shit in the bed scene in *Trainspotting*? Yeah? That's what made it worse. I wasn't even fucken original.

The quilt was heavy and light at the same time. The feathers crunched expensively as I rolled over, woken by the distant embarrassment of farting in a strange bed. The white quilt cover, the crisp white sheet I lay on, my clothes, me – all smudged with brown.

The room was twice the size of our living room, with a high ceiling and one wall made almost entirely of glass. Wintry sun shone through the window wall's drapey nets, making the white bed glare and the whole room squinty bright. The floor was a pinky white wood and a thick white rug snuggled up to the mile-wide bed. On the wall above the bed hung two huge flat blocks of abstract art. Even the frosted blue glass wardrobes and drawers scattered round the room seemed to have been created, not just made. There was a frosted glass door on either side of the room.

I threw back the quilt, ran to the windows and pulled back the nets. I was two stories up from a long mature garden which sloped down to a quiet, elm-lined road. I turned back to look at the bed. Shit.

I could smell bacon. Bacon and something sweet. Wait a minute, I could smell bacon and something sweet and I couldn't smell shit. I looked at my streaky brown hands, then sniffed at my fingers. I licked them. Chocolate.

I had to get out of there. The first door I tried led to a *Star Trek* bathroom. Light blue, dark blue, stainless steel, chrome, full bottles of shampoo and shower gel and a flat silver dish holding a pyramid of unwrapped soap. Thick fluffy white towels hung over a heated silver rack and a thick fluffy white dressing gown sat folded on the toilet seat. I swept it aside and had a quick deep orange piss, a guilty Goldilocks, then went back to the window. There had to be some escape. Maybe I was in the loony bin.

Definitely no way down from the window. I'd have to try the door. Prince's coat lay on the floor. I remembered taking it from his room before I left the party, but I didn't remember taking it off or getting into bed or even how I got there. I still had my clothes on and my bum felt fine so I figured I hadn't been introduced to gay sex. Yet. I shrugged on the coat and opened the bedroom door. The smell of bacon was stronger.

I was on a balcony that overlooked a wide, open

staircase, just like the one we had in school. If I leaned too far over the balcony I'd fall right down to the hall, two floors below. On the right, the glass wall stretched from the top of the house down to the ground, woven through with steel. To the left, more glass doors lined the route to the stairs. Mounted on the red walls were the kind of guitars I only ever read about, crucified for visual stimulation.

The whole building shook with an overwhelming wave of choral music, the kind you hear in museums about medieval times. I clamped my hands to my ears and looked about in panic. Speakers were mounted in the ceiling corners. Too many voices, holy and sanctified, too too loud for my hungover head. I couldn't escape it. I charged down the stairs, down one flight, then the next, where more doors led off another balcony, then down into the hall.

The front door was set in the middle of the glass wall, made of heavy studded steel, like something you'd see on a ship. I pushed at the handle but it wouldn't open. The noise went on, the red walls pressed down on me, the guitars hung in silent agony. I pushed and pushed at the door.

A small female hand settled lightly on top of mine. 'Don't you want breakfast? And maybe a shower? You're supposed to eat the chocolate.'

Ever been stoned? Not that kind of stoned. I mean the biblical stoned. With rocks. Lindsey Scott competed in shot-put and had an incredible throw for a girl. A skinny girl, at that. Surprisingly strong arms, astounding brute force and a machine gun cackle that could demolish walls. She found it funny to see me run. I wasn't born to run. I was born to sneak and if I had to, mouth off and slam down the phone. Running went against every law of my physical make-up. I ran like Big Bird, all straight legs, sticky-out feet and nodding from the waist. My brother was the same. He was lucky though. His height seemed like explanation. Me though. No excuse.

I hated PE and PE hated me. I was always good at the obstacle race though. I could squirm my way out of every difficulty but we only had that in primary school and once I reached secondary squirming still got me out of a few difficulties, but not all. Like the bin, for example. It was too narrow, I was upside down in a shallow layer of filth and the fall had dislocated my shoulder. I was pretty much stuck and in a lot of bloody pain. Lindsey Scott and her mates waited outside, cackling, rocking the bin and kicking the sides so I stayed there until a teacher ordered them to get to class. When it was quiet, I started calling for help.

Girls were monsters. They ran in packs and they couldn't just kill their prey, they had to torture it first. Cruelty increased their appetite and gave them team spirit and I dreaded being anywhere near them. It's not that I didn't like women. God no, I loved women. I wanted women. Unfortunately they weren't in the habit of wanting me. Wonder Woman was a goddess. Angelina Jolie was supremely wankable. Xena could kick my crap in any time she liked. Josie Baps was, well, Josie Baps was Josie Baps. But if a member of the opposite sex wanted me it was generally a bad sign. I fully intended to put Lindsey Scott out of her misery. Or at least, make her much more miserable.

The girl at the door was like nothing I'd ever seen in real life before. I guessed she was about eighteen but she looked younger and somehow older at the same time. She was smaller than me, open, relaxed and confident and she smiled to show perfect American TV teeth. Her reddish hair was chopped boyishly short and her clear skin was flooded with freckles. She had full unIrish lips, was spindly thin and dressed all in black.

'Do you have a headache?' she said, in a mongrel American accent. It had a European inflection and an Irish infliction. 'Paracetamol. Breakfast. Bed. The simplest things work best, you know. Come on.' She tugged at my arm.

'Will you let me out? I have to go home.'

'Boo'll take you home. Come on.'

'Would you open this door?'

'Don't look so scared. I'm not going to eat you.'

'It's not you. It's ... that music.'

She looked up at the speakers in the corners. 'It's how I get Boo out of bed. I'll turn it off. Come on, have breakfast.'

'Who the fuck is Boo? Where the fuck is this? Let me out. I have to go home. I have stuff to do.'

'Oooh. Grumpy in the morning, aren't we?' She turned away and walked to another frosted glass door at the end of the hall. She pushed it open with her backside and the smell of cooking drifted out, stronger than ever. My stomach was so empty I felt sick. I followed her, like Tom floating away from Jerry, on the waft of a freshly baked pie.

The kitchen was huge, all blue and black and modern with stainless steel everything. In the middle was a wide – well, I would call it a breakfast bar but that's far too working class. It was a wide, block-table thing, with a black and silver marble surface and high stools set round it. Mounted in the corner, up by the ceiling, was a TV showing *Friends* with the sound turned off.

The girl fiddled at a slim stereo slotted under the TV and the heavenly voices disappeared. The only sound was the bacon popping and cracking in a frying pan on a wide gas cooker. Fresh coffee filtered through a machine that choked and puffed steam into the air.

She waved at the stools. 'Have a seat.'

I slunk over to the stool furthest away from her as she swung open the door of a massive fridge, pulled out a bottle of mineral water and whacked the door shut with a foot. She spun round to a cupboard filled with glasses, took one out and slammed the water and glass down in front of me. She rattled round in a drawer and tossed me a pack of paracetamol.

'What is it you Belfast guys say?' she said. 'Work it?'

'Work away.'

'Yeah, that's it.' She picked up a tiny mobile phone and smiled at me as she thumbed at it. I swallowed the painkillers and heard a mobile ringing upstairs.

The ringing stopped and the girl spoke into her phone. 'Morning, asshole. I think your little stray needs attention.' She clicked off and smiled at me. 'You want some bacon?

We got eggs too. And soda bread and potato bread and croissants and pancakes and fruit and pastries and oatmeal and ...'

'Yeah OK. No wait. No I bloody well don't.'

She whistled something familiar as she opened a door to my right and actually walked into their larder. And flicked on a light. I have never seen so much food in all my life. Layers and layers, shelves upon shelves, multi-coloured cartons printed in foreign languages, assorted packs of every size, jumbo catering jars, dark, gloopy bottles, millions of tins, big fish, little fish, cardboard boxes. Announcing Lord and Lady Stash of the Republic of Bulimia. She stood on tiptoe and lifted a box off a high shelf, brought it out and used the contents to mix up batter in a bowl. 'Waffle mix,' she said, smiling. 'Waffles are great, aren't they?' She went on whistling and then stopped suddenly. 'You were pretty drunk last night.'

'Look, I have to go home. I have stuff to do.'

'Boo took you home but your house was all boarded up so he brought you here. You wanted to sleep in the car but he made you come inside.'

'I could sue you for kidnap and holdin' me against my will, y'know.'

The kitchen door swung open and the man with the annoying habit of shovelling me up off the floor padded in, in silent bare feet. He was late thirties, maybe forty, tanned and toned, with short sandy grey hair, bed-swept into mini whirlpools. He wasn't much bigger than me and was dressed all in black too. He was a fucken kitchen ninja.

'Good morning,' he said. His Belfast accent had traces of

other places. 'How's it going? You want some breakfast?'

'No I fucken do not.'

He looked at the girl.

'Don't look at her,' I said, sliding off the stool. '*She* said your stray needed attention but she's a headcase and you, mate, you're scary. Scoopin' me off the floor in my own house and then scoopin' me off the road? I *wanted* to lie on the road. I didn't want picked up to join your ... I dunno, fucken ninja food cult? And that cop let you do it! I want out of here and *she* wouldn't open the door. That's after she tried to kill me with medieval music torture. And guitars on your walls? I wouldn't like to see what you do to your enemies. And what's this whole fucken Boo thing? Boo? *Boo*? That's not a name, that's a fucken ... whaddya-macallit, a thing, a fucken *presupposition*, that's what that is! Let me out I have to go home!'

They both stared, shock blanking their faces.

Boo rubbed his hand through his hair, letting out a whispery laugh. 'Presupposition?' he said. 'I'm not exactly sure what ... well, you know, Boo's just a nickname. I didn't mean to ... I didn't intend to scoop you up, it's just, I couldn't leave you lying there.'

'What the hell were you doin' at my house in the middle of the night anyway?'

He sat on one of the stools but I stayed on my feet.

'I grew up in Weirtown,' he said. 'I went back one night to, you know, have a look and that's when I heard them ... and you.'

'Oh. Right. Well. What about last night? Why were you there?'

'You were lying on the pavement outside my restaurant.

You were putting customers off. I was as surprised as you were.'

My mouth clamped shut.

'And the door?' the girl said softly. 'You should have pulled.'

My hand tangled itself in my hair. 'I have to go home.'

'I'll give you a lift,' Boo said.

'I'll get the bus.'

'It's no problem.'

I got up and turned for the door.

'Presupposition,' he said, following me into the hall. 'You should become a lawyer. Or a copywriter. That's my advice. How are you at lying?'

'Your advice and your shitter are well met, mate.' I stalked towards the door – and pulled.

'You've got quite a mouth, y'know,' he said as I marched outside and down their lengthy driveway.

I turned back at the bottom of the garden. The house was a glass block, like a 1960's school building. I saluted him with one finger. 'Suck my dick, you wanker!'

He stood at the door, stared for a second, then reciprocated.

I looked left and right. The road was lined by tall bare elms and high hedges in both directions, as far as I could see. Behind them huge houses slept privately, each one different and worth more than the next.

Left felt right so I headed that way. It was a bright morning but cold. Decemberish. I walked for about five minutes and came to open gates at the end of the road where a sign said Malone Park.

Malone Park. Belfast's Kensington. Oooh, don't think so.

'Is that shit on your face?' Bonehead said.

'Would you still give me a lift in your ...' I leaned back to have a look at his long black car.

'It's an ex-police Granada, y'dick. Is it shit or not?'

'What do you think?'

'Get in. And keep the window down.'

I fell into the passenger seat. 'It's chocolate by the way.'

He screeched away from the high Malone Road kerb, his sudden overtaking flinging me about the car before I could click in my seat belt.

I'd called his house from a phone box, reversed charges, to see if he would pick me up. Big Julie answered.

'Have you left the estate yet?'

'No, not really.'

'Will you stop actin' the big man and just get out,

Cookie? They won't stop till you're either out or dead.'

'Just a wee while longer.'

'Christ, Cookie, y'stupid wee cunt ...'

I held the phone away from my ear and when she finally finished, I said, 'So canna speak to Bonehead then?'

I nodded off on the pavement as I waited for him. I was thinking about my next target. I calculated I would need around four hundred pounds – an ambitious plan but a master stroke. Invest and conquer, that was my new mantra. I could have, maybe should have, attempted something simpler but I wanted to enjoy it. And I wanted to get away with it.

I was hoping to get some kip on the way home but I should have known. I sat with my skull pinned back against the headrest, neck muscles strained like guy ropes, fists gripping the dashboard as Bonehead weaved through the traffic, cutting up, handbraking, donutting and sliding wherever he went. It was scary with Bonehead. But it was good scary.

He bumped the Granada up onto the green in front of our house, floored the accelerator, yanked on the handbrake and spun the steering wheel with his palm. We slid up to the bottom of our garden, perfectly parallel to the house.

'Right, bale, quick,' he said.

'What's the rush? I told yuh it was chocolate.'

'Just get out, will ya?'

'Why?'

'Geddout!'

'You don't want to be seen with me.'

''Course I don't want to be seen with ya. They want you out. I want in.'

'Why, Bonehead? You could do anything. You could be a fucken stuntman or anything y'wanted.'

'What the fuck are you talkin' about?'

'Drivin',' I said, turning to him earnestly. 'It's like ... a gift you have. You're wastin' it.'

'Get out before somebody sees.'

'I'm tryin' to help yuh.'

'Cookie, would you ever just get fucken out!'

'Well, fuck yuh, Bonehead!'

'Look, I brought yuh home, didnah?'

I got out and gave the door a good slam.

The passenger window wound down with an electric hum. 'Here, Cookie.'

'What?'

'Incredible medical freaks dot com.' He half-grinned. 'Glen Donaghy's scalp.'

'No way.'

'There's a rumour your ma done it though.'

'Put it on the internet?'

'No, y'dick. Shit in his helmet. But sure she's a nutter so you're OK, mate. You're OK there.'

When she first left, I was curious. Then I got a bit worried. When eight weeks went by and she didn't come back, I decided I couldn't wait any longer. I'd have to do some investigating myself. Not that I couldn't function without her. I just had to be more resourceful, and left to my own devices, I discovered just how creative I could be. I was much more skilled at shoplifting. I played guitar a lot more. I had more ideas for songs. I had more ideas in general and decided mobile phone theft was driven by mobile phone companies to make sure people kept buying them; human bodies should be recycled because the human soul obviously was; and all Ulster Way signs should be changed to Ulster Fry. Without her around to pass comment, I became more and more inspired.

Other than her best friend who died, she didn't really have mates – just people she knew from the shops or the courses she did. The closest she had to friends were the fellas in the band and I started with Paranoid Stuartie because he was more or less on my doorstep. He drove the poke van these days and would let you have a poke for as little as 20p. He also sold everyday essentials like cigarettes, milk, bread, pre-packed meat, Pot Noodle, poteen, Es, counterfeit CDs and Kelvin Clein jeans.

He did a couple of laps of Weirtown every night, playing a loud, fast, jangly version of 'We Are the Champions' then he parked near the Stop'n'Shop. The van was ancient and rusted with two flashing ice cream cones mounted above the windscreen like the horns of a comedy demon. It was covered in stickers of ice cream exotica like oysters and sliders and signs that warned people to beware of children. Three barefoot kids jittered around as I approached, their heads barely reaching the van's counter window. They turned and ran straight into me, clutching their chewie bars, 10p crisps and mix-ups in their grubby fingers. They yelped at me to fuck off you big fucken fucker and skipped away across the green, laughing and squealing at each other. Beware indeed.

Inside the van, Stuartie stacked cigarettes onto shelves by the window. Behind him was a slim bunker of potatoes, racks of lemonade and more tight shelves packed with anonymous and cheap lookalike brands. There were boxes and boxes of sweets and crisps, a small beer fridge filled with milk, butter and Weirtown Meats products and of course, there was the ice cream machine, just inside the window, with its constant companion, the box of mini Flakes. The interior was so crammed that if you wanted bog roll or the latest Celine Dion effort, Stuartie had to perform a spidery Tai Chi move over his stock to get it.

His skin was wrinkled and yellowed with cigarette smoke and he still had his long mullet but these days it started from ear-level. His beige shirt was saggy round the chest and strained round the middle and he sang quietly to himself, feg hanging out of his mouth, as he set packs of cigarettes on the shelf.

'Hiya Stuartie,' I said.

'Alright son?' he said, straightening the packs with both hands. 'What can I ...?' The feg dropped out of his mouth as he turned to look at me. He bent slowly to pick it up. 'Cooh ... Coohoo ... Cookoo ... Lizzie's wee fella?'

I nodded.

'I knew this would happen,' he said, staring. 'It wasn't me.'

'Wasn't you what?'

'I'm not your daddy, son.'

I searched for the right thing to say. Anything to say.

He lit a cigarette with the one he was smoking. 'Did she say I was?'

I shook my head slowly, jaw hanging down. 'That's not what I ...'

'Child Support's already chasin' me for two and they're not mine either. I'm gettin' the results the marra.'

'Yeah but ...'

'We were friends like, but you couldn't be my kid.' He

dragged his hands down the hair on either side of his head, a cigarette in each hand.

'But ...'

'I know, she was a good-lookin' woman and we were ... close but y'see, it just wasn't ...'

'No but Stuartie ...'

'I haven't spoke to Lizzie in a long time. Haven't seen her in ages. What did she say? What did she tell yuh?'

'Stuartie, listen ...'

'No, *you* listen. I've been impotent for twenty years.' His wrinkles suddenly smoothed out as he whispered, 'I said it.'

Somebody in a shiny tracksuit and baseball cap gave me an almighty shove and I went sprawling sideways. They leaned into the van, grabbed a huge handful of twenty B&H and the box of mini Flakes and slipped away as quickly as they'd come.

Stuartie leaned out over the counter and roared after the tracksuit sprinting across the green. 'Bastaaaaaaaaaa-aaaaaard! Waidy I get ye, bastaaaaaaaaaaaaaaaaaard!'

I scrambled to my feet and he looked at me, hair swinging round wildly. 'Were you in on this? You were in on this, weren't ye?'

'No!'

He leaned out over the counter, grabbed the collar of my jacket and swung me round.

'Geh-het off me-he-he!'

'Y'wee bastard!' He started slapping at my head. I yanked his hair on both sides, ducked under his elbows and ran. He hung out the window, roaring after me.

'Was that her? Was that her in that baseball cap? You

tell her I said she's a looper! You tell her that! She's a fucken *looper*! And y'can tell Ocean, or whatever the fuck his name is, he's not mine either! Yiz are all fucken *loopers, every one a yiz!*'

And that was all I got from Paranoid Stuartie.

I sat on the camp bed on the floor and thought hard. Work for the money? Nah. That would take too long and went against everything I stood for. I wasn't feeling the best anyway. My hangover was still hanging round and I hadn't eaten since Prince got me the chicken and chips. My head was airy and heavy at the same time. I picked up mum's guitar and mucked about with minor chords, high up the fret board.

I looked around my room for something to sell but it was hard to see in the dark. I wasn't surprised to find the electricity had been cut off. I couldn't turn on any lights but I could see my breath whirl across the daylight that slotted in through the sides of the boards covering the windows. The only thing I owned was a load of old books and nobody wanted books. Nobody reads these days.

I read everything. I read the back of the bleach when there was nothing else to read on the toilet. I read the ads for hearing aids and stair-lifts in newspapers. I read the textbooks from the linguistics degree mum did for one whole term. I read her philosophy books, her self-help books and her slimming magazines. I read the wee paragraph at the back of newspapers about where it was printed. I coveted the *Reader's Digest* and *Take a Break* in hospital.

I had a library of classics, mostly nicked from Bargain Books. I had a load of contemporary stuff too, mostly nicked from Tesco. Inbetweeners and lots of total crap – mostly nicked from the library. I had a couple of volumes of Seamus Heaney and Martin Mooney – mostly nicked from No Alibis bookshop on Botanic, where they wouldn't let me in any more. But nobody would want any of that. Even the kids who'd got into the house while I was away left them untouched. The wee bastards must have been disturbed because a big hairy dick they'd started to spray-paint in the smudgy, charred hall was only half finished.

They'd spray-painted big hairy dicks all over the downstairs walls and furniture. Not that I could've sold any of the furniture because it was all cheap shite anyway. The living room wall was sprayed with the words YOOR FUCKEN DED. The sentence was continued on the settee below COOKIE CUNT. I liked that. That was good. That would be my stage name.

The stereo was on its side. The turntable's arm had been amputated and lay nearby. Records were stepping stones across the floor. In the kitchen, the table was still in one piece but was on its side and another huge dick was sprayed underneath. There were dicks all over the cupboards and the meat was scattered everywhere. It smelt ripe and fishy at the same time. It reminded me of the day Prince lost his virginity.

I went on strumming the guitar, dying for a smoke but there was nothing smokeable in the whole house. I fiddled about, higher and higher up the fret board, picking out tighter and tighter notes. I sang a bit, low and mumbly. Wake to the glare of white. That was all I could think of. No wait. There is no easy way out, you know. Yeah, that was good. I sang it again. I liked it. I'd play it to Prince and he'd fuck it up well and good. Everything turned to angst when he joined in.

Americans paid big money for angst, he said, and when he got his shit together he was going to head over there. I said he'd be going without the talent then. He said he'd feel guilty leaving me in quarantine anyway. He'd been planning to go to the States since he was eighteen, when he spent the summer with a mate in Edinburgh – and the mate shared a flat with a couple of leggy tanned American birds. They loved Prince, although he went by Oisín over there. He told them he was about to join the priesthood and sang rebel songs about his mammy sitting by the ashes and his daddy the hunger striker, all made up as he went along.

Prods generally don't learn traditional Irish folk songs. If you consider yourself British, then you won't want to sing about what a sadistic and oppressive bastard you are, will you? So Prods made up their own songs. About oppressing Taigs, ironically enough. Not very romantic.

Pretty unfashionable too. So in Edinburgh, Oisín donned a crucifix and was holier than thou. He sure as hell wasn't punk then. He didn't dye his hair or anything. He did whatever he had to do to get what he wanted and right then he wanted lots of sex with leggy tanned American birds. His Celtic roots were a means to his end. Now that Kloot had joined the band, he had so much angst he looked up flight prices to New York every day.

But for all the slagging I did, I had this sneaky suspicion that I wasn't punk either. I couldn't sing punk. I couldn't even write punk. Everything just came out sort of wistful and folky. I could play my instrument, for God's sake. I couldn't help it. I tried sounding harder but I just ended up writing songs that had already been written. Once I thought I'd got it right only for Dave to tell me I'd written a song by Bon Jovi. I asked him to kill me. One time I even wrote a thrash version of 'My Favourite Things' without knowing it. That kept Prince and Dave entertained for days.

I heard a car outside and I stopped playing. It was a diesel. Not Bonehead's thing. It beeped twice – short, abrupt. I set the guitar down and stood at my bedroom window, peeking through the slot where the light crept in. It was a taxi. Value Cabs. The driver, in a friendly blue Value Cabs jumper, stood beside his car squinting up at our boarded up windows. He leaned back inside and spoke into his radio. I heard a crackly reply, then he ducked out of the car again and stared in confusion at our charred door frame.

He started for the house and I went downstairs and yanked and yanked at the swollen door. He stood on the overgrown path, totally bewildered.

'Hiya,' I said, nice and friendly like, when I finally got the door open.

'Taxi?' He frowned.

'You should know. You're drivin' it.'

The frown turned sharp. 'Is this 667 East Green?'

'Yip.'

'You ordered a taxi.'

'No I didn't.'

'It's been paid for an' all. 667 East Green, drop off city centre.'

'I never paid for it.'

'I don't care who paid for it,' he said, looking round our blind windows. 'D'y'want it or not?'

'Radio through and see who paid for it.'

He leaned back on one leg. 'If I get into that car, I'm not gettin' back out. You can get in if y'want.'

'I'm not gettin' in till I know who paid for it. You could be the taxi to the River Styx.'

'If you're on drugs, you're not gettin' in my car.'

'Fine.' I closed the door but he stayed there, looking up and round the windows. I opened the door a little and wiggled my fingers through the gap. 'Cheerio then.'

'You sure you don't want a taxi?'

He looked alright. About forty, short short hair, tanned hands, short short nails, plump spare tyre. He probably worked every hour to escape a catalogue-addicted wife and the kids who demanded every slice of shite they saw on TV. But he was self-employed which, if you were going to work at all, was the only way to do it. If he didn't want you in his taxi he could just tell you to fuck right off. If you started giving him lip he could drive you straight to the cop shop. He faced dangers, like getting shot or robbed or heart disease, but he had freedom too.

'Gimme two minutes,' I said.

He nodded once and went back to his car. I headed upstairs slowly, went into mum's room and opened her wardrobe. Floor-length denim coat, metal hangers tingling together, strappy sandals, stiff dead handbags, her smell. Nothing I could sell. I rattled open her dressing table drawers. Old greying clothes, slimming magazines, crumbling make-up, a photograph of granny sitting out the back in the sun, junky jewellery, a glove, a tin-opener.

A tin-opener. Jesus Christ.

I looked in Prince's old room. The bed had been donated to the boney years ago. The wardrobe doors were open and more of mum's clothes hung inside like tired flags. Prince's Nirvana poster was still on the wall. Nothing else.

I went into my room. I didn't want to look down. I looked everywhere but down. The taxi beeped outside. I scanned the bookcase again. I pulled out the drawer in my bedside cabinet. Books, magazines, fanzines, pens, crap.

I looked at the TV and watched my boot rise up and kick it, good and hard. It crashed to the floor and the casing broke away from the guts. My heart thumped oddly and I felt sick. The taxi beeped again.

'Fuck *up*!' I looked down and lifted her guitar by the neck.

I accepted two hundred pounds. He originally offered one hundred pounds for it so I actually did really well. I knew it was worth a lot more. I sat on the kerb outside the second-hand shop on the Dublin Road as late Saturday afternoon shoppers rushed home through the dark, clattering by on foot or thundering along in cars and buses. One way, out of town, busy busy busy. Get home with new stuff, dump it on the bed, don't look at it, watch shallow TV shit, splash water, spray deodorant, head out, drink and laugh and piss, drink and laugh and miss the pisser.

I sat for a long time, elbows on knees, hands in hair, arse frozen. Nobody looked at me. I wasn't there. I was in the town with mum and Prince. I was nine, Prince was fourteen. She'd just got the money through from granny's endowment policy and she bought me a duffle coat. I didn't want a duffle coat. I wanted a CD player. But I got a duffle coat. From British fucken Home Stores. She said that's what granny would have wanted. She got Prince big, sensible shoes from Clarks and enrolled herself in a ballroom dancing class. Because that's what granny would have wanted.

We trailed behind her as she whizzed through the crowds towards Bridge Street. Prince nudged my elbow, leaned in close and said, 'Look.'

I stared through my tearful huff at his red plastic lighter.

'We'll burn it,' he said. 'Just make sure you aren't in it.'

Two hundred pounds. I could get a CD player. I could get CDs. I could get ... well, I could get a CD player and CDs. I could go to the army surplus or the Doc Martin shop and get new boots. I could get chicken and chips from the chinkie's. Twice. Loads of times. Fuck the campaign. I could get stuff. I could get ... a CD player. And CDs! I tucked my feet under me to get up but somebody sat down heavily beside me. An arm went round my shoulders. The arm's owner smiled at me, cheery pink and wavy drunk.

'Merry Dickmas, Chrishead!'

She was mid-forties, with short, glossy brown hair and too much make-up. She smelt of vanilla and money as she nuzzled into my neck. She raised her head with a frown. 'You're fusty.'

I tried to stand but another woman pressed down on my shoulder from the other side. She was mid-twenties, with shoulder length fair hair and small oval glasses. 'We thought you looked lonely sitting here,' she said. She'd been drinking too but wasn't as far gone as her friend.

'Here,' the older one said, pulling a selection box out of one of the bags that lay abandoned around them. 'I have a Chrissy prezzie for you.'

'It's not Christmas yet.'

'Don't be so anal. Here.' She offered me a Snickers, a Fudge and a Bounty. 'So what's your name, baby?'

I took the Snickers. 'It's ... Nicholas, *baby*.'

'I'm Judith,' she said. 'This is Aoife. She's a wonderfully buxom, flaxen-haired virgin.' She flashed Aoife a beautifully mean smile. 'She's my PA.'

'Happy days,' I said, standing up. 'Well, cheerio then. I have to go. Stuff to do, y'know.'

Judith suddenly wrapped her arms round my thighs. 'Dear Santa, please bring me him for Christmas.' Her over-made up eyes were almost tearful. 'Look at your skin. Not a spot, not a wrinkle. Aoife, love, take a note. From now on, it's total neglect for winter skin.'

'Come on, Jude.' Aoife got to her feet. 'Leave him alone. He's only a wee boy.'

'My feet are size nine though,' I added.

Judith let go of my legs and put her head in her hands. 'Fuck it.'

'She langered?' I asked Aoife.

'We were celebrating,' Aoife said. 'She just sold the family business. Made a mint.'

'Confectionery business?'

'*Bellefest*.'

'Well, fuck me.' *Bellefest* was a local glossy magazine, popular because it printed millions of photographs of every social event in the country, from school formals to the Pig Farmer's Ball. People bought it to see if they were in it but anybody with any sense would just go to the doctor once a month and read it there. 'Why would anybody buy that shite?'

Judith looked up at me. 'I knew somebody would find me out.' She wobbled to her feet, crashing into Aoife who crashed into me as she struggled to hoist her boss. I chucked the Snickers over my shoulder as I stalked off but Jude followed. She was taller and heavier than me, with a wide, angular face. She swung me round and gripped my elbows.

'Tell me why *Bellefest* is so shite. C'mon, tell me!'

'Get off me, y'bloody mad woman! Get off!'

She shook me by the arms and I could easily have stamped on her high, pointy boots and ducked and twisted to escape but that would have been letting her off too easy. And being small and skinny and looking like a girl has its advantages, you know.

'Help!' I called to passers-by. 'Help! Kidnap! Child abuse! Help!'

If you're going to choose anywhere to fall or faint or be abused, you won't do better than Belfast. People still have a village mentality. They pride themselves on it. Two old ladies and a man in his thirties came to my aid. Behind them came three studenty looking girls and a well-off couple in their fifties.

Judith pressed me to her breast and covered my head with her arm. 'It's OK!' she laughed. 'He's my son. We had a bit of a fall out. He's in theatre. You understand.'

I was right in there like. Right up against her black

cotton shirt, right next to her gaping pearly buttons, tight against her warm vanilla skin.

'Mother and Nicky are always fighting,' Aoife said. 'Thanks now, really, it's OK, bye now, bye.'

I stayed right where I was. I knew when I was well off.

Bonehead's ma had paid for my Value Cabs taxi from Weirtown. She was determined like, I gave her that. She'd even sent me a ticket for the ferry in the post and when I didn't use it, she put an envelope through my door with one hundred pounds in it and a note that said 10 O'CLOCK MONDAY MORNING BELFAST CENTRAL TO DUBLIN. TICKET RESERVED PAY AT DESK. I took a breath, ate the note and pocketed the money.

I wouldn't have said she was mum's friend but they knew each other. I asked mum did she not like Big Julie and she said she thought Julie was dead on. She just preferred not to associate with Julie's husband or his mates from the factory. She said when that Catholic taxi driver was murdered years ago, everybody knew it was the PPA. But nobody talks beneath the parapet. That would just defeat the point.

I remember heading out to play on a Sunday morning. I stopped suddenly as I passed the TV. There's our shops! Look! That's where we live! On the TV! Look! Granny was peeling potatoes in the kitchen, Prince was still in bed and mum hadn't come home from the night before, so I think I was just talking to myself.

I was amazed and delighted when I went outside and it was still sunny and misty like it was on TV and I went to Buckshot's flat to tell mum. I could hear church bells in the distance, tiny but definite, but it was quiet like I'd never heard before. Sort of thick and heavy. People looked at each other too long as they passed in the street. They didn't seem to see me.

The door was never locked so I let myself in. Buckshot was perched on the edge of his crusty blue velour settee and mum was stretched out behind him, asleep in a heap. I remember the smell of his dog mixed with cigarettes, glue and Savlon, which he slathered over a flaky PPA tattoo on his calf. He didn't look up. I was only about six but I remember being annoyed.

I never liked him because he told me you could get pregnant from eating beans and everybody laughed so I knew there was something fishy about it. I knew I shouldn't care what he thought but I was still too embarrassed to wake mum and explain the whole TV thing in front of him. And that made me dislike him even more.

I sat on the hearth and waited for her to wake up, listening as he rattled off a long loud list of obscenities to nobody in particular. He went on rubbing in the Savlon and I developed a thick sickening headache. I still get phantom headaches if I even think about glue. He staggered to the window, one trouser leg up, the other down, and I started to think I was still in bed and dreaming. His sentences came out like machine-gun rounds interrupted by Sunday morning silence. Fucken dirty *fuckers* fucken dirty *fuckers* chased itself around the room and shot out the window. I wasn't sure if I was there or not.

It was only when he sat down and brought the fissly plastic Stop'n'Shop bag up to his mouth that he looked at me. But he still didn't see me. I definitely wasn't there. He fed on fumes and she groaned herself awake and struggled up behind him like a drugged lab rat. She stumbled off the settee, took my hand and trailed me out, whacking her shoulder off the door frame as she went. It might not have been on a hair trigger, but my mother did actually have a bit of sense.

Which I didn't inherit.

Jude and Aoife took me to an Italian on the Dublin Road and we drank white wine which was so dry it made my gums recede. I ordered a pizza and tried to eat it but Jude had slipped off a pointy ankle boot and kept nuzzling her toes along my thigh. She wouldn't let me drink the water so I had to keep nipping out to the bog to lap from the tap, fingers grasping at the porcelain, eyes swirling at reflections in the chrome.

She bought me daiquiris, choc pops and fuzzy navels and in gratitude I showed her my whipping the tablecloth from the table and spilling everything on the floor trick. She showed me her removing her bra just by wriggling trick and I rallied with the old fling your bra across the restaurant trick. Her amazing disappearing courgette routine almost beat my ability to eat anything and every-thing trick, but in the end my involuntary regurgitation all over the floor was a showstopper. She showed me her fight with the management trick, Aoife showed us her pay for damages and loss of trade trick and the police showed us the door.

We hit the air of night time Dublin Road carousel lights and taxi upside down trick, oh no, it's me! Face first on the pavement. Up, wey hey, m'OK, m'OK! Look, see? Fall into taxi, giggle. God I'm snoggin' her how? Aoife's in the front tellin the driver where to go and I want to go to Prince's house too drunk tired but I'm snoggin' this woman in the dark in the back and I don't want to go to Prince's house

Where's this? Nice, fancy new apartments. Cul-de-sac, hey that's me! S'me, so it is! Lift up to her apartment like antique shop *House & Garden* cover pic, izzen it lovely baby? Snoggin' in lift snoggin' in doorway my balls her hand and Aoife smiles, retreats, wave night night children, nice friendly nurse

I'm in the bath such a boner oh God oh God don't I will don't I will. Follow her shivery wet. Wrought iron bed, wide window, lights from the street, cool hot vanilla skin, taste, eat the courgette, Jude I will don't Jude I will don't Jude fingers move don't I do

How much? Whuh?

Woke up and tried to turn but I was stuck. I laughed. I thought it was a joke. This is funny ha ha Jude this is funny. You can uncuff me now. No really. Jude.

The room was lit by grey Sunday morning light and I was face down on the bed, naked and getting cold. The cuffs were linked behind the wrought iron frame at the head of the bed and my ankles were tied to the frame at the bottom with silky scarves. And such a headache. Blind squashed eyeballs.

'Jude?'

No answer.

'Jude?'

I looked round. The open-plan apartment was like a French Revolution film set. Ornate candleholders on high white walls, huge curly gold-framed mirrors, wide couches draped with velvet throws, thick woolly rugs on a deep red carpet.

'Jude?'

Nothing.

'Jude!'

I pushed myself up onto my elbows and looked at the cuffs. Heavy, sturdy and tight. They were real. I tried pulling my hands through but my bones would only squeeze so far. Pulling and pulling, I started raking off skin.

The apartment erupted to deafening techno.

'Hey, baby,' she said, appearing by the bed.

I twisted round to look at her. At least, I think it was her. She wore a black rubber mask, all shiny and squashing her mouth through an odd hole, like a dodgy American wrestler. From what I could see of her skin, it was flushed pink. Her hard brown nipples were forced through a black, strapped and buckled corset thing and she had a big rubber strap-on chap on.

'*Techno*?' I said.

She climbed onto the bed.

I asked her not to. I asked her quite a lot. But I was stuck and she did it anyway.

I walked down Stranmillis Road with five hundred pounds in my pocket, my fingers hooked round a litre of Sunny Delight and a mini CD player in a plastic bag. I had a thick wad of toilet roll wedged between my cheeks and I could hear the airy whistly noise that our window frames made. It came and went. It shouldn't have done either of those things, seeing as I was miles away from Weirtown and nowhere near our window frames. I looked around the street but the sound kept dodging me. If it wasn't our window frames, then it must have been something falling in the distance. Must have been.

The sky was seamless grey and my boots scuff-shuffled through the final few leaves on the pavement. Twenty minutes would take me to Prince's house. I couldn't go very fast and I knew I was walking funny. Restaurants and cafes had coloured Christmas lights round the windows and people drank coffee and read inside. Catholics headed to mass and Prods bought the papers. A trendy dad pulled up outside the newsagents and jumped out of his Merc, engine still running. He ran into the shop, leaving a wee girl in the back shaking a finger at the scruffy terrier beside her.

The Sunny Delight was good. Fresh bread smells were drowned out by diesel fumes as buses shuddered past. I followed the road downhill, past the Ulster Museum and through the gates on the right into Botanic Gardens. Families and dogs and drunks sloped about the shady green. I could smell the trees and breathed in pine fresh damp. Out the other side of Botanic Gardens at the top of Botanic Avenue, all downhill. The street was having a day of rest. People wanted coffee, papers, nothing more.

Past Dunkin' Donuts where a small skinny girl came out, carrying a cardboard tray with tall paper cups. There was a paper bag balanced between the tray and her barely-there chest. She was dressed all in black. She stopped to smile at me.

I looked left where the whistly noise was coming from but it was gone before I could see. I felt around in the plastic bag and popped open the CD player and handed her the techno CD. I felt her watch me as I turned into India Street, then knocked on Prince's door.

Somebody thumped down the stairs inside. Satanic Hearses opened the door and looked above my head and around the street. I slipped in by him and took the stairs one at a time, holding onto the banister. Turned right on the landing and into Prince's room at the back of the house. Dark and sleepy warm. There was a blonde toss of hair on the pillow beside him, facing away from the door. I knelt beside the mattress, Sunny Delight and CD player on the floor beside me.

'Prince.'

He didn't move.

'Oisín.'

He twitched, rolled over and looked at me, unfocused and bleary blank. His squashed hair was pink.

'Can I sleep in your bed, Oisín?'

My favourite fire engine is the one with the extendable ladder. That's glamour. That's anticipation. Help help! Our hotel/hospital/block of flats is on fire! And firemen. They're class. If they thump some kid for lighting fires, you'll never actually see them do it. They're very professional. It pisses me off when people brick them just for helping, the way they do here.

I stayed in Prince's bed for a couple of days. He wanted to get a doctor and Josie made me drinks called Sideshow Melons and Strawberry Succubus but I assured them I was absolutely fucken fine and they could just fuck away off and leave me a-fucken-lone, thanks very much. I was thinking. I was recharging. I was making plans. I had my money and I had the third wave to take care of. The only thing that distracted me more than they did was the postcard, still in Prince's rucksack.

I would have been happier knowing nothing. When you know something, even when it's almost nothing, your brain will try to make more of it. Maybe the letters stood for something. Dabbling In Calvin Klein. Don't Incite Commando Kids. Dutch Idiots Come Kwick. Maybe she *did* mean Prince was a dick. Maybe she meant she was a dick. Maybe she meant King Billy was a dick. None of that was new.

Prince slept on the settee and I knew I was cramping his style but he didn't complain. He said when I got my money through from the Criminal Injuries Board we'd head over to the States. When he asked what was happening with Wilson McCullough and the hoods, I said I hadn't heard back from the cops yet. I couldn't tell him I dropped the charges. McCullough and his team deserved a much better form of retribution than that. It would mean extending the campaign but I'd enjoy it. I couldn't tell Prince though. He wouldn't understand. He wasn't a strategic thinker.

I finally got out of bed when the smell of curry got to be a bigger distraction than Prince, Josie and the postcard put together. I love curry. Not big, mad, burn-the-face-off-you-curry or anything like that. I love it when you can taste loads of different layers and that was the kind of curry Dave made. He was self-appointed King of the Kitchen and made potato waffles and chicken burgers for Prince and Alex, meat and two veg for Satanic Hearses and ventured into the ethnic whenever Josie was there. Ever see a map of the tongue? Dave's curry toured it wearing flip-flops.

Josie and Prince sat in the living room and watched as I bypassed them for the kitchen. Dave stood by the cooker, stirring and poking at a battered silver saucepan, swaying to a tune in his head.

'Hnnh, alright, ugly?' he said.

'Would there be enough for me?' I nodded at the saucepan.

'Pilau or naan, peshwari or plain?'

'Fuck your mantra, mate. I just want somethin' to eat.'

'See? See? I told them!' He grinned and folded his spoon round the pot, swaying double time. 'Hnnh!'

I sat in my usual corner on the settee, Josie sat the other end and Prince had slid down in an armchair, tartan bondage trousered legs stretched out across the room and crossed at the ankles. The local evening news was whining away on the TV.

'Anything else on?' I asked.

'We're watchin' this,' Josie said.

A reporter stood in front of a smouldering building, frowning into the camera. 'Police have not yet established whether the blaze which gutted the Weirtown Meats factory was accidental, although there is speculation that it was a deliberate attack by loyalist paramilitaries. The fire is part of a run of bad luck that has included investigation for fraud, the loss of a major order to supply a mainland grocery chain and most recently, a further round of pay-offs.'

'Class,' I said.

'You're heartless,' Josie said.

'Fuck 'em.'

'All those people are out of jobs and it's probably over

protection money or somethin' daft like that. They're just ordinary people. They don't deserve that.'

'Capitalist bastards.'

'Jesus, Cookie,' she said. 'You have no idea.'

'I have lots of ideas.'

'That's his fucken problem.' Prince rapped his knuckles off my skull. 'It's fucken dangerous in there.' He stood up and called out to the kitchen. 'Dave! When'll the curry be ready?'

'I'll put it on low, will ah?' Dave called back.

Prince disappeared up to the bathroom and Josie continued to stare at the news. Her shoulders were stiff and her eyes occasionally slid over to me.

'Say it before you explode!' I told her.

She crossed her legs and swung a DM towards me, smiling and shifting her chest round in my direction. 'I was just wonderin' did you have any thoughts yet, y'know, about the wee song?'

'What wee song?'

'For the festival. Only two weeks away, y'know.'

'Oh aye. I've thought of somethin'.'

'Brilliant! It's awful hard gettin' people to commit.'

'I was thinkin' you could tell Kloot and his Weirtown inbreds to go and fuck.'

She looked at me like I'd just run over her pet rabbit. Twice. Forward and back.

I lifted Prince's cigarettes and sparked up. 'Look, it's not you, alright?'

'I'm not doin' this for me,' she said. 'If we're goin' to move on in this country, everybody needs to show a bit of generosity.'

'Kloot's not bein' generous, Josie. It's community service. It's punishment. And you're gettin' on like it's a new dawn. It's not.'

'Even the community leaders are joinin' in,' she said. 'Even they see it's a good thing. People are beginnin' to see that this is the only way forward. Kloot included.'

'The whole thing makes me suspicious.'

'When people's eyes are opened, their minds are opened too.'

'Who writes that shite?'

'I do. In the sponsorship pack.'

'Oh right, well. I don't want anything to do with it.'

'Prince'd like you to do it.'

'He can do it well enough without me.'

She bit her lip. 'I don't think he can.'

I felt my head tilt as I listened to the noise again. Window frames. No

'You alright?'

'Couldn't be better.'

The front door opened and Alex jigged into the living room. 'Bursting for a pee. Back in a minute.' She bounced up the stairs two at a time and rapped at the bathroom door. 'Prince? You in there?'

'Fuck off.'

'I'm going to wet myself!'

'Use the alley like everybody else.'

She hammered on the door with both fists. Dave wandered into the living room, eyes turned up to the ceiling. 'Is that a chinook?'

Alex flew down the stairs, sprinted through the living room and kitchen and slammed the back door on her way out.

Dave squeezed himself onto the settee between Josie and me, lifted the remote and put the Discovery Channel on. We watched elephants humping in silence. 'Are you growin' dreads?' he asked me.

I lifted a strand of matted hair. 'Dunno.'

'Is he growin' dreads?' he asked Josie.

She didn't answer. She just held her head in her hand.

There was a polite tap at the open front door and a small voice said, 'Anybody home? Hello?'

Josie went out to the hall. 'Help yah?'

'I'm lookin for somebody. Little punk guy? Does he live here?' She had an odd, half-American accent.

'Cookie? You want Cookie?' Josie said. 'You'd be the only one, love. Come on in.'

She showed the small, skinny girl into the living room. She was dressed in a neat, knee-length black coat with a high neck and wore a reflective record bag the same way I wore Prince's.

'Want some curry?' Dave asked her.

'I've already eaten,' she said, smiling. 'Thanks.' She opened her bag and brought out a cow's tongue aargh whistly noise fuck. No, she brought out a badge. 'I just came to give you this. You left it in Boo's guest room.' It was Prince's Stiff Little Fingers badge. Actually, it wasn't Prince's Stiff Little Fingers badge, it was *my* Stiff Little Fingers badge, because he gave it to me. Formally, like, rather than me just taking it. He knew I liked them. And I didn't even know I'd lost it. I was glad he wasn't in the room.

I took the badge. 'Thanks very much.' I had Barry

McGuigan's voice.

'Boo?' Josie turned to me. 'You know Boo?'

'Boo who?' Dave said.

'The restaurant fella.' Josie said.

'We kind of met by accident,' the girl said.

'D'y'think Boo would be interested in sponsorin' a very worthwhile community event?' Josie launched into sudden sell mode. 'All kosher of course. Partly government funded. Banks and bars and businesses have already committed, so they have.'

'I think he might need more information,' she said.

'Here. Take a sponsorship pack.' Josie leaned down behind the settee and almost whacked the girl with the DM she stuck out to balance herself. She handed over a thin transparent folder. 'I'll ring him at the restaurant and say I was talkin' to you, would that be OK? What's your name? Seein' as Cookie was too ignorant to do the introductions.'

'I'm Jay.'

'Brilliant,' Josie said. 'I'm helpin' to organise it, Dave there, and Cookie and Cookie's brother, they're all doin' their bit. The theme's The New Sound of Ulster.'

'Sure, I'll say to him,' Jay said. 'He's into music. It is music, isn't it?'

"Course,' Josie said.

Jay smiled again, her perfect smile. 'Well, nice meeting you guys.'

'And you,' Josie said. She pulled me up by the T-shirt and pushed me after Jay as she headed for the door. 'Say cheerio then!'

Jay turned on the doorstep and smiled again. 'Bye then.'

I flicked away my cigarette butt and turned the badge over in my fingers. 'Thanks for bringin' this round.'

'I thought it might have sentimental value or something.'

It did. He liked Stiff Little Fingers even more than I did.

'I still have that CD you gave me,' she said. 'I didn't know what you wanted me to do with it.'

Whistly noise. 'Bin it.'

'Best thing for techno. What is it you guys say then? Safe home?'

'I say it to you. 'Cause I'm already home. Sorta.'

'Oh, right. You say it to me then.'

'Safe home.' I tried out her name. 'Jay.'

She walked half-backwards down the garden path. 'Bye then. Again.'

'Yeah, bye.'

Satanic Hearses charged up to the house, stonewashed legs scissoring fast. He pushed past her and skirted by me into the living room. 'There's fire engines out the back!'

'No way!' Dave was ecstatic. They thundered up the stairs behind me as I stepped outside to watch Jay. She glanced back at the bottom of the street but she didn't wave. Well, I didn't wave either.

Back inside, I followed the voices up to Prince's room where Josie and Satanic Hearses stood by as Dave opened the window. 'Maybe it's a suspect device,' he said. 'I miss bombscares.'

The backs of the neighbouring terraces pulsed with blasts of blue. Rattling diesel engines echoed round the alley. A fireman came through into the rubbishy yard and looked up at our window, wide and stiff in his yellow and black waterproofs.

'We got a call about a potential suicide.' He nodded towards the bathroom window, where Alex was dangling from the ledge by her fingertips. 'Is she committin' suicide or what?'

Alex peered at us past her taught shoulders. 'I just wanted to see if Prince was using one of those dick extenders! I nearly made it!'

Prince joined us at the window and called down to the fireman. 'Let her go w'dignity, mate!'

'You could write a haiku about this,' I said to Satanic Hearses. He ignored me. I went on. 'See a lone woman, the wrong move is bitter-sweet, more men come around.'

He looked at me. I pulled my T-shirt over my head and jumped around in self-congratulation. 'You Beauty!'

Alex screamed as one hand lost its grip and she jerked and twisted about wildly.

'Jump, y'wanker!' somebody called from another window.

She slammed the hand back onto the ledge to a chorus of boos. A fireman bravely jogged up the ladder they'd leaned beside her.

'Wish I was Alex!' Josie jumped around in excitement.

The first fireman squeaked and creaked into the room behind us. 'We could prosecute you for this, y'know.'

'What for?' Josie demanded. 'Alex was the one committin' hari-kari.'

'That's not what y'called him,' Prince said.

'Who?'

'Spiderman. That was Peter Parker, y'eejit. Jesus, what did you do as a kid, Josie?'

'Went to school. What did you do?'

Prince stiffened. 'None a your fucken business.'

Josie gripped my wrist, painfully tight. She knew I wanted to run. Boo's restaurant was a wide dim room with a sunken floor, jammed with low square block tables. The bench seating was so low it seemed purposely designed to test the effectiveness of Windeze. The bar was a raised area to the left of the entrance, separated from the main restaurant by a glass brick wall. It was made of the same reddish wood as the tables and benches in the restaurant, except the bar area was for giants, with extra high stools at a chin-level counter.

Brigid, the maître d', introduced herself at the door and was so efficient I felt as if I'd been scalded. She was tall, broad shouldered and muscley, in a gleaming white sleeveless shirt not tucked into baggy black jeans. Her hair was cropped with a Tintin tuft at the front and her wide mannish face was coated in a dark even layer of make-up. Her lips quivered in a smidgen of a smile as she clicked her heels together. 'I'll let Boo know you're here. Have a seat at the bar. Albert will fix you a drink.'

It was early evening. Boo had asked us to come before the first sitting. I shuffled to the bar after Josie, where a man organised glasses below the counter. He was in his fifties with sharply pointed silvery sideburns and receding white hair shaved close to his scalp. He wore fine black-rimmed glasses and had a suspiciously yellow tan.

'Yes, folks?' he said, spreading his fingers calmly across the bar.

'Just water thanks,' Josie said.

'And you, sir?'

I shook my head.

'Nothing for sir?'

I felt my teeth grind. 'No.'

We hitched ourselves up onto the stools and I leaned Prince's guitar against the bar as Albert poured mineral water into a fucken vase or something. The glass opened out from a heavy base and stretched about a foot into the air. It actually looked down on me.

Josie sighed, slightly shaky, patting my thigh. 'Relax!'

I couldn't. I didn't belong here. It was all money and gleaming cutlery and thick cotton napkins and fucken vases. It was like being dropped in Japan with no yen, no guide and no idea.

'Boo isn't normally the sponsorship type,' Albert said.

'Is he not?' Josie forced a smile.

'A lot of people ask him for sponsorship.'

'Do they?'

'People seem to think when you leave here and make some money, you owe this country something. He doesn't owe anybody anything.'

Josie stared for a second. 'Well, thanks.'

'Forewarned is ...' Albert looked into the distance and then shrugged. 'Forewarned is just forewarned.'

'Boo.'

I turned too quickly and toppled my stool but he caught me and pushed me up again. He wore another ninja outfit.

'You growing dreads?' he said.

Josie jumped to her feet and fawned and curtsied, eyebrows dancing all over her face as she grinned and held out her hand to shake. 'Oh, Mr Boo, thank you so much for agreeing to see me. Us. This is brilliant, so it is.'

'Just Boo. Mr Boo sounds ... well, it sounds like a glove puppet or something.'

Josie fell around in disproportionate mirth.

'Shall we sit?' Boo said, indicating the sunken restaurant floor. He walked ahead and we sat at a munchkin table.

'So you're organising a cross-community festival then?' he said.

'Mm-hm, yes, uh-huh, yes.' Josie nodded.

'Why don't you tell me what you're proposing?'

I felt my hands go up to my head and press themselves against my ears. Why did he have to say that?

Josie launched into her spiel, an off-by-heart explanation of benefits to the community and goodwill towards sponsors and the open eyes, open minds bit and then the song bit where we all get together and create something to remember the day by and hopefully, of course, it's still in the negotiation stage, we'll record a CD and sell it and all the proceeds will go back into community development.

'You OK?' Boo asked me.

I nodded.

'You're covering your ears.'

I peeled my hands away. 'No I'm not.'

'And our *pièce de résistance*,' Josie said. 'Is Cookie's song.'

'Right!' I said, swinging Prince's guitar onto my knee. 'This is an electric so you'll just have to put up with the tinniness. But you know that, ha ha ha. Ha.'

But my fingers wouldn't find the chords I'd been playing back at the house. Wake to the ... Wake to the ... Wake ... What ... What you're proposing. What you're proposing? *Bloody Status Quo?* All I knew was that line and I couldn't even explain how I knew it. What you're proposing what you're proposing what you're proposing. I looked at Josie. 'I'm havin' a wee technical hitch.'

'What?' I've never heard her voice so high.

Boo looked mildly entertained.

'Look, there is a song,' I told him. 'I wouldn't fuck ya about. Swear to God, there is a song.' What you're proposing what you're proposing ...

'Stage fright?'

'No, not that. Though it is sort of scary.' I looked at Josie and she glared back, panic making her eyes crisp 'n' dry.

I tried again. I tried placing my fingers high up the fret board but they wanted to slide down and play Status Quo. What you're proposing what you're proposing ...

So I just fucken played it. Didn't sing the words like. Just typical 12-bar blues in A and a bunch of mumbly words on top.

And it sounded just like Status Quo.

'Actually,' Albert said without looking up. 'That already unites the people.'

Boo nodded slowly, running his fingers over his mouth. Josie looked on in wordless pain and I stared at my Judas fingers.

'Well, as you heard,' Josie gushed. 'The song's ah, not quite finished. But it's a collaborative effort, so it is, Mr Boo, Boo. I promise this will be worth your while.'

He went on nodding. Very, very slowly.

'Thanks anyway,' she said, standing up. 'Thanks for your time.'

The door of the restaurant opened and Jay drifted in. She dumped a black umbrella on the floor in the doorway and flashed us her perfect teeth. 'You made it then.'

I surprised myself by smiling back. 'Hiya.'

'Hi, Cookie. Or ... *hiya*.'

'We were just goin',' Josie said, backing away as Jay approached.

'So Boo, is it a yay or a nay?' Jay asked.

Josie made for the door. 'We have to go now! Thanks! Bye!'

Boo got to his feet. 'Would a grand be enough?'

Josie turned back and was transformed into a pillar of salt.

Jay touched the strings of the guitar. 'You play this thing?'

'Now an' again.'

'You being modest?'

'No, I only play it now an' again. It's not mine. It's m'brother's.'

'You have your own though. You play that?'

'No, I sold mine. Although that ... wasn't mine either.'

I stood at Billy Dick's door in the dark and the rain, as his twelve-year-old daughter leaned back inside. 'Daddy! D'y'want the driveway tarmacked?'

'I just wanna talk to Billy,' I said. 'An' I'm not a bloody gypsy.'

The outside of their house was a nightmare fairground of flashing Christmas lights, rocking reindeer, luminous snowmen and motion-activated Santas who ho-ho-ho-ed as you walked past. The Dicks lived in one of Weirtown's 'nice' houses in Glen Drive, the older part of the estate. Ten years after they started building Weirtown, the Troubles began driving more people to the outskirts of the city and more flats and maisonettes were needed to house them, so as the estate developed east, it got more and more built-up. Glen Drive had fewer flats, the roads were wider and the semi-detached houses were bigger and less sardined than where I lived. It still had some of its original residents and it was where Sir Fusty of Stop'n'Shop lived.

'Who is it?' Billy Dick called down the stairs.

'Who are yuh?' She was in the black and green Weirtown High uniform and her orange hair was in long fine plaits all over her head, just like Lindsey Scott's. She wore a thick layer of foundation but no eye make-up or lipstick. She looked a bit like my granny when she was dead.

'Tell him it's Lizzie Fitzpatrick's son,' I said, loud enough for him to hear.

She yelled up to him. 'He says he's Lizzie Fizzy's son.'

'Bring him in,' he called.

She stepped back and let me come into the hall. It smelt like they'd just had a fry. Their tea. My granny used to make the tea. But when she died, mum didn't make the tea, she made *dinner*. And we had *dinner* at seven. Although I'd filled up on so many brown sauce sandwiches by that time I usually couldn't eat it. The smell turned my stomach to a tight brick.

The girl went into the living room and closed the door over, leaving me at the bottom of the stairs next to a mass of coats on hooks. I could hear *Neighbours* on in the next room. A wee orange-haired boy, about six, peeked round the door at me. 'Gypsy cunt,' he whispered. He let out a harsh squealy giggle before disappearing again.

Billy Dick thumped slowly to the bottom of the stairs. He was taller than he appeared on TV but his hair was just as bright and wild. His skin was splatted with wide purplish freckles and his tie skimmed out over his stomach like a ski slope. He turned to the hall mirror and looked at me in the reflection.

'Two things,' he said, smoothing down his tie. 'One, I'm sorry y'were told to get out but I can't help ye. Two, it wasn't me.'

'What wasn't you?'

He turned to face me. 'This would look good in the Sunday papers. The last place y'are before they do ye is here. Why are you here?'

'Who's goin' to *do* me?'

'I'm not playin' your game, son.'

'Son?'

'Figure of speech. There's a bus stop across the road.'

'But I have a question.'

He started rifling through the layers of coats. 'Nobody ever puts anything away in this bloody house.'

'I'm doin' a bit of research.'

'You're puttin' yourself at risk and you're wastin' my time. I'm about to go out.'

'Where y'goin, daddy?' The wee boy had come out into the hall. He had on the trendiest of gear. Nike this, Reebok that, Tommy the other.

Billy picked him up and held him tight against his paunch. 'Just a wee meetin'.'

'Can I come?'

'Ach, no, sure, it'll be all talkin'. You stay and watch the TV. I won't be long.'

'Will y'get me sweets?'

'For God's sake, the house is comin' down w'sweets.' He put the kid down. 'Aye, alright.'

The kid scooted back into the living room, slinking his eyes over at me as he went.

'So how's your big brother keepin'?' Billy asked me, delving in behind the coats again.

'He moved to LA.'

Billy tweaked at his nose and went on searching. He trailed a blue jacket out from under the pile of coats and shrugged it on. 'Right, listen. I'm gettin' picked up any minute. And see when I do? You don't even look outside till I'm away.'

'Why, who's pickin' you up? Santa Claus? Medusa?'

'Jesus, is it any wonder you got a hidin'?'

'Are you goin' to answer my question?'

Billy pushed his hands into his jacket pockets. 'What is it?'

I handed him the postcard. 'What does this mean?'

He shook his head as he turned it over, his eyebrows so high they were beyond innocence. 'Don't know. What does it mean?'

'She sent it.'

'Who?'

'My ma!'

'Alright! Jesus! Shut up! I don't know what it means.'

'It's your name.'

'It's not *only* my name. God knows what she meant. How can I say this? She doesn't think the way other people think.'

'Nicely put.'

'Thanks.' He looked at himself in the mirror again, sucking in his belly. He turned sideways to admire his slim physique, then turned back and let it out with a puff.

'Get on the bus. There's one in . . .' He looked at his watch. 'About ten minutes. Get on the bus and don't come back.'

'Can I have the postcard?'

He looked at it. 'No, I'll hold onto it. I'll ask around for yuh.' He tucked it into his inside pocket.

'But I need it.'

'I'll give it back when I find somethin' out.'

'No you bloody won't.'

'Right, there we go,' he said, as a horn beeped outside. 'That's my lift. You stay outta sight.' He snaked his head round into the living room. 'See yiz all later then. And you be good for your mummy, Stallone.'

There was a ripple of lazy seeya laters from the living room and he turned back to me, holding up a finger. 'Get on the bus.'

'Forget about us.'

He snapped off the hall light, stepped outside and closed the front door. The Christmas lights flashed as he dodged through the rain and got into the passenger side of a long silver car. Tommy McCullough was driving.

I opened the door and ran out into the rain. A round of cheery ho-ho-hos rose up from the garden. I gave Billy and Tommy a friendly wave as I darted up the road – in the direction that didn't lead to my house.

Sense? Well, I was learning.

In the dark, the demolition crew's machinery looked like model dinosaurs. They'd started knocking down our block but were still at the far end. The house itself was cave black. It smelt damp and unlived-in. It smelt like somebody had pissed in it. It smelt like the rats were having fun having children. I couldn't hear them for the whistly noise windows something falling, but I knew they were there. I lit a Consulate and the click-hiss of my lighter was distant. The flame flickered about the blackened hall and I used it to guide me up to my room. Where I'd left everything I needed.

The money had got me one shiny blue Kappa tracksuit, one dark blue baseball cap and one pair of blue and white Nike trainers (size nine, extra trendy), one pair of super-modern kitchen scissors, one pair of hair clippers, two small fluffy blankets, one pair of motorcycle gloves and a six-pack of household candles (all from Argos), one ham shank (now nicely on the turn), one party pack of Wotsits (from the Stop'n'Shop) and one McLaren buggy with matching rain covers (told the woman in the shop I'd got my girlfriend pregnant and got strangely broody).

I lifted the strappy sandals out of her wardrobe and dropped them in front of the wardrobe in Prince's old room. I used them as candleholders and doubled the candlelight using the mirror inside the wardrobe door. I gathered up the scissors and hair clippers and sat cross-legged in front of the mirror. I started at the front and lifted the strand that kept falling down over my eyes. I chopped it away and let it drop. Then the side. Lift snip drop. Then the top. Lift snip drop. Then the other side. Lift snip drop. Big chunk at the back almost stab myself in the neck ow lift snip drop. Lift snip drop all over, long chunks of matted black hair coated my legs. I brushed it all away and lit a cigarette off one of the candles. When I looked up, Bonehead was hovering in the mirror. I screamed.

He stared at my reflection, his chin above my head. 'I called yuh down the stairs. What the fuck are you doin'?'

'Disguise, mate.'

He put his hands round my neck and shook. I choked and fingered at his long bony hands. He let go and I laughed. He laughed too. Then he stopped and looked round.

'I've been in classier boney huts, Cookie.'

'Fuck off, it's lovely in here.'

He sort of grinned. I liked his missing tooth.

'I saw the lights,' he said, nodding at the candles.

'As opposed to The Light?'

'Whaddyamean, the light? Them lights there.' He gripped the back of my neck and turned my head to look at the candles.

'The Light. A revelation. An epiphany. Did you have an epiphany? And you didn't tell me?'

'Right, just fuck up. Look what I brought yuh.' He set a three-litre bottle of cider down beside me and held up a bottle of something called Fekkov, two thirds full. 'This is for me. They're sellin' it round the houses. How much?'

'Ninety percent meths.'

'No, guess how much it was.'

'Don't know.'

'Guess.'

'Fuck's sake, Bonehead, I don't know. A quid.'

'Wise up. A proper guess.'

'Jesus, I dunno. A fiver?'

'Four quid.'

'You were done.'

'Brought me own glass and everything.' He slid down onto the side of his ass. 'Probably catch somethin' off yours.'

'Well, your ma gave me them.'

'Well ... just fuck up.' He poured himself a pint of Fekkov and Coke and opened the cider for me. I sank a few sweet fizzy mouthfuls and looked at my tufty head in the mirror.

'I'll be with yuh in a minute. I just have to do this.'

'What for?'

'She deserves it.'

'What da fuck for, Cookie?'

'She picked on me. They all did.'

'You're a wanker, Cookie.'

I looked at myself again and lifted the scissors. Lift snip drop.

'Y'know what I get?' he said. 'I get all night parties, Cookie. I get cheap drink. I get loads of it and I get drugs as well. And CDs, Cookie. Whatever the fuck I want. That's what I get in Weirtown.'

'You've got contacts.' Lift snip drop.

'We *all* get it. Everybody gets it. It's *normal*.'

Lift snip drop lift snip drop.

He looked away. 'Drink the cider, y'cunt.'

'Gypsy cunt,' I said.

His lips moved. I looked up at a dark corner spidery hand shadows gone.

'You can't beat it, Cookie.'

'Michael Jackson did.'

'I mean it, y'tit. You can't beat this place.'

My scissors froze. 'That's a bit profound for you, mate.'

He whacked his hand off my head. 'Drink the cider, fuckwit.'

I tipped the heavy bottle back and looked at him in the mirror. 'Sorry haven't got any sounds, mate. No electric.'

He drank the whole of his pint in one go. 'If I help yuh ... do whatever it is you're doin'.' His eyes were watery from the vodka. 'Will y'just go? Will yuh?'

'You goin' to help me?'

'Didn't I just fucken say I would?'

'Alright then. Welcome to the Weirtown Rats' first big gig.'

You know the smell of the elephant house? Our kitchen. The candle wax ran down over my fingers. It was a funny feeling. Really painful for a second and then you get the fun of picking it off. I swapped the candle from hand to hand as Bonehead scattered Wotsits over the floor. The candle showed their route – through the cupboard under the sink. We uprighted the table and sat on it. I melted big blobs of wax on the table and pressed the candle into it.

'You don't have t'stay,' I whispered to him.

'I know, y'wank stain.'

We waited. And drank. And waited. And drank.

'Wish they'd hurry up,' Bonehead whispered. 'I have to piss.'

'Piss where yuh are,' I whispered back. 'This table's seen worse. Prince lost his virginity on it.'

'Fuck off.'

'Listen.'

Scratchy scratch. Nibble ee scratch scratch ee ee. My

heart hitched. A wee whiskery nose poked out from behind the cupboard door.

'He'll do,' Bonehead whispered.

'No, wait.'

The rat fell out of the cupboard and another one followed. Then another. And another. Sleek and shiny, long and thick, wormy tails. Lovely Wotsits for a hungry rat family. I counted six in total, scurrying, swerving, nibbling at the Wotsits yum crumbly yum.

I pulled on the motorcycle gloves and lifted one of the fluffy blankets from behind me. Then I launched myself off the table and danced and screamed and roared in the middle of the kitchen. The rats scattered everywhere, squeaking in terror and Bonehead disappeared into the living room, arms and legs flailing.

'Well, thank *you*,' I said, peering into the dark living room after him. I took the candle and used the dripping wax to set it on the floor, then I shifted the cupboard door away and pushed the bottles of cleaning stuff aside.

I crawled in, trailing the blanket with me. I hooked a gloved hand under the shadowy chewed hole at the back and yanked. Part came away. I yanked again and again, breaking and tearing at the chipboard, right through to the dusty grey outside wall.

I pulled at the last bit, low down by the floor, and there she was, snuggled up in a messy nest of papers and rags and rubbish, her ugly squirming brood suckling at her tits. She eyed me with crazy distrust.

I set the blanket over her nest.

*

I shouldn't have drunk the cider, not after that. Or maybe it wouldn't have made any difference. I sat in the corner in the living room with a candle and listened to the rain hit the boards and broken glass of the window. I lit more candles. I thought I could hear the rats so I started to sing. Beat it beat it beat it beat it. Get on the bus forget about us and put the blame it on the boogie don't blame it on the sunshine on my shoulder keeps me happy days are here again I made you believe we're more than just friends

There was somebody outside. Daddy Rat. Where's my children? In the buggy, where else? That's why I can't go upstairs, stupid

Please don't come in. Oh but I will by the hair of my chinny chin chin

The front door opened.

I blew out the candles.

'Jesus, *smell*!' Daddy Rat's voice.

I know it smells bad I know it does I know it does

'Fuck me. There coulden be nobody in here. They musta been wrong.' Daddy Rat again.

'Aye right, you gonna tell them?'

Don't come in no do do come in no don't please don't

They stepped into the living room, freaky long thumbs lit by streetlight beaming through the window slots. No not thumbs. Baseball bats.

'I can smell candle smoke. Can you?'

'Jesus Christ, this *place*.'

There was no streetlight outside our house but it shone through the boards and got brighter. And louder. Streetlights don't have engines. Yeah they do. No they don't.

Closer and closer and louder and louder. Daddy and Uncle Rat looked round.

'What da fuck?'

The dinosaur's nose came through the window first. It roared and screeched and grunted and pushed and thundery clouds of dust puffed up as the wall below the window collapsed. Daddy and Uncle Rat fled.

I covered my shaved head with my arms.

'Cookie!'

I peeked through my arms.

'Christ, Cookie! I'm gonna die I'm gonna die!' Bonehead's face was shocked white. The dust still rose behind him, lit by the digger's single headlight.

'They won't go after you,' I said. 'You've got contacts. Here, you always wanted to drive a digger, didn't yuh? Class!'

He held up his left hand. A rat had sunk its teeth into his middle finger and was still clamped mid-digit with a blankly determined stare. Bonehead's blood flowed and soaked its fur.

'Oh,' I said. 'Well, we can rebuild you. Or at least, casualty can. Wait till I pack up the buggy.'

Bonehead's ma actually chased me away from their house and I had to push the pram up the street at ninety miles an hour. I went back to our house even though I didn't want to. It was raining and the house was crumbling and I was cold and wet and knackered.

But I needed to prepare for the next day. Family allowance day.

I bumped the buggy backwards up the dark stairs and left it in Prince's room. Then I went into my room and lay on the floor.

After a breakfast of stale Wotsits, me and the rat babies headed out to the shops. I waved to the workmen who looked at me like I'd just got off the space shuttle as I pushed the pram out of the house. I left at about half ten, in my new spiderman outfit, which was bloody cold compared to combat gear. Lindsey went to the shops at half ten on family allowance day. She wrapped her new baby up in pink and packed her into the buggy like a doll, carefully pulling the rain covers up to protect her.

Lindsey didn't look like she'd had a baby at all. She was still tall and droopy thin and had smoked the whole time she was pregnant. Her favourite outfit, probably her only outfit, was a shiny white tracksuit, a bobbly creamy coloured fleece and lime green trainers. And that laugh. I was sure I heard it as I pushed the buggy through the square. I kept going, eyes pinned to the Stop'n'Shop under my baseball cap. My timing was immaculate. She was outside the shop, trying to manoeuvre the pram round Mrs McAteer, who was determined to talk.

'Aye, it is rainin',' Lindsey said. 'Cheerio now.'

'Hi's your mammy keepin'?' Mrs McAteer said, stepping into Lindsey's path again. I pushed my pram by them, went inside and held the door open for Lindsey. I nodded at Mr Fusty behind the cash desk and he stared back, suspicious. I was a new face round here. God, I was good.

Lindsey did the old double-dodge round Mrs McAteer, pretending to go one way and then steering the buggy the other. She followed me inside and I pushed my buggy away and looked at the tins near the door. Scotch Broth. Oxtail. Fascinating.

'Cheers big ears,' she said distantly, lifting a basket and pressing it down between the buggy's hood and handles. She pushed on by me.

Tomato. Chicken. Mushroom. Cock-a-leekie. 'No prabs.'

She moved onto the cereals and I went back for a basket and put it in the same place as hers. Then I followed.

The Stop'n'Shop smelt of pine disinfectant and rose air freshener with a definite undercurrent of Mr Fusty. It had no windows, only buzzing fluorescent lights, and was divided into two halves by a frame around the walls and ceiling, as if it had originally been two shops, now knocked into one. But you only noticed that if you really studied it. Tins, cereals, fruit, veg, bottles and biscuits were in the first half, bread, buns, bog roll, cleaning stuff, butter, milk and a meat counter were in the other.

She would park the pram in the bread aisle and run about lifting the bits and pieces she needed. When she went to the meat counter, she would get mince steak, sausages, chicken burgers and vegetable roll. I'd done my reccy thoroughly.

The Stop'n'Shop was always busy on family allowance day so I had to be extra careful. A young bloke with a pram wasn't so unusual though. I filled my basket with the same things she did and parked my pram just down from hers. Her baby was by the soda bread. My babies were by the baps. She chatted with the fella on the meat counter and oh God, that laugh. It tore through the Stop'n'Shop like a wicked spell. Old folks clutched at their chests. Children cried. Dogs howled.

I nipped across to the pan loaves and looked at the prices. I lifted the cheapest loaf and put it in her basket, then I reversed her buggy back and pushed it by my rat babies. Bye kids. My heart was thundering away but I wasn't Andy McNab anymore. I wanted to abort the mission. I wanted to swap them back but she was saying cheerio to the butcher fella and I couldn't stop now.

I pushed her baby down to the buns and cakes and parked her there. I abandoned the pram and headed for the biscuits in the next aisle down. A tall bloke, early twenties, sloped by. A mean looking dusty Jack Russell pattered after him, all high mongrel ears and clippy claws on the tiled floor.

'Here, Lindsey, givvus summa yer money,' the bloke said.

'Away an' fuck, Gary. Whadda we gonna eat if you take

it?' She put her meat parcels in the basket on top of the rat buggy.

'Givvus some money, Lindsey!'

The dog sniffed round the buggy. Oh, time to go time to go time to go.

'Hi's yer mammy keepin?' Mrs McAteer touched my arm and swallowed me up in her cloud of piss. I glanced back at Lindsey and her boyfriend as they argued in the middle of the shop.

'D'y'see that rain last night?' Mrs McAteer said. 'Thon was wile, wasn't it?'

Lindsey's boyfriend bickered on. 'I only need a Pavarotti. Come on.'

'No, we need it. What's wrong w'the dog? Get him away from the chile's buggy.'

'Diesel! Over here!' he barked at the dog, but the dog wasn't going anywhere. It went on sniffing and put its paws up on the covers. Lindsey bent down to brush it away and it wrinkled its lips at her.

'Get him away, Gary!'

'Are yuh havin' a wee cuppa tea in the house then?' Mrs McAteer looked at the Hob Nobs in my hand. 'Wee cuppa tea's always good, isn't it? Here, the vegetable roll's on offer, so it is.'

'Have to go now. Cheerio.'

'Gary, get the dog away from the pram, Gary!'

The dog jumped onto the pram and began to nuzzle in. Gary pulled it by the collar but its teeth were caught in the covers and they came off as he yanked the dog back. Gary fell into the pan loaves and the dog jumped up on the pram again and tore into the rotting ham shank. It was

Diesel's fucken birthday. Decaying meat and a fat milky squeaking rat and all her wriggling hairy babies to chomp on. Blood flew and bits squirted as Diesel ripped into them, head twisting, teeth tearing, guts growling.

Lindsey screamed and Mr Fusty came running over and all the old folks crowded round and young mothers pulled their kids to them and Mrs McAteer was saying something to me but there was just the noise and it whistled into silence and I knew something was coming and then there was a big metallic clang. Like one end of a girder hitting the ground. I felt my head jerk.

Nobody else seemed to notice it. They were looking from the bloody buggy to Mr Fusty, twitching on the floor. He stopped twitching.

Uh oh.

I killed Mr Fusty.

Redemption. My ham shank redemption. Yeah good, nice one. I shared a black taxi from Weirtown shops to city centre, crammed into the backseat between two fat ladies we looked like 818. Every now and again I tuned in, the way you do when you're drunk and you have a sober moment. I'd hear the radio in the front and then I'd go away.

Got him to stop at the Art College. Oisín would be at The Collective. The fat ladies' hips had me jammed in. They pushed me out, being born again into diesel air fume street. I think I needed something.

Sat on the low wall at the back of the art college and lit myself a Consulate. Spidey clothes not fucken warm enough. Right. Think. Shit OK. Right. Shake. OK. This wasn't right. I needed. Right. OK OK OK.

I breathed deep. My Nikes were light and uncertain on the cobbles. Downstairs in The Collective, Josie's mates watched me closely, a spiderman in the inner sanctum, oh no, oh yes

Unwelcome looks upstairs. It's me, for God's sake, it's me it's me it's me. Into the cafe.

'Hey you.' Mark the skinhead got up from a table of tie-dyed people and their kids. 'That's the kitchen. Y'can't go in there.'

'Lookin' for Oisín.'

'There's no Oisín here. Away outta here, you're off yer face. This is just a wee cafe. Go on, out.'

'Oisín!' I called. 'Oisín!'

'Out.' Mark grabbed my collar and walked me backwards to the stairs. I lost my baseball cap as he shovelled me out the door.

'Oisín!'

'Mark!' My brother's voice came from the kitchen. 'Mark, houl on a minute!'

Thank you God I do believe I do I do I do.

'Fuck's sake, Cookie.' Oisín clattered across the wooden floor towards us. 'What the fuck have y'done?' He looked at my clothes and shaved head. His hair was plum. He pushed me back onto a chair. 'What're y'doin? What's the Hob Nobs for? Relax your kacks.' He tried a grin. 'Can y'spin me a web then spiderman?'

I gripped the waistband of my Kappa top and went to pull it over my head but he caught my hands and pulled it down again. 'We'll go home, alright?'

The bandwagon was gaining momentum. Josie and her friends put up posters on every wall and in every window in central Belfast. I didn't go back to Weirtown but I guessed Kloot had plastered them around there too. The posters showed the standard samba band, stilt-walkers, Chinese dragon, lambeg drums, bodhráns and Irish and Scottish dancers in a circus collage of clashing perspectives. Right slap bang in the middle was

EXPLORE DIVERSITY THROUGH!
The New Sound of Ulster!
On!
22 December!
Have a Multi-Cultural Christmas!

Jesus Christ.

Jesus Christ indeed.

Below that were details of the procession! a day of demonstrations at St George's Market! world food stalls! an inter-denominational carol service! and a performance of the specially commissioned Song for Peace! At the bottom were tiny reproductions of the sponsors' logos. The whole thing looked like a trifle thrown at the wall.

Josie went on Radio Ulster and delivered her spiel to the people at large and we stood around in Prince's kitchen and listened. She was good, like, she really was. Persistent and persuasive to the point of intimidation. She got photographs and features in the local papers and set up a website. She couldn't think or talk about anything else. I just nodded and said OK a lot, but the song hadn't progressed any further. She hinted and nudged and pleaded as I watched MTV. All I had to do was come up with a melody and a few words and everybody else would sing, bang drums, sample, scratch, mix and stilt-walk all over the top of it. But all I could play was 12-bar blues in the key of A.

I wasn't able to figure out a plan for Wilson McCullough or his two mates either. I didn't know his mates and had nothing to go on for them but then sometimes my best ideas came out of nothing. So I stared at the TV and thought. I still wasn't feeling the best and wasn't half as inspired as I had been. The more I thought about it, the worse it got. I'd hit a wall. Literally.

It happened the night of the sponsors' reception, a couple of days before the festival. Boo was into this thing big time. He gave over his restaurant for a couple of hours early one night so everybody could meet before the event. He said it was time he gave something back to the community, which made me wonder if he'd actually been put out of Weirtown for being a Catholic. It sat neatly with my theory: Catholic = republican = socialist = community. Mum said Catholics have a more developed social conscience than Prods, the difference being, they actually have one. That explained why it was underdog eat underdog in places like Weirtown.

I was having real problems eating. The idea of something sitting on a plate and then going inside me, it was just too fucken weird. I'd dig into something, say, for example, champ. A mountain of buttery mashed potato and scallions. I'd dig in and I'd see it disappearing off my plate but I couldn't see where it was going. It wasn't on the floor. It wasn't down the back of the settee or in the pot plant. My God, it was inside me! Sometimes I'd have to puke it up just to see it again.

I didn't eat anything before I went to the sponsors' reception and that was part of the problem. Josie told Prince not to worry. She'd been making me Take My Cherry Sweeties and anyway, he could cram fancy nibbles into my face once we were there. He pretended everything was fine but he'd spent days making me anything-on-toast, while Dave stood around in the kitchen looking lost.

The bar in Boo's restaurant buzzed with middle-class, middle-aged civil servants and Northern Ireland's new army of community workers. Business people in tired suits drank water and mixed with wannabe DJs, couldabeen rock stars and Irish, Chinese and Indian musicians. Local press took pictures of the least scary kids. The piped music was distant and squeaky. Free champagne made the small talk huge.

I didn't want to but I liked the champagne. It was like the best cider I ever had – smaller, more energetic bubbles and it fizzed all round my mouth and the whole way down to my shrunken stomach. And such a good drunk. It wasn't like vodka or beer which sent me to sleep. It was just like cider but much much better.

Champagne made me a brighter, lighter person. You can keep your herbal and chemical highs. I'd found my drug of choice. If anybody left down a half-finished champagne glass, I poured it into my lemonade glass and carried it around with me. Oh, I was on form. What a fucken charmer.

Josie introduced me to Molly, a greying government type who was talking to Joanna, who worked for a local paper and looked drained in a crumpled business suit. An impatient photographer called Neil hovered about behind them.

'Molly, Joanna, Neil, this is Cuchulain,' Josie gushed, pronouncing it Cookoolin and getting nine out of ten for effort. 'Cuchulain is writin' *our song.*'

Neil flashed the camera before I had time to salute him with a finger. Molly's smile looked honest but Joanna's face didn't change. And I'd made a special effort with my personal hygiene too. A bath, Prince's smelly stuff, new combats (there *must* be a pygmy army somewhere in the world, swear to God, go to the army surplus if you don't believe me), a skinny shirt and tie from the Cancer Research shop and a woolly beanie borrowed from Prince. I was looking pretty damn swank, even if I do say so myself.

Boo took Neil away to snap and flash at groups of people around the bar, although he never appeared in any photographs himself. Probably against ninja law. Josie latched onto Joanna and Molly turned to me.

'I have sons about your age,' she said. She had a kind, open face but she'd obviously got a taste for the champagne. Her cheekbones were pinched red. 'They wouldn't be capable of writing a song,' she said. 'They can barely string two words together.'

'You have kids my age?' I said. 'You must have been a child bride.'

She grabbed my arm, leaned into my face and laughed without making a sound. I carried on, even though she obviously didn't believe a word I said. In the civil service twenty-two years? No way! Didn't go to the gym? Having me on! I astounded myself. I really liked her.

'It's so good the young people are getting involved,' she shouted at me over the din. 'It's the future, don't you think?'

'Bollocks.'

'What?'

'That's shite. The young people are poisoned. It's too late.'

'Gosh, you're so cynical. But that's good.' She took my hands, drunkenly enthusiastic. 'It's good that young people from the street have licence to express themselves. I don't mean that in any offensive way. Everyone comes from somewhere. It's all valid. It's healthy. That's what creativity is all about. That's the future.'

'Where do you live?' I asked.

'Bangor. And where do you live, Cuchulain?' Cuckoo

Lane. One out of ten for that, and only because I liked her.

'Are you not drinkin' that champagne then?' I asked.

Prince swung his arm round my shoulders. His hair was bleached white and he looked far too good. 'Introduce me to the nice lady then.'

I whispered in his ear. 'Fuck off, she's mine.'

He whispered back. 'She wants to tuck you in with a hot water bottle.' He flashed her his drop dead smile and returned to me. 'You fuck off.'

'Molly, this is my brother Oisín. He's a prostitute.'

She smiled kindly and patted my arm. 'Oh, some day you'll have a mortgage too.' She turned to Prince. 'So what are you, a designer? No, don't tell me, you write advertising jingles, don't you? No, you sing on them, don't you?'

'Yeah! I do!' Prince said, genuinely surprised.

'No but ...' I started, but she was engrossed in Prince, who was already onto – 'Whaddyamean mean you don't work out? There's just no way, look at yuh. Two big sons? You're havin' me on ...'

I was out of the picture. I looked around for Jay but she still hadn't arrived. And I'd had a bath for her and everything. I swayed through the people, minesweeping glasses along the way. So many people, so much neglected champagne.

Neil went on snapping and flashing and I went pretty much unnoticed until challenged by Steve, a suit who worked for a bank.

'Oh, sorry,' I said. 'This yours?'

'Yeah. And you're too young to be drinkin'.'

'Oh for God's sake, this happens to me all the time.

I'm thirty. It's a disease, alright?'

'Oh. Sorry, mate.'

He was thirty as well and into motorbikes. We gushed over the Dunlops, planned to ride up to the North West 200 together and talked about the fun of speed – that's the motion, not the drug – and the thrill of narrowly escaping death. We really hit it off.

We were joined by Ciaran from Glengormley who needed a light. I got a free cigarette as well. Ciaran was a peer educator, a sort of official big brother for local kids. Steve told him about my terrible age affliction and we talked about the fun of speed – that's the drug, not the motion – and the thrill of narrowly escaping death. We promised to keep in touch.

Eventually I got back to Dave. My cheeks were on fire and my fingers had puffed up like baps but I felt brilliant. Neil took our picture and moved on.

'Dave! I want to be a photographer!' I said. 'No! I want to work for the civil service! No, a bank! No, the community! No! I want to own a restaurant and drink champagne all fucken day!'

He frowned at the stringy chicken thing he was tearing at. 'Taste this.'

'Nah.'

'Why not?'

'It's ... well, it's really ... orange.'

'What, is that like, a political objection?'

'Pluck the Protestant chickens!'

'It tastes ... I don't know, like perfume or somethin',' Dave said.

'Don't eat it then.'

'No, I like it. Here.' He held up a plate of more stringy orange things, soft whirly cheesy things and thin red meaty stuff on midget cracker things.

'Nah, you're alright,' I said. 'Here, is Prince a fucker or is Prince a complete fucker?'

Prince's hands were wrapped round Molly's wrists and he stared into her eyes. His long eyelashes flicked down shyly and he looked at the floor. How can eyelashes lie? Jesus, I dunno.

'How do you stick him, Dave?'

'Whah?'

'How do you put up with him? His ... thingywhaddya-macallit.'

'His *whah*?'

'His ... what's the word, it's comin it's comin' it's comin' ... here it comes, whhhuhhh, ahhhmm ... am-bivalence! How do you put up with his am-fucken-bivalence?'

'Where'd y'get a word like ambliva ... ambulan ... ambipur ... amblivvalanch ...'

'But he is, isn't he?'

'I dunno.'

'But man, you're so ... pure.'

'*Whah*?'

'No, but you are, Dave.'

'He's just like ... he's alright. He's dead on. He's alright.'

'But he's all over the show.'

'So're you. You watch MTV all day.'

'But I'm mental.'

'I know you are, mate.'

I wrapped my arms around him. 'I love you, Dave!'

'Hi, you guys. Or *hiya*.'

My stomach wrung itself into a knot. 'Hiya, Jay!'

She was all in black again, supernaturally thin. 'Having fun?' She tapped her champagne glass against her teeth.

'What's this here?' Dave held up the half-eaten chicken thing.

'Deep fried testicle of something,' she said. 'It's very orange, isn't it? Have you tried the Paddinis?'

'The whah?'

'It's a panini with a Paddy slant. The chef's creation. He worked for Marco in London and came back to Belfast with Boo. It's a tiny bite-sized panini made with potato bread, brie, bacon, sundried tomatoes and spring onions. Sorry, scallions?'

'That's the one.' I nodded.

'You ought to try them,' she said to me. 'You've lost weight. They're high in saturated fat and loaded with cholesterol. Very popular locally I believe.'

I opened my mouth but nothing came out. Neil's camera flashed at Josie, Kloot and Billy Dick.

'Keep your head back,' Jay said. 'It'll stop eventually.'

I pressed the hankies and ice-filled towel to my nose. Cool bloody snot ran down the back of my throat.

When I saw Billy Dick smarming up to the camera, I did a quick about-turn. And walked right into the glass wall that divided the bar from the restaurant. Clang. Everyone flocked over as I sank to the floor, blood gushing out of my nose, all down the front of my new shirt and tie.

Josie and Jay sat with me at the bar as the staff arranged

taxis for the thinning crowd. Brigid clicked her heels at the night's first paying customers. My brother had disappeared in a taxi with Molly long before I busted my own face. Billy Dick disappeared soon after.

'Josie.' I touched her arm as she said cheerio to the singing jugglers on roller blades. 'Josie.'

'Yes, wee love.' She turned to me, pink and light like Angel Delight.

'I'm not doin' the festival.'

She laughed. 'Y'wee messer. Y'near had me there.'

'No, I mean it. I'm not doin' it.'

Ever pour cold water on Angel Delight? Not pretty. She planted a fist on her wide hip. 'Why not? Because you just made a tit of yourself?'

'You never said Billy Dick was involved.'

'Ach Cookie, not this again. The only way we can change things is if we can get everybody on board.'

'But Billy Dick's a fucken terrorist.'

'*Was*. So he might have been in prison. So's half the bloody country. So's half the people here. Billy's moved on and he's willin' to show other people we can do things another way. We have to give people the benefit of the doubt.'

'No we don't.'

'Frig yah, Cookie! Did y'have to wait till now t'tell me?'

'I didn't fucken know Billy Dick was involved and as I re-fucken-call, I never actually said I *would* do it.'

But she'd already spun away, shoulders stiff, tassels whipping out violently.

Jay watched her go. 'I understood most of that. I'm getting better at this.'

I peered down my nose and over my hankies. 'Are you married to Boo?'

'What do *you* think?'

Well, I didn't know what to think. That was why I was asking. But I didn't want to look even more stupid than I already looked so I didn't question any further.

Boo materialised in front of us, arms folded over his black ninja outfit. 'Maybe we should take you to casualty.'

'Nah. I'll just have another glass of champagne. I'll be dead on.'

'You were drinking the Moet?'

'Fucken presuppositions.'

Boo frowned and laughed at the same time. 'You little show off. You're just like her.'

'Who?'

'Lizzie.'

So. My dad. It wasn't a constant concern or anything but I was curious. And I did ask. It had turned into a game, one of those insider games where you end up just using key-words and codes that nobody else understands. When I was wee, if I came across somebody she liked, or some-body I liked, I would ask if he was my daddy. And she'd say I was too special to have a daddy. At one point she actually said I was a gift from God, which was really embarrassing when I let it out of the bag in primary three and got into trouble with the school principal.

'Mrs Fitzpatrick, did you tell your son he is the Messiah?'

'Actually,' she said. 'It's Ms.'

When I was ten, I stopped asking. It didn't bother me any more. But I started asking again when I was fourteen because I'd got these really huge feet and gingerish pubes and they did bother me.

We were sitting on the front doorstep on a warm September afternoon, skinning up. She wore her sandals and was warming her tattooed ankles in the sun. I still hadn't got the hang of rolling up and I'd made this big loose joint that looked like an Egyptian mummy's finger. We smoked it anyway and one minute I was sitting up, staring across the green towards the shops, and the next minute I was lying on my back, staring up through the hole in the paper lampshade that hung from the ceiling.

'Mum?' I asked the back of her head.

'Mmm?'

'Jamember you said I was the Messiah?'

'I did not, did I?'

'Wait a minute ... you mean ... I'm not?'

She swung round in a flash of panic and I pointed and laughed and pointed and laughed. She dug her fingers into the flesh above my knee and called me a wee bastard. I squawked and squirmed but she wouldn't let go.

After that, if I came across somebody she liked, or somebody I liked, I would say, 'Is that God then?' Sean Connery, Liam Neeson, Terry Wogan, Nelson Mandela, Bono, Tom Waits, Father Ted, Father Jack, Batman, Ghandhi. All of them gods, but none of them mine.

Prince never talked about it. I only ever asked him once, when he was sixteen. He'd just come out of the bathroom and I lay on his bed, watching him squeeze blackheads and rub his orange hair dry in front of the wardrobe mirror.

'Prince, who d'y'think your da was?'

He looked at me in the reflection, then he jumped on me and tried to strangle me. All in fun like. I think.

So when Boo said he knew Lizzie, I should have been curious. But funny things were happening to my head and I wasn't curious. I was furious. I took a swing at him. Oh, messy. My bloody nose. His bloody nose. People rushing to hold him up, people rushing to hold me back. Josie flapping, Jay laughing. Wait a minute. Jay creased over with breathless laughter. I stopped struggling and stared.

Two community workers trailed me outside to the damp, four-lane, Great Victoria Street, bursting to practise what they'd learnt in their conflict resolution classes. Customers skirted by us, unsure whether to go in, in case I was an escaped raw ingredient.

'You just calm down, alright?' the beefier one said. Probably late fifties and short, with a shiny black quiff and droopy wobbly jowls. He pressed his arm against my chest and held me against the wall.

I shook and sweated and tasted blood from my nose. I held up my trembling, painful hand. 'Fucken bloody *ow*.'

'Did yer man Boo just hit you?' The younger one bobbed about, eyes bright with excitement. He was taller than me and well-built, with a close-shaved receding hairline. He looked like he'd sucked the Levi Store dry.

'Do you like his jacket?' I asked him, nodding at Jowly's leather jacket.

'Whah?'

'Do you *aspire* to his leather jacket?'

Denim Boy looked at Jowly then back at me. 'What are you on?'

'I'm sort of embarrassed to say.'

'It's cool,' Jowly said. His rubbery lips looked dubbed. 'We won't tell the peelers ner nothin'. It's harm minimisation. We can help yuh.'

Ham minimisation.

'Do you eat meat?' I asked.

Jowly looked at Denim Boy. 'Is that a new E?'

'Where d'y'get the speed?' Denim Boy asked me. 'Was it somebody here?'

'Why, is this your patch? Can I go now? I have to go home.'

'Where's home?'

'Up the road.'

'I'll give you a lift,' Jowly said.

'Fucken sure you won't,' I said. 'You could be a child molestor.'

'I have a certificate in child protection,' Jowly said.

'I have a certificate too,' I said. 'Twenty-five metres butterfly stroke. It means I can swim, it doesn't mean I can fucken fly.'

Denim Boy pulled Jowly off me and I staggered away, trying to laugh. But I wasn't really laughing. I didn't know what I was doing. I couldn't control my face and I wanted to find a bin and throw myself into it, upside down.

I headed for Shaftesbury Square, busy with people, glittery with Christmas lights. I knew it was coming. The girder, not window frames. Whistling down through the air, louder and louder. Don't let it land, don't, don't. I pressed my ear into my shoulder.

Shaftesbury Square is a massive star-shaped crossroads with a bright advertising screen flickering down to distract the drivers. Cars, taxis and buses come and go in constant streams, skimming pedestrians who ignore zebra crossings, generally because they're drunk. A pack of Celtic supporters scattered across the roads, dodging traffic and guldering at each other. Young fellas from Sandy Row eyed them from outside the KFC, bristling with adrenaline. A bunch of Chinese hurried into a Chinese restaurant, shouting at each other. Studenty types sloped around thumbing at mobile phones, counting money and sweeping hair out of the way. There were girls dressed up as angels and devils out on a hen night. Office Christmas partygoers snogged people they didn't fancy. A flock of party hats drifted past in the nasty wind.

I took the traffic island route, quick-quick-slow as I scooted in front of cars and stopped on each island. I joined the other slow-walkers, judging the speed, lights and noise of the traffic, looking for a long enough gap to cross. Mid-island lamp-posts were looped with fine rope and stained with eggs and flour from another hen night. The traffic stopped one way and found another way to come. Every direction, more and more streaming lights.

I stood in the middle of Shaftesbury Square and looked up at the advertising sign. Happy local people drank local lemonade. Thirsty. Foreign Jay people drank Coke in red scarves and hats cold red. I had a red moustache. My nose was fat and rattly. Ow. The advertising sign changed like somebody turned the page. Technicolour lights tainted pedestrians purple meat I didn't see that walked on and made it to the Botanic side.

I was under the covers with coloured filters over my torch stuffy but the bed was cold no I was at the bottom of Botanic Avenue my nose was stuffy and I was cold shit tune in tune in but the noise, my nose, my noise

Up to the left I avoided why was everybody coming this way why couldn't anybody walk in my fucken direction dodged whiskery old man doubt on his face onto road and girder BMW lights I planted my hands on the wet bonnet.

Jay stared out at me, tiny behind the wheel. She lifted her eyebrows and pointed to the passenger seat. The car behind blasted its horn. I heard that, you. She turned to offer them a short, sharp finger, then swung back and pointed again.

I got in. The car was stuffy hot and smelt of new leather. The dashboard looked Christmassy, even though it wasn't, and the stereo played low. She opened the glove compartment, brought out a small pack of paper hankies and dropped them in my lap.

I used one to scrape lightly at my nose crust. Only water was going to take it off. Very gentle water. The car hummed along smoothly and she was all mirrors and indicators as she drove.

We pulled into India Street, double-parked outside Prince's house and she looked up at the dark windows. 'This is it, isn't it?'

I got out. 'Hanks.'

Her window went down as I walked round the car. 'You be OK then?'

I nodded.

'He'll be OK about it, you know,' she said.

I walked away from Prince's house, deeper into the

student district, and she crept the car alongside. 'Where are you going now?'

'Would you just go away?'

'Do you want a ride?'

'Do you know what that means in Belfast?'

'I do now. I'll take you wherever you want to go. Get in.'

I looked ahead. More bleak student houses, then Republican lower Ormeau. They wouldn't want me wandering their streets with my bloody face and shirt. Or maybe they would. With a name like mine it would look like a sectarian attack. Perfect. Somebody take a picture.

I looked back. I could walk into town but even if I made it past Shaftesbury Square, where then? Just walking and walking, a moving target. I felt weird and wobbly and far too cold. I couldn't sleep outside. I'd die of exposure, a sore hand and a very sore bloody nose.

I got back in and we hummed along, swerving close to parked cars as she felt about in the glove compartment again. I wanted to get in there, with its wee snug light. She pulled out a crinkly bag of sweets and clapped the glove compartment shut.

'Might rot your teeth but no fat worth mentioning,' she said. 'Like Frosties. God bless Mr Kellogg.'

I unwrapped a sweet and put it in my mouth. My head thumped and it hurt to suck. I started to cry but that hurt too. I stopped crying and let the sweet dissolve slowly on my tongue. Strawberry sherbet.

'Where do you want to go?' She pulled out onto Botanic again.

'Dunno.'

'We'll go to my house, yeah?'

'I'll get out here.'

'Come on. You can get cleaned up and I'll get you a fresh T-shirt. He won't be there.'

'Is that Blondie?' I nodded at the stereo.

'I just play whatever's in there. It's his car.'

I looked at the side of her freckly face. 'You're mad. Why'd you pick me up?'

'Mad, I guess.' She looked everywhere as she drove.

'You shoulda drove on. Run me over and drove on.'

'I couldn't do that.'

'Yeah, you could.'

'No I couldn't.' Eyes everywhere, up and down the road and in every mirror. 'I don't have a driver's licence.'

It was really sore to laugh.

N ot long before mum disappeared, I was sitting on the bog, skimming through one of her old books. I started reading about these researchers who trained a monkey to sign, years ago like. Something to do with proving that humans are pre-programmed for language. The monkey was only able to learn a limited number of signs but the experiment scored a million out of ten. I thought it was bloody terrible.

Monkeys don't think like people, even I could've told them that. Those researchers didn't think about the consequences. When you teach a monkey to sign, what's it meant to do when it's returned to the other monkeys? What happens when it starts signing to the other monkeys but the other monkeys think, well, you're one freaky monkey, you are. Whack. What is that bloody monkey meant to do? Forget it all?

Mum said nature always won over nurture and the monkey would re-adapt. But I wasn't sure. I tried to talk to Prince about it but he said the only thing I should bring into the toilet were magazines I could read with one hand. I went to the library and read up on the nature/nurture argument. And suddenly me and mum started having a real argument. And that just wasn't like us. I mean, how do you argue with somebody who *likes* your hair green? She threw her toys right out of the pram. She thought I was getting at her for bringing me up different to everybody else. And I was.

She huffed for days and she was an expert huffer. Much better than me or Prince. We couldn't keep our mouths shut. But when she huffed, the silence was huge. It drenched the whole house and got worse the longer it went on. When I came back from the library, she would still be in bed and she wouldn't get up. I heard her singing and I heard her crying. She wouldn't talk to me so I just sat in the living room on my own, trapped with my own thoughts.

Her. Weir High. Every fucker who ever took advantage of me. It got to the stage where I couldn't think about anything else. I wouldn't let myself think about anything else. Because I started to realise it wasn't just them, it was me. I *let* things happen. Me. Cookie cunt. Anybody could come and fuck me over. And I started to think about redemption. It wasn't just about revenge. Redemption was like a new start, a real clean slate. It was time I took control. I'd fuck them all up well and good. Oh, I was going to be busy. I had a whole campaign to roll out.

I picked the mushrooms from the green in front of our house. Low September evening sun filtered through the fine, rich grass and each blade cast a spiky shadow across the next. The small, pointed, light brown umbrellas hid no fairies but well, you never know. We were the only people who indulged although she used to gather them years ago with the fellas in the band. But now she was Norma No Mates. I made oven chips, buttered bread, brewed up mushroom tea and brought it all upstairs on a tray for supper.

I watched her sandals move along to my singing in the bottom of the wardrobe. I watched her clothes pack themselves into her holdall. I could see my voice. I had to remember the song. The words came out fast like an upside down cascade. Look the monkey mum! Mum! Mental monkey monkey swinging screaming monkey do your head in mum!

When I woke in the morning, still inside her wardrobe, she was gone.

Along with the holdall I'd packed for her.

Shit. I only wanted to make her think.

'I know what you need,' Jay said.

We sat in Boo's kitchen in near darkness. Hidden lights made the stainless steel glint and hurt my eyes. Complete blackout would have hurt my eyes. My head was stuffed with marshmallow, forcing itself out through every pore in my head. Maybe I should've gone to casualty, at least to get some serious drugs.

She nodded to the drawer. 'Work away.'

I found the painkillers among the kitchen junk and swallowed three. She let me clean my face in their clinical downstairs bathroom and I noticed I was getting a nice set of matching black eyes. And for all the fucken pain, there was only a tiny mark across my nose. We put my shirt and tie in the bin and she gave me a soft black T-shirt to wear instead.

She heaved a hundredweight of oven chips out of their giant freezer and thudded it onto the cooker.

'Where's your accent from, Jay?'

'France.'

'France?'

'And Australia.'

'Australia?'

'And Brazil.'

'Brazil?'

'And Scotland. And Belfast.'

'It sounds American. Did y'live in America?'

'No.' She scattered generous handfuls of frozen chips over a baking tray. 'I watch a lot of TV.'

'Can I have a coupla them?' I asked.

'I'm doing them for you. I've had my carbs for today.'

She was making enough chips to feed the whole of the Dublin Road at closing time. I'd either make pictures on the plate or regurgitate them and I was already embarrassed enough. Maybe I could take them home and keep them in a box.

She slammed the chips into the oven, whacked the door closed with a foot and sat down opposite me at the breakfast bar. 'So tell me about this song.'

'What song?'

'The song you were writing for the festival.'

'I'm not doin' it any more.'

'But you had a song, didn't you?'

'Sort of.'

'Can I hear it?'

'Nah, it's shite.'

'What if I got Boo's Lowden out of the basement for you?'

'He keeps his Lowden in his basement? What did it do, bite somebody?'

'That's where he keeps the favourite pieces from his collection.'

Materialistic bastard! I wanted one!

She grinned. 'You look funny when you fight with yourself.'

'You're mad, Jay.'

'Why?'

'You're really nice. To me like.'

'I'm a nice person,' she smiled.

'I just don't see why you're bein' so nice to me.'

'You're very distrustful.'

'You're dodgin' the issue.'

'Do you challenge every girl this way?'

'No, but ...'

'What?'

'You're too nice ... to have time ... for me.'

'Oh, look at you,' she said, sticking out her bottom lip and leaning forward, her elbows on the tabletop. 'What is it you guys say? Wind your head in?'

'No, kick your head in. Or wind your neck in.'

'Wind your neck in then,' she said, straightening up. 'I'm not too nice. I'm playing a role. I'm pretending. I'm a good actress.' She flashed me her completely symmetrical smile. 'My mother was a French prostitute. Addicted to crack cocaine. She died on the street when I was three. I was with her. She was wearing a fur coat and no knickers. That's funny, isn't it?'

'Fuck. Me.'

'Don't know you well enough and anyway, I think I might be celibate.'

I fiddled with the hem of my new T-shirt. What do you say after that? 'So Boo's into French prostitutes then?'

She looked at her hands. 'We never checked if I was his. He just took me with him. You know what?' She gave me a small smile. Just a little one. And she didn't mean it. She didn't mean any of those smiles. 'I haven't told anybody that before and I wish I hadn't said it.'

I crawled across the breakfast bar and wrapped my arms round her in an awkward, desperate kind of hug. And she hugged back. My hands and arms and shoulders fizzed like Alka Seltzer. My skin breathed her in, a first draw that went on and on. Then I started to appreciate her fine, reddish hair and her warm, bobbly bony neck, her freckly even skin and the tiny hairs that pointed down the back of her top. And then I felt guilty. And then I felt horny. And then guilty. And then horny. Then guilty. Then horny. Then she pulled away, accidentally hitting her head off my nose.

I squealed like a girl. I held my hand under the heavy drops of blood as she dragged me off the breakfast bar and leaned me over the round sinks. Blood spladdoinked onto the steel and tears stung my eyes. She handed me sheets of kitchen roll.

'I guess that hurt.' She stood close behind me, a hand on my shoulder blade. 'Can I do anything?'

Hug me. Snog me. Jump into bed with me. Run away with me. 'Check duh chips, wouldja?'

She said Boo was a chef on a French yacht when he

found her. He wouldn't leave her behind and they wouldn't let him take her on the yacht so he took a job as a pizza chef in Nice. But he worked his way around and two years ago, he set up his first restaurant in Edinburgh. She'd never been to school. She'd always had a private tutor. She was thinking about going to Oxford. Her friends were the children of Boo's clients and she was very nice to all of them. She knew bulimia would ruin her skin and teeth but she couldn't stop it. She was good at languages and bad at maths and talked to people she didn't know on the internet. She loved Hollywood, Bollywood and Burt Bacharach but she couldn't hold a note and she had no rhythm.

She complained her butt was getting sore on the kitchen stool so we left the cold chips behind and went into the living room. It looked like they'd just moved in and dumped the furniture wherever was handiest. Antique, high-backed leather armchairs lurked about behind two soft black leather couches on either side of a low glass table. Huge blocks of art like the ones in the bedroom hung next to a flat widescreen TV on the white walls. The windows were part of the house's glass wall. There was a rough pile of logs in a hole in the wall, but no fireplace or grate. On either side, small metal lamps sat on towers of magazines. It was all too haphazard. It had to be planned and I didn't know where to put myself. I was messing it up just by being there. Jay slapped one of the couches and I balanced on the edge, afraid to move.

She left me in the room on my own and I stared at the paintings. They were abstract. No they weren't. Yes they were. No they weren't. Oh yes they fucken were. Red flicked and smeared across the child's buggy and I stared hard at the logs. 'Will Ye No' Come Back Again', learnt in recorder class and useful at last. I hummed it. Please come back Jay, please come back, please come back. I was about to launch for the door when she finally came back, holding Boo's Lowden out by the neck. She said something.

'Whah?'

'I sure as hell hope *somebody* can play this thing.'

She dropped onto the other couch and I turned the guitar over on my knee. It was a Lowden 025 which means fuck all to anybody until I say David Gray plays one. Made down the road in Newtownards but coveted every-where. It was a pale sandy colour and plain to look at but it sounded and felt like somebody I knew in a previous life.

I rested my chin on the body and breathed in its warm, woody, dusty smell. I ran my stiff fingers over the strings. Clear and sweet. Long drops of runny honey. I loved it. I closed my eyes to feel the sound shut out mad paintings.

I couldn't stop. My already sore hand ached and the fingertips on my left burned. I just played any old shit, just to play it. And not even any Status Quo either. She asked me to play something she knew, anything as long as it wasn't about Jesus, and I played Nirvana, Bob Dylan and Simon and Garfunkel so she could sing along. Her flat voice was incredible. It really made me laugh, although that meant I had to literally spite my face. She laughed too, and told me to fuck off, show off. When she smiled for real she got a single dimple low down in her right cheek.

She opened a bottle of champagne and said she wanted to hear the songs I wrote. I sang the one me and Prince made up about Mr Fusty, which was originally upbeat and fun but I slowed it way down and made it kind of sad and poignant. I picked up the pace with the bouncy school protest song, 'You Can't Get High on a Trampoline', words by Prince, music by me. Then the lumbering, grungy 'Beethoven's Filfth', words by me and Prince, music by me and Beethoven. Then I slowed it down and got all soft and sea swelly with 'In the Bin', words and music by me.

She lay on the other couch and stared at the cold logs, her head on her arm. I put my chin on the body of the guitar and slid my fingers high up the fret board. Clean, crisp sounds. I felt them in my teeth. Tense intense. No strumming. Just simple picked out notes to get the flavour. All soft and warm and Dairy Milk and then you shocked your teeth on silver paper. Fuck, it was there. I remembered it.

Wake to the glare of white. There is no easy way out, you know. Blood red walls to keep me in. If you could just open up and let me out, I would let you in

'Your voice disappears when you sing,' she said. 'Your age, I guess.'

'Shut up.'

'No, it's really cute. I could eat it up.'

'You'd just boke it up again.'

'So you're in a pink band? What is that, gay?'

'No, a punk band. I write the songs but I don't sing.' I yawned a wide frog yawn so as not to hurt my stupid face. 'My voice isn't right for it.'

'I like your voice. I like your songs. I can't imagine Johnny Rotten singing songs like that.'

'Prince sings them different t'me.'

'I see now why Josie wants you to take part.'

I snorted down my nose and felt everything shift. I shoved the kitchen roll back up again.

'You should do the song for her,' she said. 'I'd go to hear it.'

'Wouldja?'

She yawned with a high-pitched squeak and covered her eyes with her arm. 'Maybe we should do some speed or coke or something.'

I set the guitar down and sank back, champagne drained. 'I have to go home.'

I could smell bacon.

You know that contented feeling you get sometimes, just after you wake? Especially if you've slept for a long time. Then way back in your head somewhere, this general unfocused worry surfaces. You feel it approaching a corner in some synaptic corridor. You can't see it yet but you know it's coming. Then it slides round the corner and speaks to you through your own lips and you groan out loud as it shows you its ugly face.

I sat up. My face was stiff and heavy, my right hand and wrist needed oiled and my left fingertips were dented and sore. I was still on their couch with a quilt over me. The guitar was still there but Jay was gone. I looked round for an escape route but the ninja stood in the doorway.

'Boo.'

I stared at my boots.

'Is that my T-shirt?'

I looked down. It said Boo on the left breast.

'How's your nose?' he said. The skin on the inside of his right eye was dark and puffy but it wasn't anywhere near what I'd done to myself.

'S'pose I should say sorry,' I said.

'I suppose I should say the solicitor's letter's in the post.'

'Shit, no, look, I really am sorry.'

'Come out to the kitchen.' He stood up. 'Have a coffee. We'll talk.'

Satanic Hearses looked about the street above my head. 'People are just dyin' to be in your company, you harbinger of doom,' I told him.

I dodged inside and picked up his paper from the living room floor. I'd seen the headlines plastered outside the newsagents as I made my way back to Prince's house, trying to absorb the cold winter sun as I walked. Vitamin D, apparently. I needed vitamins. Or something. Sunshine would do in the meantime. I was drained and shaky but I'd turned down Boo's offer of a lift. Just sitting through a cup of coffee with him was punishment enough. He told me he grew up in one of the streets off East Green and if he'd known it was an offence worth a punch in the face, he never would have brought it up.

And as if ordinary run of the mill hangover guilt wasn't bad enough, I got paranoid that he thought I thought he was a Catholic and maybe he thought that was why I hit him. And if he thought that, then he was thinking about me thinking about his religion, and I wanted him to know that I didn't punch him because I thought he was a Catholic, in fact I *liked* Catholics, and I definitely wasn't thinking about his religion but I didn't want to bring it up because that was proof that I definitely was. And I wanted to seem above that kind of thing because that was such a wanky Weirtown thing to do.

I squirmed through the coffee and his silent stares and left as soon as I could. But I was sure he watched me the whole way down the street.

Prince's house was cosy-warm with the smell of baking and I guessed Dave was making his organic biscuits and cakes for the festival's world food stalls. I settled in my usual corner on the settee and looked at the photograph on the front of the paper. White tents covered the ruins of Weirtown Meats. The headline read BODY HUNT AT WEIRTOWN. They weren't looking for people killed in the fire. There weren't even any casualties in the fire. They were looking for missing persons, disposed of within the building. Jaysus. Not just any old factory fuck-up. A serious one this time. I intended to enjoy my evil glee.

My legs were numb and dead after the long walk and I didn't have the energy to pull them up under me. I left them, stretched out and knackered on the floor and pulled the settee's worn throw over me. I skimmed through the article until I came to Billy Dick's name. They'd quoted him. 'Of course they won't find anything. This is all based on rumour. This is a Protestant area and naturally enough the factory employed Protestant people. This is just another attempt to blacken the name of Protestantism. It's terrible unhelpful to try and score political points from something like this.'

I tried really hard to concentrate on my evil glee. I tried helping it along by looking at the photo of Billy Dick, his hair flipping up like a bin lid. But something gnawed vaguely at the back of my head. The headline said Weirtown, and not Weirtown Meats. And Weirtown included me. That sort of meant I was being blamed too. Oh, I knew exactly what was gnawing at the back of my head. It was guilt, big fat embarrassment and that sneaky bastard frustration again. Evil glee didn't stand a chance.

I rattled through the paper, fiercely looking for something, anything else, to distract me. Man fined for driving without insurance. Fasci-fucken-nating. Santa arrives in one-horse town on a horse-drawn cart. Wheels of commerce grind to a halt. Cattle bring M2 to a standstill. First recorded incident of road niceness. Two paramilitary punishment beatings – house breakers or joyriders. Bastards. Serve them right.

I crinkled the paper onto my lap and stared at the blank TV. I should know that paramilitary beatings aren't always for burgling pensioners' houses or stealing DLA cars. You can get one for parking your car in the wrong space. You can get one for disagreeing with 'connected' people. You can get one just for sticking your head above the fucken parapet. I should fucken *know* that.

I flicked through the pages and counted two more beatings and a shooting. It had fucken well happened to me and I still assumed they were guilty. I still couldn't control my own thoughts. Well, I wasn't going to take it any more! I, the newly declared fucker-upper, was going to ... what was I going to do? *Who* was I going to do?

In the furthest darkest corner of my head, beyond guilt, embarrassment and frustration, sat helplessness. It shuffled round and invited me to kick its soft flabby ass. The newspaper launched itself across the room and disintegrated mid-flight. 'Fuck!'

Prince leaned in the doorway and stared at the sheets of paper floating around the room, frowning. His hair was still blonde.

'What's wrong w'your bake?' I said. 'Molly give yuh a dose or what?'

He looked at me, cool and distant. 'Why'd yuh let Josie down?'

'You can talk.'

'That's different.'

'No it's not.'

He contemplated the far corner of the ceiling. 'Why am I even talkin' to you about this?' He looked at me again. 'I got your name on the emergency housin' list.'

'Am I not livin' with you then?'

'You can live w'me if you earn your keep.'

'What, like get a job?'

'Play in Josie's festival and you can stay w'me.'

I stood up too quick. The ceiling was falling on me. Black shadows crept in the sides of my eyes. 'You'd put me out? Over her?'

'I didn't mean it like that.'

'Fuck you.'

He grabbed my wrist as I went to pass. 'Come on, mucker. Do her a favour. She's a good mate. Doesn't she look after yuh?'

I prised my fingers under his. 'Oh fuck aye, she looks after me, alright. Ask her about the time we tried out your bed when you were out earnin' *your* fucken keep. She was lookin' after me alright. Don't know about you though.'

His eyebrows were so screwed up they must have hurt. His pale eyes were too dry.

'Fucken let go, Oisín.'

'Cooh'oolin ...' 10 out of 10 out of 10 out 10

I sank my teeth into his hand and thudded upstairs to get my stuff. It wasn't until I looked round his room that I realised I didn't have any bloody stuff. All I owned was that CD player, still in its plastic bag. My shaky legs wanted to drop me onto his mattress but I wouldn't let them. I searched through his pockets for change, took his combat jacket, gathered up the CD player and left.

I was still wearing his hat too.

Have yourself a merry Belfast Christmas. Pick a sunny day in December and squint at the power-washed city centre. There's real yuletide spirit in the air if you have a lunchtime drink. Streets are packed and bags of shopping rustle and bust off each other as they're dragged to car parks and bus stops. The air is saturated with roast chestnuts that nobody buys and onions and burgers that smell better than they taste. Skinny Santas ring bells and offer dollies for boys and guns for girls – well whaddya want for a pound, for fuck's sake. Thieves run with arms full of clothes, whipped from a rail too near the door. Buses puff out diesel clouds and the pavement shudders as they pass.

I was in the best mood ever. I'd had an epiphany on

the bus. I swear to God, I did.

I had to take two buses. One from Botanic to the city centre because I didn't have the energy left for the walk, and one from the city centre to east Belfast because Sound as a Pound FM was on the Newtownards Road. It was time I talked to Pete Fleming. It was worth a try. He was the only other member of the band I knew where to find and I owed it to her to at least talk to him. The fact that it meant I wouldn't have to go back to Weirtown for another few hours didn't influence my decision at all.

I bet everybody remembers where they were when they had their first epiphany. Mine happened on the bus from Botanic, in the no man's land of Shaftesbury Square. Didn't I tell you the best ideas come out of nowhere? I sat down and started counting the change from my fare. Twos, ones, fives. I pressed the coins into my palm and stared out the window, drifting, empty, half there, half elsewhere. When I wasn't dodging guilt and frustration over Prince, I was dodging guilt and frustration over everything else. I focused on the coins. They were just lumps of metal that didn't really mean anything. Lumps of metal that represented value, counted in numbers so the system had order. A system everybody could understand.

And then it happened.

What the fuck was I doing counting the waves in my campaign? First, second, third, fourth – their value had nothing to do with numbers. They had no order. Nobody else had to understand. I didn't have to do the fourth wave fourth. I could do the millionth wave fourth if I stopped fucken counting. I wasn't ready for Wilson McCullough and that's what the blockage was. Well, all I had to do was fuck up instead. I could come back to the fourth wave later and call it the zillionth.

The way I'd been thinking was crap! I was limiting myself. I was imposing order on my ideas. It was like forcing a flock of sheep down a U bend. And there's me running about with an anarchy sign on my back. I blushed on the bus. Mum would have pointed that out straight away. Well now I was back on form! Now I had purpose. Now I could get on with things.

I got a surprising eighty pounds for the CD player in Cash Converters because it was some fancy Danish make. Then I rang Bonehead's house from the phone box in Castle Place. Nobody uses phone boxes these days. Pull open the door of a phone box and people look away to preserve your dignity, like you're a hospital patient who got more than you bargained for when you squeaked out a fart. People would rather walk about and shout in the rain Hello! Hello! Hello! You show me the mobile phone that comes with its own shelter and perfect reception every time and that's the one I'll buy.

Big Julie answered abruptly. 'Yiss!'

'Hiya, Julie. It's Cookie. Have y'got another job yet?'

'What? Oh my God, Cookie. Are yuh up at your brother's house then? Are y'alright?'

'I'm dead on. Why?'

'I just wanted t'know if y'were alright.'

'Why wouldna be?'

'Jesus, you are one wee fucken pain in the *hole*!'

'Well, canna speak to Bonehead anyway?'

'Robert! Cookie's on the phone! *Robert!*'

I heard him take the phone and I crowed at him cheerfully. 'Bonehead! Fuck ye!'

'Cookie, I need to talk to yuh.' His voice was low.

'I know, I need to talk to you too. I need yuh to help me out.'

'But I *really* need to talk to yuh, Cookie.'

'OK, well, I just have a wee message to do over in east Belfast but you could come over and meet me, coulden yuh?'

We arranged to meet outside Wyse Byse at four and he agreed to try and get what I needed.

I caught another bus at the side of the City Hall and sat behind the driver. I didn't know the east side of town at all so I asked her to let me know when we reached Holywood Arches. I wished she was my big sister. She was big like. She was bursting out of her pale blue Translink shirt, obviously not made for women.

Her shoulder length black hair was pulled back into a shiny pony-tail with a celtic design clip and her face was scraped clean. The sharp December sun lit the hairs on her chin. Her short arms circled the wide steering wheel and I liked the way she drove. So patient as we moved through the chaos.

Out of the shiny city centre, past the glassy Waterfront Hall on the banks of the Lagan, past Maysfield Leisure

Centre and the too-tall Hilton and its non-identical BT twin, through monster junction after monster junction, all so confusing I kept swallowing in fear. Twice I had to cover my eyes. Good job I wasn't driving.

I read the street signs. East Bridge Street. Albert Bridge Road. Terrace houses, Orange hall, barrack-style bar with boarded up windows but an open door, Presbyterian church, charity shops, drop-in centre for the unemployed and/or recently paroled, fly posters for singles released by bands that never played in Belfast. Must think we're daft.

The people looked run down and tired like the people of Weirtown but their skin was different. Dull, like they needed to move to the outskirts where the air of damp grass and distant sea and rivers would clear their tubes out for them. They should get on the bus. Buses were brilliant. I wanted to be a bus driver. I wanted to be her.

She glanced back at me. 'This is Holywood Arches here.'

'Thanks.' I turned to her before I got off. 'I hope you have a really nice Christmas.'

She smiled to show badly capped teeth. 'Same to you, pet,' she said. I loved her.

A mother and three psychotic kids tried to flatten me as I got off but I decided to be generous. I could share the bus. I ignored the pedestrian crossing and dodged across four lanes of traffic to Wyse Byse, the everything shop that sat on the outer edge of the sprawling Connswater Shopping Centre. Next door to Wyse Byse was an anonymous dark glass door with a small sticker beside an intercom and buzzer. The sticker said Sound as a Pound. It was hand written. So this was Belfast's Newest Coolest Music Station.

I got their address from the Yellow Pages but there was no number on the door to confirm it. I'd worked out where it would be by asking Dave what else was on the Newtownards Road and using their door numbers as a guide. I stepped back and looked up at the building. A tall, plain white architectural lump with a couple of rain-stained satellite dishes on top. It could have been a giant bookies or anything. I don't know what I was expecting – pop stars, naked girls, limos, *something*. A fucken sign at least.

I pressed the buzzer and heard the rattle of a handset being lifted at the other end. I could hear shouting and laughter and a childishly high female voice answered. 'Yes?'

'Could I talk to Pete Fleming?'

'Do you have an appointment?'

'No.'

'You'll need to make an appointment. Do you want to make an appointment?'

'Fuck me, I only want to talk to him. What's he want to do, feel my balls and get me to cough?'

'Sorry?'

'Yeah, I'll make an appointment.'

'What's the name?'

'Cookie.'

'What's your whole name?'

'I call mine arse.'

'Sorry?'

'Look, it'll only take a wee minute.'

'He's very busy.' I could hear more laughter in the background.

'I came right the way across the town. I only need two minutes.'

'Well, he's not available right now.'

'Well, when would he be available?'

I heard her flick through pages as the fun went on in the background. 'Second week in January?'

'*Whah*?'

'Do you want to make an appointment or not? I'm quite busy myself, you know.'

'Sounds it.'

'Either make an appointment or, not to put too fine a point on it, fuck away off. I know you're a kid.'

'Look, it's a disease. I'm thirty alright?'

'Listen, love, I wrote the book on that one. But I am thirty. Now piss off.' She hung up.

I turned away from the door. 'For fuhhhh-four calling birds, three French hens, two turtle doves ...'

'Ach, luck, Aggie, a wee carol singer.' Two oul dolls passed me on the footpath, rocking along towards the shopping centre. One stopped to smile at me.

'Lucks like he's ready for war, Sadie,' her friend said, taking me in from head to foot. She had a voice like a bag of coal being dragged up a path. 'Fact, lucks like he's been in the wars arready. Is that two black eyes you have? You're no carol singer.' She linked with her friend and went to walk on.

'It's ah, the children's army,' I said. 'Like the Salvation Army. Only we help people prepare for ... redemption.'

'Are yuh collactin' then?' Sadie asked me. She had a much softer voice, decades deep.

'Yeah.'

'Wuhr's yer wee collaction bax?' Gravelly Aggie said. 'An have y'no identification ner nathin?'

'No, we collect, ah, prayers. Yeah, we just ask people to pray. And light a candle.'

'What for?' Aggie asked.

'For peace.'

'Sure we have peace.'

'I think you'll find we don't.'

'Wait a wee minute.' Aggie fished in her shopping bag. 'Wait dee I phone our Ricky. He says there's a ceasefire. They're not killin' Taigs no more, so thuhr nat.' She brought out a tiny mobile phone and held it a mile from her face as she whacked at the bleeping buttons.

'That's not what I meant,' I said. 'Anyway, I have to go. The Lord's work is callin' and shit. Cheerio.'

Sadie caught my sleeve as I went to slip away. 'Here, wait, love,' she said. 'Here.' She pressed something into my hand as Aggie quizzed Ricky in the background. Sadie wore powder on her soft, lined face and had smeared shimmery pink lipstick around her mouth. 'Put that in your wee collaction bax,' she said.

I felt the shape and weight in the palm of my hand. A pound coin. 'No, look, I was only jokin'. Don't. Keep your money.' I tried to open my hand but she held it closed tight.

'I know, love. You put it in your wee collaction bax anyway.' She squeezed my hand and her eyes disappeared into her loose skin as she smiled. She linked her arm back into Aggie's and they dandered on, Aggie still hounding her Ricky on the phone.

I turned back to the door of Sound as a Pound as a limo

pulled up outside. Well, hoo-fucken-*ray*! This was more like it! A uniformed chauffeur got out and opened the door. Bet Lynch, Marilyn Monroe and Cher poured onto the pavement, all fishnet legs, lipsticky fegs and sweaty champagne glasses.

Englishy sing-song voices startled birds from rooftops as a swarm of local TV 'personalities' rushed up the street to join them. Cher pressed the buzzer and grunted, 'It's me.' They all crushed inside shouting, 'Can't believe it's been a year!' 'You look fabulous!' 'I know!' 'I'm gonna get me some young firm flesh!'

I followed them in, dodging champagne glasses as the queens tossed them back over their heads. A newsreader I recognised from TV latched onto me as we made our way along a long, dark, narrow hallway. He was big and oily and red-faced, with a loud Ulster–English accent.

'Who're you then?' he boomed, spittle flying.

Bet Lynch turned back to us. 'Who're you callin' a hoore?' She flung her knotted pearls back violently and trailed me forward. 'He's my apprentice. Annchuh, chuck?'

'Who will he be when he serves his time?' the newsman asked.

'Phil McCracken.' Bet pushed me ahead. I almost head-butted Cher in the ass and she scowled round at me.

'You're not Phil McCracken yet.' She had the voice of a sixty-a-day docker.

At the end of the hallway, a huge sign, lit from behind by shifting multi-coloured fibre optic lights, announced:

SOUND AS A POUND FM
Belfast's Newest Coolest Music Station
The Greatest Place to Place Your Ad
Est 1996

Not that new. Not that cool either. To the left, an open reception area pulsed with Christmas lights and the kind of cheesy Christmas music I hated and loved at the same time. One wall was made of frosted white glass but the fading sun that filtered through was nothing compared to the glare from the sign and the decorations.

Clumps of middle-aged suits and twenty-somethings in tight T-shirts and baggy trousers stood around with glasses of champagne, chatting and laughing with people I recognised from TV. In front of the frosted glass wall, a tiny blonde woman draped herself over a wide black desk, waving a glass of champagne in each hand.

'Welcome to Sound as a Pound's Christmas parteeeeeehhhhhh!' she squealed in a cartoon voice, evidently the one who wouldn't let me in. 'Help yourselves to a drink because I cannot be *arsed*!'

Bet was at the drinks table already, wobbling in her tall platform boots as she bent to pour champagne. I aimed myself towards her but a small fella with loose black curls and heavy black glasses caught my sleeve.

'Are you Andrea's son?' He pronounced it An-dray-ah. His friends, one girl and two blokes, all dressed like him in cool trendy gear, smiled at me with forced affection.

'Is your mum really setting up on her own?' the girl asked me. She had incredibly straight and shiny black hair and wore small, horn-rimmed glasses.

'My mum?'

'Yeah.'

'Her own ... whah?'

'Her own ad agency, duh.' Curly bloke shook his head. 'He doesn't know anything.'

'Well, that depends on what you're talkin' about, mate.'

'See!' Horn-rim girl said. 'He does know something! I knew it!' She smiled at me slowly. 'Can I get you a drink? Water perhaps?'

The small blonde squealed as more people arrived and the trendy types swung round to see. I joined Bet and she handed me a glass of champagne, lightly clinking hers against mine. 'A thousand million comes, Phil.'

'Ahm ... yeah, OK.'

A round of ecstatic shouts and screams erupted from the dark hallway and a bunch of people, including Marilyn, bowed and scraped in front of somebody who must have been even smaller than me. I couldn't see anybody though.

'Who's the invisible dwarf?' I asked Bet. 'In fact, where's the invisible dwarf?'

'That's Pete, you silly wee thing.' She wobbled her piled-up hair towards the hallway and frowned down at me. 'Have you not met Pete before?'

'Not really.'

'C'mon w'me.' She propelled me across the room, one muscular hand on my back. 'Pete, love!' she said, bending to kiss him on the cheek. He was still tanned and good-looking but his skin was saggy and he was much thinner than he was in the old photograph. I couldn't see him from across the room because he was in a wheelchair.

'How's you, Seamus?' he asked her. 'Who's this?' He

looked at me. 'Not another apprentice?'

'This . . .' Bet looked down at me. 'This is . . . what is your name anyway?'

'Cookie.'

Bet swung me round by the back of the neck. 'Jesus, Mary and Joseph! That's better than Phil McCracken!'

'It's short for Cuchulain! Aargh! Cuchulain Fitzpatrick!'

Pete opened his mouth but Marilyn spun his chair round, smothered him in a hug and chatted at him furiously.

'Pete and Mo go way back,' Bet said, propelling me back to the drinks table. 'I always let them have their wee moment.' She poured more champagne. 'Y'know Cookie, when I look at you, I see a wee star. And that's not a come on. Come on. Drink up. I see me in you. And that's not a come on either. Holy Mary Mother of God, I can't help it. Let's get blocked. It's free.'

We knocked back our champagne and refilled. I glanced back across the room. Marilyn had moved on and Pete was already talking to somebody else.

'Do Edith Piaf again! Go on, go on, do Edith Piaf!'

We stood in Sound as a Pound's small, smoky, window-less kitchen – me, Bet, Cher, horn-rim girl, a stocky sound engineer called Micheal (pronounced Mee-hawl – black looks for those who got it wrong) and a tall, drunk, middle-aged advertising man in a glossy suit who staggered on the spot and said nothing. He was good friends with the fridge though.

How I loved the champagne. How I loved Edith Piaf.

Now that I knew I could do her.

Bet leaned out into the reception and guldered across the room. 'Hey Marilyn, chuck! Marilyn! Mo! C'mere d'y'hear this! Mo, fuck ye, c'mere!'

Marilyn clattered across the reception's tiled floor and swung round the doorway into the kitchen. I swigged from a bottle of champagne, held it out and sang into it.

'Nonnnnnn, regrette rien, non, je ne regrette riennnnn ...' I even did the down-turned French lips and shruggy shoulders. I was so good! I wanted to be a drag-a-gram!

Marilyn looked at Bet, surprised and slightly doubtful, then she spoke in that whispery voice. 'What's your name?'

'Je m'appelle Edith.'

Marilyn's breathy voice transformed into a low, easy listening County Antrim accent. 'No, what's your real name?'

'Sacre bleu!' I slapped my hand to my chest. 'Edith Giovanna Gassion!'

And you thought piano lessons were bad? I swear to God, I had to listen to that one record, every minute of every day, for four weeks solid. She'd just got her tattoo.

Bet clapped her hands and laughed like a hiccup. Mo nodded with a lopsided smile. 'I could have some work for you, if you're interested. How's your Cleo Laine?'

'Boo-doo-doo-dee-doop. Bah-daaaahp-a-doo. Doo-doo-doo-doop-a-daaah.'

'Good God. What's your name again?'

'Coo-ee. Sorry, drink does that. Cookie.'

'No!'

'Yup,' Cher growled, waving her champagne glass

around delicately. 'It's short for . . . what did you say it was short for, bird?'

'Cooln fizzparrick.' Jesus Christ. Minus nine million out of ten. 'Bit drunk now.'

'Wait a second,' the horn-rimmed girl said. 'You aren't An-dray-ah's son?'

'Nope.'

'Why'd you say you were?'

'As I re-fucken-call. Good word that. As I re-fucken-call, I never said I was.'

'So I've been standing here plying you with drink for nothing?'

'Not *all* for nothin', cause like, I'm fucken drunk now.'

'A fucking hour I've wasted in here! *You*'ll hardly get me into Andrea's new place!'

'An-*dray*-ah wouldn't want you. 'S your attitude.'

She pushed her ass off the counter and made for the door. 'Fuck you, fruit.'

Cher grunted after her. 'I'll fucken dig you, love.'

Pete wheeled into the kitchen and I blinked hard and tried to look sober.

'Micheal, get us a Bud there.' He rolled up to the advertising bloke and nudged a wheel in his leg. 'Away home, Gary, for God's sake. Angie'll get you a taxi.'

Gary closed one eye and squinted down at Pete. 'These women are all very . . . big.' He closed his eyes and concentrated but when he opened them again the clouds were still there. He looked at me. ''Cept for the one in combats. Are you a lezzer?'

Pete reversed up a bit. 'Micheal, put Gary in a taxi, would you?'

Micheal handed Pete a beer and gave another one to the advertising bloke, before shovelling him towards the door.

'I don't want to go home yet,' Gary said. 'She'll be waiting for me.'

'Seeya, Gary!' Pete called after him.

'Uz a goo party, Pete ...' Gary was distant.

'You keep paying the invoices, I'll keep supplying the drink.' He turned to me and the ladies. 'Did I hear singing in here?'

'Oh, you wanna hear Cookie's Edith Piaf, Pete!' Bet swung her pearls.

Pete looked at me. 'Bit young for a female impersonator, aren't you?'

'There's none too young for me!' Bet looped her arm round my shoulders and squeezed the breath out of me. 'You're my wee star! Annchuh, chuck?'

'Pete,' I said, struggling to stay focused. 'Pete, here, listen, I wanted to ask yuh somethin ...'

'Can't offer you a job. Sorry.'

'No, wait, you know, you know Lizzie Fitzpatrick ...?'

'I *knew* it,' he said. 'I just bloody knew it. Soon as I saw you. Then the name. And when I heard you sing. She could sing. Not Edith Piaf like, but she could sing. God, I just bloody well knew it.'

'You're Lizzie's wee fella?' Marilyn's eyes glittered with delight. She studied me. 'Right enough!'

Bet jumped up and down, pearls bouncing on her hard boobs. 'Everybody knows everybody!' She handed me another glass of champagne.

'Pete, I just came t ...' Felt sick. I needed food not champagne but the thought of food made me feel worse.

'Oh, I get it now.' Pete shook his head. 'I know what you're here for. What age are you? Fourteen?'

'Sixt ... no wait, Pete ...'

He held up his hands. 'I was in London for fifteen years. I've been back for four. Hopefully that answers your question. How is she anyway?'

'Welluegh.' I choked on a small burny burp. 'She took off. Split. Done a runner. September.'

'Ach no.' Marilyn was disappointed. 'I'd love to see Lizzie again.' She turned to Pete. 'Jamember the heels she used to wear? She gave me my first pair. I was like King Kong standing on a couple of Mini Metros. Wee Lizzie was brilliant.'

I liked Marilyn. Everything she felt just plastered itself all over her face. I really, really liked her. Him. Her. I wasn't sure about Pete. I turned back to him.

'I thought maybe you'd know why she'd go to Amsterdheugh ...' Another painful burp gurgled up. 'Jeeesus.'

'How much champagne has he had?' Pete looked at Marilyn.

Bet fluttered her eyelashes. 'He's alright. I've taken him under my wing.'

Cher spluttered into her champagne. 'Ballicks.'

'Well, if Lizzie turns up, tell her to give me a shout,' Pete said. 'The production department needs session singers. Good ones.'

'What would she be singin'?' I asked.

'Trails. Jingles. That type of thing.'

Trails Jingles Prince Molly Prince. I looked up to the left but couldn't see straight

Pete took the glass out of my hand. 'Did you have to let him have so much?'

Bet filled a pint glass under the tap. 'Drink that, wee star.' She handed me the pint glass. It slipped through my fingers and exploded on the floor, loud enough to make me tuck my ear

Soaked my legs. Cold hot cold. Bet leaned into my face said something. Ceiling. Her face again. Her make-up was so thick. Josie was not a man I knew that. She said.

Drink up play Prince's guitar for me, in his room, come on you're better than him come on he's never here I'll show yuh come on

What you say?

I never fainted before. I never knew what fainting felt like. But I knew I was doing it. Heard a black drill. Saw the tiles close up. Red speckled stiletto dented lino not limo

Light under her bedroom door pass a fiver out to me, lowdown hole in the wall. Away and get chips, Cookie, me and Buckshot's busy in here busy in here

I'm away then

'Sit him up! Sit him up!'

'Sorry.' I tried to catch the watery vomit in my hand. 'Sorry she did sorry.'

I was on a low red settee next to a mixing desk I'd seen on MTV. No not this one. Similar. I trailed my legs round to the floor. 'Sorry OK sorry.'

Bet dabbed at me with a tea towel, already saturated with champagne vomit. 'You're alright, wee star.'

The studio was cramped with just three other people.

Bet propped me up, an arm behind my shoulders, the hand with the tea towel under my chin. Her make-up was shiny hot. Pete sat in his chair behind her, supremely pissed off. Marilyn stood beside him, arms crossed over her waist, vomit on her white dress.

No not cry stupid I refused, shivered, set my teeth.

'Will y'be alright in a taxi?' Bet said. 'Where d'y'live?'

I took the tea towel and wiped at my face. 'What time is it?'

'Quarter past four,' Pete said. 'Time you were out of here. Micheal! Order a taxi! And cancel the ambulance!'

I sat for a second, then tried to get up. Bet caught me as I toppled forward. I turned to Pete. 'I'm sorry. Really. Really sorry.'

He shook his head. 'You're just like her.'

'I'm *not* like her. How can a bloke be like a woman?'

Marilyn and Bet lifted one eyebrow each.

'Let us have a minute, lads, would you?' Pete said.

Bet put a finger under my chin. 'You drink plenty of water now, woncha?'

'Yeah. Sorry for ... doin' that on yuh.'

Marilyn pulled me to her in a one-armed hug. 'When Lizzie comes back, tell her to give me a ring. As for you, well, there's still an opening ...'

'Ooh eck.'

'... for an Edith Piaf or a Cleo Laine. When you're eighteen.'

They left and I sank down on the settee again.

'What the hell are you playing at?' Pete asked.

'I said I was sorry.'

'Look at you.'

'I have to go.'

'Are you on your own, you know, since she went?'

'I'm meetin' a mate.'

'Does nobody know where she went?'

'She sent a postcard from Amsterdam. I was sorta hopin' you'd know somethin'.'

He shook his head blankly. 'Well, other than drugs and porn ... Anyway. Have you talked to anyone else?'

'Stuartie. Billy Dick. Not Buckshot. Nobody knows where he is.'

'What about Paul?'

'Paul? Who's Paul?'

'Buckshot's wee brother.'

'Where does he live? Do you think he'd know somethin'?'

'You could try him. I don't know where he lives but he owns that new restaurant, what do you call it now, I haven't been to it but I hear it's good.'

'Where?'

'Bit of a daft name. He's a chef. Left here years ago and came back last summer, a wee ginger bird on his arm.' He squinted, unfocused, at the mixing desk. 'God, what do you call the place? I keep meaning to go. Blue? Boot?'

Name that restaurant in oh fuck. 'Would it be called Boo?'

'That's it.' He nodded. 'Try Paul. He went out with her a couple of times.'

Paul just said he grew up in the next street. *Paul* didn't tell me he was Buckshot's brother. *Paul* didn't tell me his name was Paul or even Buchanan. And he didn't even mention green velvet soup.

And he sure as fuck didn't tell me he went out with her.

He was checking me out. He was checking me out before deciding whether he wanted me. Bastard.

Oh, I'd *try* him alright.

It was only half four and I had a terrible hangover. I slid along Sound as a Pound's hallway, grateful for the darkness of the street outside. The teatime rush was just beginning and I pressed myself into the doorway of Wyse Byse to watch the headlights swap and dodge along the four lanes.

I looked in every car that slowed for the lights. A small, sleek Mercedes. Maybe. A silver Ford Mondeo. More like it. Ah, a Ford Puma. No. I sank down onto the step. I needed something. I'd ask Bonehead to call into the garage. That's if he came. Maybe he wouldn't come. Of course he'd come.

I was woken by a sharp clunk on the noggin. I rubbed my head and looked about. The next one was more of a thwack, this time on the cheek. I pushed myself up. Cars were everywhere. Buses and vans and lorries, rushing to stop at traffic lights, then rushing to stop at the next. Oww! Another clunk, on my forehead. I heard a clink as something hit the pavement. A two-pence piece. Some bastard was tossing money at me.

I looked everywhere but the girder was so fucken annoying. I squinted up at the orangey-black sky. The girder was whistling down through the air, bits dropping off and falling in the shape of coins

OWWW!

He said he'd been shouting and waving and throwing money from across the road for ten bloody minutes. He was frantic when I finally made it across to his forest of vanilla Magic Trees. His mouth was flapping like a muppet.

'This is a fucken clearway!' He rammed the car into gear when I got in and screeched up to the lights. His middle finger had a Loony Toons bandage on it. It glowed on the gearstick.

'Can you not park Fiestas in clearways?' I asked. 'What's a clearway? Here, how's your finger?'

'It's not a Fiesta, it's an XR2!' He revved and revved at the lights, bobbing about nervously. 'This place is fucken crawlin' with traffic wardens and cops ...'

'Whah?'

'Open your lugs, y'wanker!'

I looked at the street sign as we turned left at the lights. Holywood Road. More Christmas lights across the street. Cheery. I looked over at him as he raked the car between each set of lights. 'What's wrong?'

'I'm late,' he said.

'Maybe we should get married.'

'Whah?'

'Take a chill pill, Bonehead. So you were late.'

'More than an hour! Could you not be fucked off for once?'

'It's not a problem, mate.'

He gripped the steering wheel and rocked back and forward, roaring.

I laughed. 'What's wrong?'

He forced himself back in the seat and drove with both arms stiff and straight, his knobbly knuckles tight on the steering wheel. 'I coulden get all the stuff y'wanted.'

'Well, what did y'get?'

'Everything 'cept the acid.'

'But I need it all for the marra.'

'Well, you think of somethin'. You're the one with all the fucken great ideas.'

'OK. I just did. Head back to Botanic. You had your tea yet?'

He roared at the driver ahead and waved his hands like an Italian. I didn't know why though. The road was jammed with slow-moving traffic so nobody could go any faster.

'What's wrong with yuh, Bonehead?'

He nodded and then he shook his head and then he nodded again. 'We're dead.' He gave me a serious look. 'We are dead.'

'There is a heaven.'

'Cookie, this is shit, alright? All this shit you're always talkin'. This is fucken real. We are dead.'

'Why?'

'We have to be down the glen the marra night, ten o'clock.'

'What for?'

'A batin'.'

'What for?'

'Christ the fucken night. They knew it was me. They knew it was you, dickhead.'

'What about your contacts?'

'I don't have any more contacts than anybody else. You can't get that into your thick skull, can ya? My contacts. Jesus Christ.'

'Don't go,' I said. 'I'm not goin'.'

He took his hands off the steering wheel and wrapped them round my neck, his bandaged finger almost poking my eye out.

'Watch the road!' I choked. The car in front had stopped at a zebra crossing.

Bhamp. The other car shunted forward, swerved left, mounted the pavement and hit the striped pole. The belisha beacon toppled off, hit the car's bonnet and trundled by. The car rolled back to its original position.

Bonehead looked at me, furious desperation draining his face. He shook his huge hands again, possessed by the ghost of an Italian grandmother. 'Right. You get out and talk. It's your fault.'

'*You* were stranglin' *me*.'

'Go on. You can lie better than me.'

'What'll I say? I don't know anything about cars. What am I meant to say?'

'Give them your name and address and insurance company.'

'What insurance company? An' I'm sort of between homes at the minute.'

'Make it up! Go on, get out!' He pushed me out the door and I walked round the front of the Fiesta. Sorry. XR2. The other car was crumpled along the lower part of its back bumper and I didn't even want to see the bonnet. Behind us, stationary lights stretched to oblivion and cars that overtook blasted their horns.

I squinted at the other car's gleaming black end. The rear lights were shaped like boomerangs and the boot was an odd, boxy shape. I squinted at the name. The car in front was a Maserati. I finally understood why Prince looked at me funny when I asked him to get me a bottle of that in the offy.

The driver stayed put but the passenger door opened and a small, skinny fella jogged round to join me. He couldn't have been much older than me. His head was shaved under his baseball cap and he wore a Celtic top and about nine million gold chains round his neck, each with a different pendant. Two crucifixes, a sovereign, a boxing glove, a mobile phone, a heart with the word MA inside and an armalite.

We stared down at the Maserati's bumper.

'Wick one,' I said.

'Yeah.' He stuffed his hands into the pockets of his Levis.

'Sorry like,' I said.

He shrugged. 'These things happen.'

'D'y'want my name and address and insurance company then?'

'Ahm ...' He ducked and looked back inside the car at

the driver. He took a tiny mobile phone out of his back pocket and dialled with his thumb, ducking again to look inside. 'Do I want his name and address and insurance company?' He nodded in through the window, then turned to me. 'Go ahead then.'

'Have y'got a piece of paper?' I asked.

'Houl on.' He dialled again and looked through the back window. 'Do we have a piece of paper?' He jerked the phone away from his ear and put it away. 'Just tell me,' he said. 'I'll remember.'

'The name's Ian,' I said. 'Ian Steele. Just use my initial. Everybody does.'

Pendant Boy nodded.

'Address is ... 175 Driver Way.'

'Right. OK.'

'And my insurer is ... Heist and Co., Belfast. Jewish. Very good, so they are.'

'Right.' He nodded.

'You goin' t'give me yours?'

'Houl on a minute.' He phoned the driver again. The side window glinted as the driver launched his phone up to the stars. Its 'Soldier's Song' ring grew distant.

'Right, well, ahm,' Pendant Boy said. 'My name's ahm, John ... Smith. Number three, ahm, this road here. Insurer's, ahm, same as yours. Same fella like.'

'Nice one.' I nodded. 'OK, well, I'll get my people to talk to ... my people then.'

'Yeah, dead on.'

I held out a hand to shake. 'All the best then, Ian.'

'Yeah,' he said, shaking. 'Cheers, John. Sorry about that.'

'Absolutely not a problem,' I said, and got back into the

car. I slid down in the seat as Bonehead started the engine again, looking at me eagerly.

'Well? Well? What d'he say?'

'I don't feel very well.'

'He looked alright to me.'

I opened the car door and puked bile onto the road.

We called into a garage further along the Holywood Road and I bought four sodas (that's the bread, not the drink), four potato bread, six eggs, a double pack of pork sausages (unrepeatable offer), a double pack of bacon (another unrepeatable offer), a bottle of water, a pack of Strawberry Sherberts, twenty Consulate and a pack of icing sugar.

We doubled back towards the city centre on the Sydenham Bypass, the dual carriageway between Belfast and north Down. We stayed in the slow lane, inconspicuous at just over the speed limit, and passed the airport and the shipyard on the right. Christmas lights hung all over the cranes.

'D'y'see the cranes, Bonehead?'

'Yeah.'

'They're sort of like rifles, aren't they? Y'know, with the beam straight across like the gun and the rope things from the ends up to the top, like the strap you would put over your shoulder?'

He glanced at me. 'What the fuck were you drinkin'? Cleanin' fluid?'

'No. Not this time.'

We crossed a strand of the M3 bridge. Sudden and addictive views on either side. On the left, city lights stretched back and lapped like a tide at the Castlereagh Hills, Black Mountain and Cave Hill. On the right, I could see down the entire length of the Lough. Escape. We came down off the bridge and headed back across town.

I kept the window down and sipped at the water. I tried sucking a Strawberry Sherbert and offered Bonehead one but he said I could blow it out my ass. I said that was optimistic. I tried a cigarette but ended up just holding it. I offered Bonehead one but he said I only smoked Consulate because nobody else liked them. I said that was perspicacious. I loved doing that to him.

Botanic Avenue crawled with taxis and every one of them had a stunted mutant Christmas tree on the dash-board. We screeched up outside Prince's house, startling some drunk students who wobbled along in Santa hats.

I got out and rapped at the front door. Satanic Hearses thumped down the stairs inside and opened the door. He looked at Bonehead.

'Yes?'

'He's w'me, Fart of Darkness.' I pushed by him with my fissly bag of shopping but he caught me by the collar.

'Where are you going?'

'To see Prince, fuckwit.'

'Prince isn't here. He's away. And I can't tell you how much I have longed to do this.' He took a better hold of my coat and flung me backwards out the door. My messages went flying as I tumbled arse over tit onto the path.

Bonehead stared down at me as Satanic Hearses closed the door. 'This was your great i-fucken-dea then?' He hauled me to my feet but I went down just as quick. I sat on the path for a minute, letting everything settle.

'I can't make out a word you're sayin',' I said.

'I *said*, we can't get into your brother's and I can't get you off on the path. Now what, Hannibal fucken Smith?'

I looked up at him. I heard the noise but it always dodged me. Cold black sky with stars dimmed by sodium lights. Dave moved in big wordy grin.

'Dave!' I said. 'Satanic Hearses threw me out.'

'Hnnh, did you come over his Xena annual too?'

'No.'

Dave nodded slowly. 'Come on.' He stepped over me and opened the door with his key. I got to my feet and pushed Bonehead away. He picked up the messages and we followed Dave inside.

The house still smelt of baking. The kitchen worktops strained under towers of plastic boxes and tins, full of Dave's cakes and buns and biscuits.

'Didn't make much, did yuh?' I said.

'Hnnh? Well, sure, whatever doesn't get ate I'll take down The Collective or St Vincent de Paul or somethin'.'

'You're full of it,' I said.

'Whah?'

'Christmas spirit, mate. You know Bonehead, doncha? Dave, Bonehead, Bonehead, Dave.'

Dave scanned Bonehead's scalp. 'Where'd y'get the scars from?'

Bonehead opened his mouth but Josie stepped in front of him. She glared at me, fist on hip. 'You.'

'Yes, me. I've come to make you all a big fuck off fry. By way of apology.'

She marched across the room and slapped me one

across the head. It wasn't that hard but I slid down the cupboards and onto the floor anyway.

'Oh Jesus, I didn't mean to do that.' She knelt down.

'It's alright. I haven't been feelin' well.'

'Ach, Cookie, why diddin yuh say?'

'Well, I didn't know you were gonna fucken hit me.'

She pulled me to my feet again. 'Why do you have to be such a selfish wee shit all the time?'

I took the bag of messages out of Bonehead's hand and held it up. 'Eight quids worth of fry materials here, y'know.'

'I had to rearrange everything.' She bounced where she stood, like she would have liked to stamp her foot but was too grown up to do it. 'With Prince away, we didn't have anybody.'

'Well, where is he?'

She shook her head, her eyebrows doing what his always did. 'His guitar's away an' everything.'

'He'll come back,' I said.

'Well, are you doin' this the marra or not?' she said.

I nodded.

'Good. But I'll believe it when I see it.' She swept over to the fridge, the tiny bells on her tassely top tinkling. 'I need a bloody drink.'

I asked Josie to put MTV2 on for Bonehead and then I set about making the fry. Dave didn't want to leave the kitchen but I pushed him out. I just wished Prince could've had some.

Tinned soup and toast. Packet soup and toast. Cereal and

toast. Scrambled eggs and toast. Microwave soup and toast. Oven chips and, wow, buttered bread. That was the extent of my repertoire. A fry of biblical proportions was going to be a bit of a challenge but I had total confidence in my abilities. I was going through my most creative period.

My eyes burned with smoking fat, I set the smoke alarm off three times and I sweated so much it dripped off the end of my nose. Still. It gave Dave and Josie a chance to get lickered in front of the TV and at one point, I saw Dave lurch back and forth by the door to Rage Against the Machine. He might have been dancing but I wasn't sure. Josie got drunk pretty fast and I put it down to stress or the fact she'd already been drinking. I think she started to like MTV2 as well.

I turned the oven on so I could fry in batches and keep it all warm. And keep Josie's fried soda and potato bread and egg away from the meat, as requested. But it was awkward as fuck and I used every pot and pan in the house and then moved onto oven dishes and baking bowls. Then when I went to put the first batch of fried bread and sausages into the heated oven, I found that was where they kept the chip pan when it wasn't being used. I grabbed the pan in panic, howled, followed it up with 'I'm OK I'm OK I'm OK!' and danced around the kitchen, screaming silently, my roasted hands between my thighs.

I got a few tea towels, wrapped them round the chip pan and took it outside, opening the back door with my boot. I rushed back inside to see smoke coming out of the closed grill. I must have turned it on by mistake. I whipped it open and black smoke and the sting of melting plastic engulfed the kitchen. I chased the clouds out the back door with a flapping tea towel.

Dave hung round the kitchen door. 'D'y'want me to help yuh?'

'I've got it under control!' I jammed the fish slice under the soda bread and two pieces tore their gooey undersides from the pan, flipped up the wall and slid down behind the cooker. I turned to Dave. 'I didn't want those bits.'

Josie called in from the other room. 'Can I have a cuppa tea w'mine?'

I opened my mouth to retaliate but Dave slapped a hand over my mouth and pushed me away by my face. He took the fish slice out of my hand and turned everything down very low.

'I'm not really very good at this,' I admitted.

He laughed. 'See? That's the difference between Prods and Taigs,' he said. 'Prods always have to get it right first time.'

'I'm not a Prod. And *you*'re not a Taig, Dave.'

'My ma an' da were.' He flipped the soda bread gently. 'I used to go t'confession an' all.'

'No way. What happened?'

'Just shit. The army. London. Drugs. California. Marriage. Y'know. Shit.'

'Fuck. Me.'

'Hnnh.'

He finished the fry but I'd made such a bollocks of the early stages it wasn't nearly as good as his usual efforts. He dished everything out onto plates as I used the scorched tea towel to dry my face.

I turned on the kettle for Josie's tea but forgot to put the water in and almost destroyed that too.

'Dave,' I said, filling the kettle under the tap. The water hissed as it hit the bottom. 'Did Prince say where he was goin'?'

He shrugged. 'Diddin get talkin' to him.'

'D'y'think he'll come back?'

'Everybody comes back.'

I filled the kettle up to the brim and noticed there was something stuck down the plughole. I leaned over to look. There was something down there looking back up at me.

'No, *this* is why you can't cook,' Dave said, taking the kettle off me. He poured out most of the water and set it back on its stand.

'Dave, would you do me a favour?'

'Hnnh?'

'Don't feel obliged like.'

'Well, like, I won't.'

'I want some acid. Where do you get yours from?'

He looked at me with half a frown. 'I'm thinkin' what Prince would do.'

'Prince would tell me.'

'I know he would. That's what I'm thinkin' about.'

We took the M5, which runs parallel to the Shore Road until they become one at Whiteabbey, then we drove along the coast to Carrickfergus, a town on the Antrim side of Belfast Lough. The first thing you notice about Carrick is the number of places to eat. KFC, Indian, Chinese, ice cream parlour, McD's, pizza place, chippies, bar food, more Chinese, more Indian, more chippies, more pizza, more ice cream and even more chippies. Oh, yeah. Then there's the huge great eleventh-century Norman castle as well. I did try eating that. One time on a school visit in primary five. Well I didn't eat it, I just licked the sides.

We drove through the town towards the towering fat chimney of Kilroot Power Station, a few miles further along. Dave sat in the front with Bonehead, and I sat in the back with my legs up. They were both so big, they'd pushed their seats as far back as they would go. Dave's dreads constantly flicked me up the face after I asked him to wind the window down but at least the cold air helped me keep my potato bread under control. Every now and again he'd go Hnnh but Bonehead only spoke once the entire journey. And that was to tell Dave to stop going fucken Hnnh. I used the time productively. I thought about Stretch Armstrong.

Me and Prince had a Stretch Armstrong. And we stretched him everywhere and every shape. Stretching was far too easy for Stretch Armstrong so we tried him in other ways. We tied him to fireworks and dropped him off the bridge down onto the motorway. We tied him to the back of Big Julie's car, tossed him into a cement mixer, melted him with a magnifying glass and launched him off the top of the Cave Hill. And still he grinned that big mad grin. We couldn't break Stretch Armstrong. But maybe we just didn't try him hard enough.

Pete said I should try Paul. Fly away Peter fly away Paul. Concentrate for fuck's sake. My next wave would try Billy Dick and Boo at the same time. It was great. Like fate. They'd both be at the festival and I had a loose plan of action in my head. I tried to imagine my exact movements but it was such a rush job, I accepted I'd have to improvise and compromise a lot of it. I turned it over and over in my head but I got to the point where the word try didn't mean anything any more. It was just an eye with teeth. I kept going back to Stretch Armstrong, lobbed off the Cave Hill, a spindly spook with a big head somersaulting over Belfast.

The road narrowed as we passed the power station and we were suddenly in the country. Black fields, skeletal trees and thick thorny bushes slid along on either side of us. Dave raised a fat wide finger and pointed to the right. 'In here.'

Tucked away and hidden like an embarrassing relative was a mini housing estate. Kerbstones were stained with faded red, white and blue and raggedy flags hung from lamp-posts outside battered 1970's terraces. Boarded up windows, loyalist murals and a web of shell suits standing by a Corsa made it all seem very familiar.

'How do you usually get here?' I asked Dave. 'Bin lorry?'

'The bus. Next left, Bonehead. Manse Park. Then down the end.'

Bonehead drove along a tight car-lined road and stopped in front of a terrace at the end of a cul-de-sac. He yanked on the handbrake like he was lifting a suitcase.

'What you stop for?' Dave said.

'There's nowhere else to go.'

'No, go up the pavement and round the back.'

'Round there?' Bonehead peered at the side of the terrace. 'You off your head already?'

'No, mate. That's where we go.'

Bonehead bumped the car up onto the pavement and we drove round the side of the terrace, where a rough track disappeared into darkness. The car's squinty head-lights flicked up and round a line of arthritic hawthorn trees as we dipped and sank through muddy potholes. My potato bread threatened to make a break for it but I couldn't get out of the car there no way fucken wee fairies don't bring the mayflower in the house aye alright granny

I stared straight ahead but I knew they were looking at me they knew I was there fuck off fuck off

Bonehead followed the track round to the right where it suddenly opened up into the grounds of an old manse. One ground-level security light shone dimly on a sturdy old block of a building with five or six cars and as many motorbikes outside. The house's grey-blue paint was peeling but there was a light on in every window. The front door was wide open.

'What da fuck's this?' Bonehead said, parking beside the other cars. Two kids tumbled out the front door and ran round the side of the house, giggling and shouting.

'This is where the Minister lives,' Dave said.

'Have you brought us here to be *saved*?' I said. 'Could you not have at least tried to convert us to Catholicism?'

'They'll get paranoid if you sit here. Come on.' Dave heaved himself out just as a man with long hair sprinted out of the house, slapping at his head and shouting, 'Scary monkeys! Scary monkeys!' He ran off down the lane.

Bonehead looked at me. 'Is Dave a Taig?'

'His ma and da were. Why?'

'Nathin'.'

'D'y'not like him now?'

'Just don't like Taigs.'

I leaned forward. 'Whaddya think we should do?'

'Maybe it's full of RCs. They'll want to kill me.'

'Dave said it's where the Minister lives. That's Protestant.'

'Aye but if *he*'s one ...'

'His ma and da were.'

'Aye but ...'

A motorbike revved like a series of explosions and I covered my ears. A chunky biker in shiny red leathers raced out of the house on a shiny red motorbike.

Bonehead was still going on.

'Whah?'

'Fuck's sake, Cookie, get your ears syr-fucken-rinjed, would ja? I'm not goin' in.'

'Dave said they'd get paranoid if we sat out here. What if they come out and dig our heads in?' I looked over at the house. The same two kids ran out the front door again.

'Fuck 'em, Fenian bastards.'

'Aye but maybe they're Prods. Paranoid Prods.'

'They'll not dig our heads in then, will they'?'

'Oh aye? Who's diggin' your head in the marra night then?'

We both jumped as Dave rapped sharply on the window. Bonehead wound it down.

'They've got a parrot called Mr Moo Moo,' Dave said.

'You tryin' to get us killed?' Bonehead said.

'I think he's tame.'

'Here, Dave,' I said. 'Is it safe?'

'Yeah. Is what safe?'

'In there?'

'Come on if you're comin'.' He turned away and sloped inside.

Half an hour later, I decided I wanted to be a drug dealer biker tattooist. The fairies approved. I had a feeling they were in the hot-press but I didn't tell anybody. They knew when I was in the kitchen underneath them as well. And these weren't the nice wee friendly fairies your teacher or your mother told you about. These were evil wee fuckers and they all had my face. I tried not to think about them as we searched for Dave.

The kitchen was in the process of being renovated. Half was sparkling red and yellow tiles, ageing range and fairytale cottage cupboards. The other half was bare brick and new plaster. Wiring hung out of crumbling holes in the walls and a pile of washing sat next to a dog's basket. The only light came from a dim lamp above the range.

The room was full of women, all having the screamy laugh of their lives. Some hovered round the range, breaking garlic bread and pizza out of packets. Others stood in clumps passing round joints, drinking beer, pouring Bacardi and Coke and showing off tattoos. The two kids ran in the back door and through to the front of the house again.

I turned to Bonehead. He was staring at a small, heavy woman whose red backless top showed off a dramatic swirl of tattoos. Her huge boobs hung like a quilt where all the feathers have worked their way to the bottom.

'Alright love?' she said to him. Her County Antrim accent had no Ts. 'Come on over for a better look. I've won competitions.' She cupped her hands under her boobs and held them up for his inspection.

When I turned, Bonehead was gone.

I thought about taking her up on her offer but I trailed out to the hall after Bonehead instead. No sign of him. Just boxes and boxes piled high against the stairs. I leaned into the living room. It was beginning to crumble round the edges. Frank Zappa was trapped inside the stereo and the bikers draped over the old settees and chairs stared at him in mild shock.

Leathers and heavy jackets were piled three feet high in the corner, even though nobody seemed to have removed any layers. One guy rolled up on a tray, his papers, roaches, blow, cigarettes and lighter arranged about him like he was about to sit an exam. A lucky gonk sat on the arm of the chair.

Mr Moo Moo balanced on the leather arm of a fat biker.

'Mr Moo Moo! Mr Moo Moo! Mr Glovey kill you now!

Mr Glovey kill yooooo!' The fat biker toreadored a gloved hand round and round the parrot. 'Eeeeerghrrgh you dieee!'

'Can I hold Mr Moo Moo?' I asked.

'Here, Geoff!' A skinny-necked biker suddenly sat up. 'Saxa Salt commandoes!'

'What?' the fat biker said. Another silent T.

'My tattoo. I was goin' to get a celtic sorta thing but my da says that's too Catholicky, right? So I was thinkin' Saxa Salt commadoes.'

The fat biker looked at Mr Moo Moo. 'Say Alan's a wanker. Alan's a wanker. Say it.'

'Geoff's a fat bastard,' Mr Moo Moo said. 'Geoff's a fat bastard.'

Skinny neck was serious. 'Anything Proddy looks hard as fuck, right? Like you're a terrorist, right? So I was thinkin'. You know the red hand of Ulster? About the two fellas on the boat that said whoever touched Ireland ...'

'Northern Ireland,' somebody growled.

'Whoever touched Northern Ireland first, they'd own it and the guy cut off his hand and chucked it? Well, it was a bit fucken mad, wasn't it? Why didn't he just throw salt in the other fella's eyes and swim for it? And then we wouldn't have the Red Hand Commandoes, we'd just have the Saxa Salt commandoes! Fuck me! That's it! I'm goin' to tell the Minister!' He jumped up and pushed past me in the doorway.

The bird stared fixedly at the fat biker. 'Geoff's a fat bastard, Geoff's a fat bastard.'

'Mr Moo Moo, Geoff kill you now.' The fat biker held Mr Moo Moo's beak shut with a finger and thumb, then he

took his hand away and puckered his lips up to the bird.
The bird sank its beak into his nose.

'It's OK,' I said above the screaming. 'I don't wanna hold
Mr Moo Moo now.'

I dodged into the room across the hall. It had clinical
modern wall lights, a pale wooden floor and three red
velvety settees. Bonehead sat on the one nearest the TV
with the remote in his hand. I stared at the screen, waiting
for him to turn it over to MTV2.

He didn't. He went on watching the thumpy hypnotic
dance channel. 'Get your big mate and come on,' he said.
'This place is full of fucken freaks.'

'You included. What the fuck are you watchin'?'

'I like this.'

'Since when?'

'I like lots of different stuff, Cookie.'

'But that's shite. That's spiderman music. Put MTV2 on.
They play metal.'

'I don't wanna listen to metal all the time, alright?'

'Whah?'

'Find your mate and come on.'

Something brushed by my legs and I looked down at a
tiny grey-faced wee me no, no, just a black mongrel which
didn't have my face. I knelt down and it tucked in its tail
and wagged its back end around, its nose snuffling at my
chin.

'Hello, doggie,' I said, tossing its ears around. I tried to
imagine what it was like to be a dog. I stopped tossing its
ears around and stroked its head instead. 'Where'd you
come from?'

It barked once.

'What's that?' I said, looking over at Bonehead. 'You know where Dave is? Is Dave in trouble?'

The dog barked twice more.

'Is Dave stuck down the well?'

The dog barked again and licked my chin.

'Show me, doggie! Take me to Dave!' I looked at Bonehead but he wouldn't take his eyes off the TV. The video flashed and reflected in his glasses and he didn't move.

'The dog knows where Dave is,' I said.

'Find him or I'm goin' without yiz.'

I followed the dog out into the hall. I wanted that dog. I wanted to be that dog. He waddled out the front door happily and I stood on the doorstep and watched him slip round the side of the house. The hawthorn trees fissled and creaked as he passed. They were in there. I knew they were in there. There was a trickly shuck below the row of trees, dug to keep them away from the house but they'd found a way to cross it.

The dog peeked round at me again and barked once more. He did know where Dave was.

I followed and felt along the wall in the darkness. It was blacker than under the covers round there. It smelt damp and weedy and I tripped over things. I didn't want to know what they were. There were fields at the side of the house, bare brambly bushes and shadowy sheds at the rear. Maybe I should go back. It was only a dog, for fuck's sake. I looked round to the front of the house again where the security light leaked out over the gravel.

The dog let out a sharp bark from behind the house.

'You better be right,' I said. But the dog was a good dog.

He wouldn't let anything happen to me. I followed him to a huddle of dilapidated buildings, then down a narrow passage between a breeze block shed and one made of corrugated iron. The loose sheets rattled in the wind. We turned left at the end where the blackness got too thick to go on.

'Where are ya?' I said. 'You've got dog eyesight. I can't see. Where are ya?'

'Here!' he barked.

I followed the sound, trailing my hand along dry bricks. I felt around a crumbly corner and saw a bright window straight ahead. The dog was on his hind legs, his front paws on the sill-less ledge. I looked in the fibre glass window too.

The building was full of motorbikes. Some gleamed new while others lacked their vital organs. On a workbench by the far wall sat a tattooed woman. Dave was pressed between her legs, his dreads moving gently. Red and blue flames wound round her thighs and forearms and wrapped themselves over his head.

'Good boy,' I said. 'You found Dave. But he's busy. Good boy anyway.'

'Not a problem,' the dog said. I looked at him. His sleek black neck stretched up into a human face. My face.

I tutted. 'They did this to you, didn't they?'

'How did you know?'

'Why don't you leave? You don't have to stay.'

'I live here.' He tilted his head. 'Where else would I go?'

'You're a dog. You'd get by.'

He set his front paws down and shook his body from head to tail. 'Nah, it's cool.'

'But you have people teeth. Whaddya eat?'

'Frosties.'

'That's no good for a dog.'

'I get by.'

I traced my way back to the house by my trail of jumbo crumbs. I had to jump some of them, they were so bloody big. I leapt up the front step and in the front door and slid up the banister along starlit stairs, no I wound my way up and under thick green tinsel and blinking Christmas lights, no what I did was, right, I took the bare wooden stairs one at a time and skimmed my hand over the soft tinsel to the long landing at the top.

I stood in front of the hot-press door, old and over-painted with a rattly black knob handle. I gripped it and whipped it open. They scattered quicker than I could see. But I saw them. I saw their dog blood teeth sheets nice fresh towels smelt clean. I leaned in and pushed the towels aside. Where are you, you bastards! How could you do that to that dog God but it was nice in there. I remembered our hot press. We had other stuff in there.

'What are you doing?' a voice came from behind me. Good solid voice, like a radio announcer. This is Radio Four. The time is four

'I'm lookin' for ... my mate,' I said.

'Well, he's not in there,' he said, closing the door. He was much taller than me, very broad but not fat. I couldn't pinpoint an age. Dad age. He wore a red and brown ethnic knitted top and leather trousers. His blonde hair shone although it was shaved almost to the scalp and his square, Scandinavian face ended in a foot-long, taily blonde goatee. He had no moustache.

'I've lost my brother,' I told him.

'Thought you were looking for your mate.'

'I've lost a couple of people actually.'

'Are you next?'

'What for?'

'Tattoo.'

'Ahm, yeah.'

We passed along bare floorboards to the Minister's vestry, the room at the furthest end of the landing. There was a comfortable old settee and a few low dentist style chairs with stools close by. Next to each chair was a tall, adjustable study lamp. The walls were covered in pictures of tattooed bodies and a wobbly warped ska record played in the corner.

Another tattooist worked on a young woman's hip bone as she lay on one of the dentist chairs, jeans pushed down to skim blue knickers. The tattooist's lip, eyebrow, nose and ears were pierced with silver and she watched him intensely. Every vein and tendon stood out in her neck. He concentrated on her skin, the pen's thin electric buzz constant.

'Miss Morrow?' I said.

The tattooee looked at me. 'Do I know you?' The tattooist lifted his pen from her skin and sat back.

'You laughed when Glen Donaghy tried to lynch me, jamember?' I looked at her fleshy-bony hip. She was lightly tanned. Smooth. Lickable.

'No, sorry,' she said. 'I remember Glen though. You one of his friends?'

'Glen's dead, did you know?'

'Oh my God. Seriously?' She leaned up on her elbows.

'He was so young. What happened?'

'Mauled to death by his own dog. Rottweiler pit bull cross. I think he was temptin' fate.'

'God, that's awful.' She lay back down.

'What are you gettin' done?' I asked.

'Loaves and fishes.'

'Whah?'

'Love and kisses. Very me. Nice to see you, anyway. What was your name again?'

'Ian.'

'Oh, yeah, I remember you now. I'm paying by time so I'll just let this very talented man carry on, if you don't mind.' She lay back, straining the tendons in her neck again as the tattooist leaned forward with his pen.

'Fill this in and sign it,' the Minister said.

I took the sheet and noted down my details. Ian Steele, 75 Driver Way, Belfast. 2/7/00. Making me considerably younger or more stupid than I hoped. No psoriasis or eczema or infectious diseases that I knew of. I gave Ian a big bubbly signature and a huge, circular dot over his I.

'Have a seat,' the Minister said, indicating a dentist chair. He drew a stool towards me. 'What do you want?'

'Just a wee thing,' I said.

'Where do you want it?'

I pointed to the centre of my forehead. 'Here.'

Crawl up on towels in the hot-press to pull sheets over my head. Close the door, handle on the inside, good God, good thinking. So dark I can hear them chatting. Still buzzing skin smarts, slide to the back where the fairies run away, you wouldn't dare now

Jamember what was in here, Prince? Do ya? We had stuff in here, we had tins, jamember? Why do we keep tins in the hot press, mum? Oh, well, you know, I want to hold onto those. I have to mind them

Permanent fixture. Fuck hungry what can we eat what can we eat what can what about those tins, Prince. But they're ancient. But they're tinned if this was a world war we would eat them. But this isn't a world war, it's just

We eat them and they're OK I like them hot press is

meant for fucken towels and sheets and shit LIKE THAT
MOTHER and not tins Christ stop it now stop it leave her
alone leave me alone

'Where the fuck were you?' Bonehead tightened his grip round my neck.

Bottles, glasses, empty pizza boxes and crisp packets were littered about the cold morning kitchen. The Minister and the flame-tattooed woman leaned on the range, arms folded, lips thin. Dave sat at the table, eyes half-closed like they were fighting daylight. His hand had burrowed itself into a bag of tortilla chips the size of a pillowcase.

'What's that on your head?' he said.

'*Hat,*' I choked as Bonehead swung me around.

'They thought you went into the estate!' Bonehead shrieked. 'I thought you were fucken dead!'

The Minister pulled Bonehead off and held him back with one long arm. The tattooed woman picked up the phone and told somebody at the other end the missing person had turned up. The two kids came in the back door and dragged themselves through to the front again.

Dave stood up and turned to the Minister, his hand still in the crisp bag. 'Sorry, mate. He's a bit funny sometimes.'

'Take them away, Davy.' The Minister froze me with his chilly vibes. 'I don't need this.'

He led us through the cold house to the open front door. There was party debris everywhere, including bodies on the settees and floors in the rooms I'd been in last night. The towers of boxes in the hall had lost a few storeys since I last saw them. I read what it said on the sides. Mole deterrents.

I turned back to the Minister as we stepped outside. 'There are no moles in this country.'

'They work then, don't they?' He closed the door.

'Merry Christmas, chief,' Dave said, holding up a hand. A few crumbs fell out of the crisp bag.

Bonehead stormed over to the car, all elbows and knees and Ichabod awkward, and we crunched across the muddy, scarred gravel behind him. The sun glinted off the few cars and bikes left outside the house. The hawthorn bushes had wrought themselves into silent exhaustion.

'Y'get your acid then?' Dave said, pressing more tortilla chips into his mouth.

'In my pocket.'

'I thought you took it last night. I didn't know what'd happened to yuh.'

'I got it for somebody else.' I strained to see him in the bright sunshine. 'You know what, Dave? I bet you're brilliant in bed.'

'I'm not into wee boys, Cookie.'

'I know! Here, Dave. What was the crack with he's a bit funny sometimes?'

'Did you get a tattoo on your forehead?'

I touched the light bandage on my forehead and felt my mouth form an upside down smile. 'Big day the day, isn't it?'

'Hnnh. I think we're late.'

I folded my fist over the wrap in my pocket. 'Nice to know you can still buy your drugs from a non-paramilitary source. Fair trade an' all that.'

'Aye, but he probably gets it from the hoods like. I don't think you can get it from anywhere else. He does cheap CDs as well if you're lookin' some.'

So. You take Stretch Armstrong's hand and your brother takes his other hand and you run through to the kitchen. Don't let go Prince don't let go! I won't I won't! Keep goin'! And Stretch stretches and stretches and you try and try and he won't give up and his arms are so thin. You yank and strain till you get a cramp in your shoulders and your jaws are sore with the effort. He's stretched so thin but he won't give in. You can't break him. But boy, does he stretch thin.

I got into the back of the car and Dave fell into the front and pulled the belt across. Bonehead stuck the car into reverse and wellied it, spinning the wheel and splashing gravel over the other cars. The force flung me forward into Dave's seat.

'Fuck yuh, Bonehead!'

'You just sit there and shut up!' he yelled, his voice brittle and breaking.

Well, I would have been happy to, except the way he drove had me all over the back and sometimes in the front as well. I slid around and bashed off Dave's seat and Dave laughed his tits off because he could see me in his peripheral vision. Bonehead braked sharply at every opportunity, took every corner and roundabout at ninety miles an hour, swung round the lanes as he overtook and changed gear like he was digging holes in dry dirt. He watched the bright road with narrow eyes and sometimes glanced at me in the mirror. I tried not to speak but I couldn't help the occasional Oof.

He finally slid to a stop in front of Prince's house. It looked quiet. The whole street looked quiet. Chimneys smoked illegally into the still air.

'Thanks mate,' Dave said. 'This your car?'

'It is now,' Bonehead said.

'Cool.' Dave held up his hand to shake.

Bonehead stared straight ahead. Dave took his hand out of the crisp pack and wiped it on his baggy pink trousers. 'Hnnh. Sorry.'

Bonehead still wouldn't look at him. I snaked a hand round and gave his diddy a big nip and he squawked and convulsed. He slowly brought up his hand and Dave gripped it, biker style. Bonehead was left staring and shocked as Dave got out of the car.

'What you expect?' I said. 'A flipper?'

Dave sloped into the house and left the door open for me.

'S'pose I'll get out then,' I said.

Bonehead looked at me in the mirror. 'The stuff I got yuh. It's in the boot.'

I heaved myself into the front seat. 'What's wrong?'

'Fucken nothin'. Get out.'

'But you're pissed off with muh.'

'Get out.'

I nodded. Then I shook my head. 'Come on, Bonehead. Mates?'

'Get. Out.'

'You goin' to call up to the house then?'

He gave me half a shrug. Not even a whole one.

'Tell you what,' I said. 'Come to the festival. Me and you could even stay here. We could live in Prince's room. There's all these German metal bands play in the town. You could go all the time if you lived up here.'

'Fuck off. Festival shite. Loada shite.'

I studied my hard fingertips. 'Don't go down the glen the night.'

The sun was behind the house and it reflected off his glasses. It made his chin fuzzy. His lips were a tight line.

'Don't go.' I said. 'I'm not goin'.'

'I know you're not.'

'Come on, mate.'

'I'm goin', Cookie.'

'But it's a loada bollocks. Why d'y'want to be part of it?'

'Because it's me, alright?'

'But it's not. You could come up here and live with us and we can all get off our faces and have a geg. Come on.'

'What about my ma?'

'She can come too.'

He half-grinned. I liked his missing tooth. 'You would

give her one, woulden yuh?'

'Yeah but I'd have to be on top. She'd fucken flatten me.'

'You're a cunt, Cookie.' He pushed his bony hands down his long thighs. 'I know you don't get it. I know what you're like. I know ya. But mate, you don't know me. This is what I want.'

'How the hell would you know what you want?'

'How the hell would *you* know what I want?' The ghost of an Italian grandmother again.

'I know more than you,' I said.

'Alright then. Where am I workin'?'

'What did I say about work ...'

'What d'y'call my girlfriend?'

'Who, whah?'

'Y'see, Cookie? Just get out.'

'Come on, Bonehead.'

He leaned across me and opened the passenger door.

'Bonehead, come on.'

'See ya, Cookie.'

I lifted the stuff he'd got me out of the boot and he tore away up India Street, skidded to the junction with Wolseley Street and indicated left. Then he took off to the right, tyres squealing. Seconds later a police bike flew along Wolseley Street, siren blasting and lights pulsing.

We never did kill Stretch Armstrong. But we did part company. Me and Prince had a competition to see who could throw him the highest up a pylon. If one of us got sparks, he got to give the other one a dead arm. I could hardly lift a fork for days. Stretch is still up that pylon, you know.

I pulled Bonehead's granny's dress over my head and nearly set it alight with the feg still in my mouth. Bloody polyester. Bloody feg. Bloody hole in my Sunday best now. It would have been brilliant if she'd been in the Salvation Army and he'd been able to get me her uniform, but then I was only divinely inspired. I wasn't actually God. I had to accept a few flaws.

She was smaller than me, but wider. A church goer. A Presbyterian, to be exact. I didn't need her patent shoes or jacket or big fuzzy hat, even though he'd supplied them. I was already too hot. The jacket was too warm, the shoes were too small and as for the hat, I needed to show off my new tattoo. I studied it closely in the mirror. Its fine black lines were perfectly executed. Let the Minister show us the way.

Soft and clingy with a shirt style neck, the dress had a thin belt of the same maroon paisley material. I turned and turned in front of the mirrored bathroom tiles. Even in the last hole, the belt was too big. Maybe there was something in this eating business. I couldn't figure it out though. I knew I needed it but it wouldn't go in. What I really needed, I decided, was a lesson in biology. Or a glass of milk. I made a mental note.

Somebody hammered on the bathroom door and I swung round and hammered back.

'Prince, is that you in there? Hurry up! I need in!'

'It's not Prince, it's me.'

'Who's me?'

'*Me.*'

'Well, whoever me is, hurry up. I need in.'

'Alex, do you have cystitis?'

'Were you in my room?' She rattled the door once more. 'Hurry bloody up!'

Yes, I had been in her room. What a delight. It smelt salty like she needed to open the window and wash her sheets. Her pink and purple tartan bed was scattered with sickly cute toys I wanted to punch. Books and folders were piled high by a narrow study table. I was looking for fishnets to complete my outfit but tampons and crampons were all she seemed to have. Which was probably lucky. I would've been walking round with a stiffy all day. Bare legs and para boots would just have to do.

I set Prince's beanie hat on the back of my head and leaned into the mirror. No wonder I was so hot. My teeth had a coat of fur. I gave them a quick skoosh over with a

brush that had sat on the window sill for as long as I could
remember. I had to make a bit of an effort for Jay, didn't I?
I squirted some pink flavour Sure in my pits, a bath in a
can, and burled in front of the mirror again. The dress
came to just below my knee. Very modest. The purple
paisley went well with my bruised face and new tattoo.

I crossed to Prince's room to drop off my clothes and
put on his green jacket. Both his guitar and rucksack were
gone. Maybe he was at the medical research centre. Maybe
he'd moved in with Molly. Maybe he'd gone to the fucken
States without me. I'd give him till Monday and then I'd
ring the research centre. And if he wasn't there, I'd call the
cops. Or maybe I wouldn't. They couldn't help much
when you drove the person away yourself.

I sat on the floor and looked closely at the two fairy
cakes I'd snaffled from the kitchen. After the previous
night's escapade, I knew this was right. I'd brought the
icing sugar, a bowl and a teaspoon upstairs too so I could
make the preparations in peace. I read the instructions on
the sugar and measured out two teaspoons, sprinkled in
the crumbled acid, dropped as much spit as I could muster
into the bowl and mixed like mad. It was a bit lumpy but
what do you want, this is buns in Belfast not tea at the
Ritz.

I used the back of the spoon to spread the icing over the
buns and set them on the mattress. Small plain buns in
patterned paper cups with a lumpy layer of snow on top. I
gave the icing a poke. I thought it was meant to harden.
The icing was hard and smooth when I bought buns in the
Weirtown bakery. I lay on the mattress and stared at them
for a while, poking them every now and again. Harden,

bun, harden. But they both refused. I looked around. Josie's hairdryer was on the floor in the corner.

The first bun shot out of my hand with the force of the blast and I launched myself after it like a goalie. It landed upside down on the dusty floorboards and I scooped it up for thorough examination. It was speckled with grit and had a half orange, half green hair and a ginger pube pressed into it. It was a delicate job but I got most of it out. The icing might have looked like a coalman's bed but at least it was starting to crisp over. I set it down alongside the other bun, which still hadn't hardened.

Well, the airborne journey must have helped the first bun along. I took a bun in each hand and waved them around. If there was ever a freestyle bun waving competition, I would win. The bun run. The bun swing. The bun spin. The bun tumble. The bun dive. When I was completely exhausted and physically sick with effort, I set the buns on the floor and fell back on the mattress, arms and legs dead as lead. I stared at the buns. Harden, buns, please please harden.

I woke up in near darkness, thirsty and headachy. The damp house was breathy cold but I was clammy hot. I struggled to my feet and stood on something soft as I flicked on the light. The best bun was destroyed! Fuck it! Well, it would just have to be first come, first served then, wouldn't it? I scoured the room and spotted a stiff, greying hankie with Homer Simpson on it, hiding behind one of the mirrors. I wrapped the bun up and set it carefully in my pocket.

I turned on all the lights as I waited for my taxi with my glass of milk. It's draughty in a dress but not entirely unpleasant. If you're too hot, you can actually waft it. I stood at the open front door so I could see the taxi coming and watched Satanic Hearses approach from Botanic. He stopped suddenly on the path in front of the house.

'What are you doing here? No wait. What are you *wearing*?'

'It's OK, I already threw it up the chimney.'

'Sorry?'

'My letter to Satan. This Christmas, please bring me a cure for dyslexia. Love, Cocky. Did you get it?'

'Just you remember this,' he said, pushing me aside and standing in the hall. 'When you die, I will be there. Think about that. I will be there.'

I sucked in a breath but nothing came out. He'd got me. He'd thrown in a bomb and he knew I'd create my own shrapnel. I *would* think about it. I'd have to outlive him for a start. He sprang up the stairs, all joy to the world.

And who should be driving my taxi but good old Mr Value Cabs himself.

'Alright, love?' he said as I slid across the plastic covered seats in the back. 'St George's Market, isn't it?'

'Hey, it's me,' I said. 'Jamember me?'

He looked at me in the mirror and shook his head doubtfully. 'I get a lot of people in the back. I thought you were a girl there. Sorry.'

'Jamember you picked me up in Weirtown?'

'No, sorry.'

We chugged through the slow Christmas traffic and I felt him looking at me in the mirror. 'What are you, twelve, thirteen?'

'Sixteen. For fuck's sake.'

'What're you doin' with a tattoo on your head?'

'Is there a tattoo on my head?'

'See if you were my kid, I'd kill ya.'

'See if you were my da, I'd kill myself. Nah, didn't mean that. Have you got kids?'

'Seven and five.'

'Santa got everything in then?'

'Oh aye.' His eyes crinkled in the mirror. 'In next door's garage.'

'Kids don't know?'

'Not at all. Santa's as real as you or me. Realer, for fuck's sake.'

'Santa is opiate for children,' I said. She said that.

'What are you, Anti-Santy League or somethin'? Is that what that tattoo is?'

I never knew Santa. She wouldn't lie to us that way. But maybe if she'd let us believe in Santa, I wouldn't have eaten her Max Factor and Prince wouldn't have burnt down the forest. She could have said he wouldn't come if we were bad. It was a nice threat really.

Granny died just after Christmas and she didn't go to the funeral. God, Church, Santa – I couldn't see her problem. All I could think about, as me and Prince stood in the rain-soaked Carnmoney Cemetery with granny's neighbours, was that God was cosy in heaven, Jesus was making the tea and Santa had parked the reindeer and was bringing Hob Nobs in by the sack.

I stared out at an old man wandering along the Ormeau Road near the junction with Cromac Street. He wore a loose beige raincoat and purple flares and had big flappy cartoon feet in red socks and Moses sandals. He gripped a plastic bag tight in his fist.

'Pull over,' I said. 'This wee man here.' I got out and touched the man's shoulder. 'Excuse me.'

He looked at me with worry.

'I just won the lottery,' I said.

'Whah?'

'I'm payin' for your taxi, wherever you want to go. Jump in. I just won the lottery.'

'Did ye?'

I gave him all the notes I had left and kept the loose nupes for myself. I leaned inside as the oul fella got in the back. 'This is my granda. Take him home, would yuh?'

The driver ducked to look up at me. 'You sure?'

'Yeah.'

'You alright?'

'Couldn't be better. Yo the Anti-Santy League. Yo ho ho.'

'Here, son,' the oul fella said, leaning forward. 'Here.' He held the plastic bag open and I looked in. Twinkling, glittering, gleaming Pick'n'Mix. I pulled out a big chocolate, all sparkly in a squeaky pink wrapper, and watched them drive off towards the centre of town.

I let the sweet melt on my tongue as I walked. Ever cry with chocolate in your mouth?

St George's Market is close to the city centre, on the corner of Oxford Street and East Bridge Street and between the Waterfront Hall and the republican Markets area. The government had forked out to resuscitate it and its red bricks had been washed down, windows un-bricked, ceilings repaired and a restaurant added. There was always some kind of community project, exhibition, food or craft fair going on. In fact, the more creative the event, the more likely it was to be held there. St George's Market, Bohemian subsidy.

Spindly tables had been organised into 'zones' – Chinese, Indian and traditional Irish, with beardy types and sheep dogs in neck scarves. Spidermen fissled round an electronic music zone. Belfast's small hip hop massive slouched round mixing decks. There was a chamber orchestra in Santa suits, students experimenting with a piano and boxing gloves, clap-happy Christian kids with guitars and tambourines, forty indie bands in forty coats, and Dave and his mates and their musical bongs. A sign that said Sounds Tasty Zone! hung above tables crammed with Indian, Chinese, Japanese, Italian, French and Greek food. Dave's cakes and buns had a whole table to themselves.

I knew it had to be loud but the girder was whistling all over the place. At one point it even sounded like it was dying down the plughole. I made a mental note to think about it later. Josie's bandwagon was pulling up.

Photographers and TV crews backed in first, followed by stilt-walkers and fire-eaters, the Samba band, the tights-and-masks brigade, the kiddie clowns, the Chinese dragon and at the rear, the squawking, spitting children's army, rounded up from youth groups to form the cross-community choir. Josie, Kloot, Billy Dick and his Catholic counterpart, Conor Copeland, were among community workers who chatted and smiled in exactly the same way Alex put up with Prince's friends.

Well, first come, first served then. I paid for a steaming cup of tea, pressed the fairy cake onto the saucer and only spilt a wee drop as I crossed the room to Billy Dick. A ripple of sneers trailed my progress. Good good good.

Kloot had moved on to the electronic music zone, Conor Copeland was at the Irish music zone but Billy Dick still stood with Josie.

'Mr Dick.' I bowed and clicked my heels. 'A gift from the Orient.'

He frowned. 'Beg your parding?'

'Cuppa tea.' I handed him the cup. 'And the bun's organic, so it is.'

Josie's hands froze mid-rollie as she looked me up and down and then stared at my forehead. 'Is that real, Cookie?'

'The tea? Cost me everything I had, I should fucken hope it's real.'

'And a dress?'

'Sunday best. It's a very special day.'

She resumed rolling. 'Well, at least you're here. That's all I need to know right now. You taught them the song yet?'

'Who?'

'The Christians. You're meant to teach them the song and they'll go round and teach each group before the finale. Come on, we'll start now.' She latched onto my wrist.

'Houl on a minute! I'll follow yuh over, alright?'

'You better.' She pierced me with narrow eyes and marched away, scanning her zones majestically.

I smiled at Billy. 'How was the bun then?'

'Ask him.'

We looked down at the collie with the neck scarf as it licked its lips. It trotted back across the market and I chased it through the people, searching my mental archives for anything I knew about doggie health. Grass made dogs boke. What kind of grass though? Blow? Do dogs take whities? They must do.

The dog glanced back and went from a trot to an all-out gallop when it saw me. It skidded outside to the six-lane

East Bridge Street and headlights swung and horns blasted as it dodged and slid between the cars. Somebody grabbed my collar. Josie's face was shipyard hard.

'I knew you'd do this.'

'No but Josie ...'

'Go on then.' She released my collar. 'Just go.'

'I wasn't goin'! There's a dog out there ...'

She walked away and I glanced back outside. The dog was gone. With any luck, a car would hit it in the next street. I turned to see cops filing into the market and Josie heading them off at the electronic music zone.

'*Whaddya doin? Whaddya doin?*' Kloot whined as computer monitors, decks, speakers and headphones were dismantled around him. Josie disappeared as soon as the cameras started flashing. Kloot was still whining as the cops took him away.

I'd completely bollocksed it. I couldn't believe it. Yes I could. Because it was me. It was fucken me. Was it. Me spinning on the Minister's ska record, up down fast slow loud

distant. Dream not fucken now

I needed

Time needed think. The Christians. Struggling with radio interference turn it off or down or something

'I'm Cookie and I'm here to do this fucken song!' I shouted at them.

They froze. Eight or so young people led by a short chunky old woman with a loud wobbly soprano.

But the shouting seemed to help. It cleared it.

'Josie said you'd be joining us,' the old woman sniffed. She even spoke in a loud wobbly soprano. 'I'm Maureen.

You'll be working with Lisa and Chris.' She snapped her fingers at two young guitar players. 'This is Cookie, as you might have heard.'

Lisa laughed as she approached. 'You're wearing a dress!' She was about fourteen and plain with dark eyes that suddenly made me self-conscious. Her brown hair was pulled back into a high pony-tail but frizzy curls escaped everywhere. 'What's that on your head?'

'Anty-fucken-Santy League.'

Chris examined me, suspicious. 'No it's not.' He was tall and serious with long fine ginger hair that swung over bony shoulders.

Maureen pointed to a circle of wooden chairs. 'You folks have a seat over there.'

'Where's your guitar then?' Chris said as we sat together.

'Don't fucken have one.'

'Have mine.' Lisa handed me her Yamaha acoustic.

Chris positioned his guitar on his knee. 'Go on then.'

'Not a fucken problem.' I played the first bar of 'Dueling Banjos'.

He repeated it.

I played the next bar.

He repeated that too.

'Gosh, you're quite good,' Lisa said. 'Chris is grade eight.'

'Grade eight what? Grade eight wank?' I played the next bar, fast and upbeat, then launched into the main, intricate, weaving duel. I used to out-play Prince all the time but fuck it, Chris kept up. And he was better than me. We attracted quite a crowd but I was out of practice and my hand began to cramp and the strings buzzed painfully as my fingers missed the mark.

I left off, my fingertips burning and stiff and Chris finished with an improvised flourish, working his way up the frets and ending with a simple shave and a haircut, two bits. It was like a big Christian poke in the eye. The audience applauded, slapped him on the back and wandered away, smiling and nodding.

Chris swung his hair over his shoulder triumphantly. 'So have you got a song or what?'

Maureen leaned over us. 'Pay attention to me now! This lovely TV crew wants to interview this nice man with you folks playing in the background. Isn't that super?'

I looked up. I recognised the interviewer from TV. Young, blonde, plastic-skinned. She was backed by a sound woman and a cameraman and they pushed and prodded at Billy Dick until he stood right in front of me and my Christian fellowship.

'Your *song* then,' Chris said.

'Right!' I fingered at the strings high up the fretboard. Wake. Wake to the . . .

'This is a great day for Belfast,' Billy said, running a hand over his hair. 'Experiencing other cultures is the only way forward for a divided community. There is no alternative. Ulster has. . .'

'One second, Mr Dick,' the interviewer said. She looked at me. 'Could you play your guitar or something? People will pay more attention to you than the interviewee if you stare at us.'

'Oh. OK.'

'Excuse me, Cootie,' Chris said. 'Or whatever your name

is. Have you got a song or what? I'm taking bible class tonight.'

I slid my fingers up the fretboard. Wake to the ... wake to the ... I really wished he hadn't said that.

'The kids are lovin' it,' Billy said. 'But we have to ensure the Protestant community receives a fair share of fundin' so we can continue to bring people together like this. It's the only way. There is no alternative. Ulster is at a ...'

'Would you ever just *concentrate*?' Chris said.

'*O fucken K!*' I stared at my fingertips. Wake ... wake to the ... wake to the ... shit ... alternative Ulster.

I disguised it like. 'Alternative Ulster' as played by Joni Mitchell. I only gave them one verse and one chorus and then repeated the verse. That's all I could remember.

'That sounded familiar,' Chris said.

'I do the odd gig,' I said.

'Really?' Lisa said.

I looked at her bright, open face. 'Nah.'

'Can you write the chord sequence and words down?' Chris said. 'It seems simple enough.'

'The next time I see Jake Burns, I'll let him fucken know.'

Chris pulled a neat black notebook out of his back pocket. It had a band round it and a stumpy pen looped into the band.

'You fucken amaze me, man, you really fucken do.'

He tutted. 'Do you have to swear so bloomin' much?'

'Keep at it, mate. You'll get the hang of it.' I handed the guitar back to Lisa and scribbled the words down as Billy continued his catchy sound bites on camera.

All I wanted was to make him feel as helpless as I did. He wasn't just involved in the PPA, he was a fucken fat controller. Well, he wouldn't have known what was happening if he'd taken an unplanned acid trip. He would have had no control. That's all I fucken wanted.

I could still improvise.

You know the high jump where you throw yourself over the bar backwards? I think it's called the Fosbury flop. You start with a curved run up and you focus all your strength in your legs. Well, if at the last minute you jam your toe up somebody's hole instead, I believe it's actually called a fucken big kick up the ass.

He leapt into the air, bent over backwards, hands clasping his arse, then he swung round just as quick to whack his palm off my noggin. I went sprawling. Josie dragged me back across the floor as spectators swarmed and I couldn't get up for laughing. But when I looked up, Josie was crying.

'Josie?'

'I can't reason with yuh, Cookie.' Tears made white tracks through her orange make-up. 'And I'm sure as God not goin' to fight with yuh.'

'But Josie ...'

'Just go, Cookie.'

She made her way back to Billy Dick, who waved people away, good-humoured, polite and embarrassed.

Embarrassed? Embarrassed ran a close second to helpless. I got a hole in one! Caught on camera for posterity! Billy Dick was going to be the butt of every joke! I might not have won but I was getting good at this!

'Here. You. Here.' A high, flat Weirtown voice came from behind me. It was a kid about twelve with dark hair and a wide pale face. 'Is your name Cookie?'

'No, Cootie.'

'Y'see my mate there?'

I looked. Monkeys always look.

'He smashed your windees, so he did.'

His mate was the same age. Fair hair shaved almost to the wood, grey face, blackened teeth.

'Were you eatin' shite?' I asked.

'What da fuck are you talkin' about, dickhead? You're wearin' a dress.'

'Did you smash my windas?'

'Aye. Whaddya gonna do about it?'

I wasn't designed for conflict. And I don't know how Roman Legions coped in skirts. But I gave it a go anyway. I felt his nose crunch as I landed my fist but then all fifty of his limbs flailed at once. His trainers took lumps out of my legs and the other one jumped on my back. They were a cloud of killer bees, jabbing and stabbing, anywhere and everywhere and I went down under them. I only had energy for survival. I didn't have anything left for defence.

And suddenly we were the most popular zone. The Sounds More Like the Belfast You Know and Love Zone. Adults and kids gathered to watch as cameramen filmed and cameras flashed. Diversity? Zzzzz. This was what people wanted to see. It was when I was lying on the floor, arms over my head, that the idea came to me. Lateral thinking really worked. I just never dreamed it could hurt so much. I suddenly knew how to get McCullough and the hoods.

I've never been so grateful for European funding in all my life. A team of community workers pulled the killer kids off and a nice middle-class youth worker heaved me up and trailed me through the disappointed spectators to the Sounds Tasty Zone. One of the killer kids called me a fucken Fenian bastard as he was dragged away and despite all my aching, stinging, bleeding and wanting to cry again, I was impressed. I was a Weirtown legend!

The youth worker pressed me down onto a chair and handed me his hankie. He was tall, studenty, with a dark spiky quiff and glasses. 'Your mouth's bleeding,' he said. 'It's dripping on your ... dress.'

The hankie was crisp white cotton. His ma must have ironed it. I gave it back, unused. 'It's OK. I'll only dirty it.'

He knelt down in front of me. 'I hate to say this but ... do you know who his da is?'

'Do you know who *my* da is?'

'No.'

'Me neither. You weren't expectin' that, were yuh?'

'Do you want me to take you to casualty or drop you at the bus or anything?'

'I can take him.' A new voice joined the conversation. I knew that voice.

The youth worker looked at Boo and then back to me. 'You know this man?'

'That's my da.'

'Thought you didn't know your da.'

'I don't.'

Boo's eyes were everywhere, my forehead, my dress, my blood. 'What happened? You're ...'

'Well, you can fuck off right now.' I stood up and staggered wave shit now here it comes again

Girder down the plughole

Weirtown window frames I'm sick of this! Walk

properly bloody idiot

Watched his lips herb teeth – I need to talk to you, Cookie!

FUCK *OFF*, YOU!

Shouting helped

A mad fairground of bleeps, buzzes and rings as every mobile phone in the place went off at the same time. Sweat prickled across my neck.

The press and TV crews suddenly ran at Billy Dick. More filed in from the street and they surged forward in a hokey cokey riot.

Josie was like Elmer Fudd, standing in mid air, looking down at strains of 'Alternative Ulster' rising round the room.

Boo gripped my arm but I wouldn't give in. To him or myself. Myself wanted to strangle him or kick him up the ass. Myself wanted to run away or lie down. Myself didn't feel very well.

'Cookie,' he said. I'd never seen him worried before. 'Do you know where she is?'

'Lyin' cunt.'

'No, it was just ... Cookie, I went to see her when I first came back to Belfast.'

'Afraid the papers would find out about me?'

'I asked her to keep something for me.'

'What, me?'

'No, not you, listen. She said she'd keep something for me, years ago. But when I came back to get them, she said she'd have to search the roof space.' He looked past me to the journalists.

'*Mr Dick! Mr Dick!*' they crowed. '*It's on the front page of the Evening News! Mr Dick!'*

'Maisonettes don't have roof spaces, dickhead.'

'This is really important, Cookie.' He held my arm tighter. 'She said she'd ring me when she found them.'

The journalists pressed forward, fighting for space. *'Mr Dick! Can you give me a comment about Weirtown Meats?'*

'I waited for weeks but she never rang, so I went back to see her. But there was only you. On the floor. In the kitchen.'

'Well, whaddya want? A certificate?'

'Cookie, I need you to help me here!'

'Mr Dick, the Evening News says you've been helping police with enquiries!'

Boo spoke quickly. 'She kept some tins for me. I need to know, did she throw them out? I need them back. I need to know what she did with the tins.'

'Are you God, Boo?'

'Mr Dick, the murder hunt at Weirtown Meats ...'

'Are ya then? Are you my da?'

'Mr Dick, the Evening News says the body was processed in the factory ...'

'No, I'm not your da, Cookie.'

'Did you buy the tinned stewing steak, Mr Dick? Did you eat it?'

'Fuck you, Boo! Fuck ...?'

'Did you know the victim, Mr Dick? Did you know Samuel Buchanan?'

'It was Buckshot, Cookie. I'm just your uncle.'

I didn't exist outside my head. I floated across to the

cameraman and touched his shoulder with a faraway skeleton hand. He hardly registered me as he flicked through numbers on his mobile phone.

'I have a story,' I said.

'Yeah?' he said distantly.

'I think I might be a cannibal. But that's not the story.'

He listened, distracted, as I reminded him of all the channels that he could sell footage of a real live punishment beating to. And then I told him where he could film it.

I was setting the next wave in motion. I could be busy for the rest of my life.

Gradually he began nodding. Finally he stopped flicking and looked up. 'This is my lucky day,' he said.

I only met Lucky twice before he had to be put down. Lucky was Bonehead's granny's poodle and he was originally white but had gone grey with age. The matted fur round his mouth was browny red and his body was barrel-thick, as if he was so constipated the shit had seeped out of his intestines and settled under his fur. One minute he was all friendly and waggy and loveable, the next he was tearing at your trousers, nipping at your fingertips and wrinkling his lips to show you tiny sharp teeth.

She only ever fed him real meat. None of that tinned muck for him. And when she couldn't be arsed microwaving it, she gave it to him raw. There was one time me and Bonehead were lying on the floor in his ma's house, watching *The X Files,* and Bonehead picked a spot on his head and it wouldn't stop bleeding. His zits and cuts always bled more than mine. It fascinated me for a while the way the blood wouldn't clot and just kept trickling down his shaved skull but I lost interest eventually. Dana Scully was in danger and I was in love with her.

And then next thing, didn't Lucky come tearing into the room and sink his teeth into Bonehead's skull and shake and tear and growl and by fuck, he wasn't for letting go. Oh no. After years of flicking and tossing uncooked T-bones and ham shanks round Bonehead's granny's back yard, he'd finally arrived at dinner nirvana. He gnawed and chomped and trailed his teeth and no matter how much Bonehead screamed and pulled and no matter how much I punched and kicked that dog, it wouldn't give up its new bone. Until Bonehead's granny quietly rattled its dish, even though there was nothing in it.

And thus did Robert earn the name of Bonehead.

Now that was a fucken legend.

I remember going to see *Titus Andronicus* in the Opera House with mum. It was mad. Murder, rape, treachery and then to top it all off, Queen Tamora's son was served up for her dinner. It didn't even put me off my Maltesers. The programme said the play was based on other plays which all fed off the same story and that made me think it was based on legend.

I realised later that I'd completely missed the point. I should have been thinking about the total and absolute horror of a mother actually eating her child. I did eventually like. It just took a while. By the time everybody else in the audience had got over Queen Tamora, she'd quietly welded herself into my head, and then I couldn't get rid of her. And maybe nothing brings the horror home better than having a long, long time to think about it.

Boo had about ten years. So did Billy Dick. The PPA thought Buckshot would give them away after they murdered the Catholic taxi driver. Well, you know what Buckshot was like. Off his face most of the time and with a habit of sticking his neck out. Saying what he thought. And so bloody loud too. It was the result of a hereditary deafness he would pass onto me, but he didn't even know he had it.

So they got rid of him. And then it all went quiet.

Except Billy Dick. He could keep his mouth shut about murder but not about a mother eating her own son. He had to pass it on. He told Boo, because she was Boo's mother too. The impression I got, sitting in Boo's car as he told me, was that Billy Dick actually wanted to do something about it. He wanted to help but I couldn't understand how somebody could justify murder and object to it at the same time.

They couldn't do anything about it anyway because then Boo and Buckshot's mother would have found out what she'd served up with the Smash, put in a pie and even gave to the dog. They agreed to wait until she died, and then they'd try to put things right. They left what tins they could find with a mutual friend. Somebody who preferred not to associate with the PPA. Somebody they knew wouldn't ask questions if they didn't explain why. Somebody who made a point of accepting odd behaviour.

Billy Dick turned to politics and Boo turned up in the

south of France, where a rich Frenchie needed a kitchen assistant for his yacht. Monsieur Dupont de Dieuleveult couldn't pronounce Buchanan. Boo was just a nickname. He *was* checking me out when he came back. But only because I was going to have to know sooner or later. But the first time he even mentioned her to me, I punched him in the face. Well, I probably wasn't going to handle it very well, was I?

As for eating my own parent, I just wasn't sure. I wondered if that was what was making me so sick. I'd had a few hours to think about it and I knew Wilson McCullough's da had something to do with me eating my own da but I didn't feel horror for me like I did for Queen Tamora or even Boo's ma. I tried. I felt it was my duty, as a human being, but all I could come up with were awful puns like family dish and you are what you eat. I couldn't help it. I lived in the Hammer House of Pun. Maybe it was because I never liked Buckshot. Maybe it was because I needed more time to digest.

I punched myself in the face as I sat on the mound that used to be our house. I was just listening to the window frames in the dark. They weren't there any more but I could still hear them. Boo had wanted me to go to his house but I asked him for money for a taxi instead. He was generous that way. He was paying for Jay's private treatment in the Ulster Clinic. She'd collapsed on the Dublin Road. She weighed five and a half stone. I imagined myself going to visit her. I'd bring her a present. Wax fruit.

There was a fence round the remains of our row but it wasn't hard to climb. The demolition dinosaurs slept close by, most of their windows now covered by steel shields. Under my ass, layers and layers of bricks and rubble and wood sat tight. I'd searched the mound like a Brazilian on a rubbish dump but I couldn't find any of my stuff. They'd either cleared out the house or it was all buried too deep. My scissors were gone.

I lit myself a Consulate and stood up to survey my home, feet sliding around, head heavy and light at the same time. I'd set the next wave in motion but even a few hours had made a difference. I wasn't sure about doing this any more.

I punched myself in the face again. Jesus, I was smarter than that. I almost let them win. And the whole point of this wave was showing the hoods that *I* could beat *them*. I took off my beanie and used the cigarette to burn holes in the worn wool.

It was the fifteen-week anniversary of my mother's disappearance and time for my next punishment beating. It was a slow dander towards the glen. I walked through the dark empty shops listening to my trailing feet. It sounded like there were three of me, one I knew, one to the left and one up on the balcony. I wondered did Jean the cabbage thrower still live up there. If she did, she'd taken to boarding up her front door and windows with wood.

The shutters were down on the Stop'n'Shop. I stood outside and looked at the graffiti without reading it. Maybe Mr Fusty had a son and he'd take over the shop. Son of Fust. Fust Junior. He'd have great ideas. He'd start an empire. He'd be young and thrusting. Fust thrust. He'd only smell a wee bit. I sloped on, through the car park and across to the path that led down the glen.

It was a clear starry night. The heat had gone out of my body and I shuddered like an old boat but my lip kept layering with sweat. I couldn't let it get to me though. I had stuff to do. This would be the final wave of the campaign. It had to be. I was getting tired. It was entirely improvised but I was pretty sure it would work. We're in demand the world over, just for fighting. McCullough and his team might even make it onto CN fucken N. But cops have TV too and they'd see it too.

A dog skittered by, sniffing along walls, and I was going to bark but I had to concentrate on walking. I liked the estate in the Christmas cold. Nobody about. No Corsas to run me over. Not like summer when people hung about the streets all night and I didn't go out if I could help it. My head was a steadicam and my view bobbed as I followed the narrow path down to the river.

This was the river that ran past Weirtown Meats, a narrow effluent flow that was once wide enough for Vikings to come up. This was the river that had been dammed to feed linen mills and that the estate got its name from. The river where she gathered nettles for soup. Where I fell on glass. Where Prince carried me across the sewage pipe before they built the pedestrian bridge. Where Prince said Even girls can walk this bloody pipe, y'lazy wee shit. Where Prince got his worst kicking for being a punk.

This was the river that smelt like garlic and sewage and I hated myself for loving it so much.

It was called a glen, but it had been interfered with. On

the left bank, the woodland had been left to run wild but on the right, the long gradual hillside had been flattened into a wide concrete slope, built up with boarded-up maisonettes. Its ghost town streets backed onto Glen Drive and were semi-lit by bricked street lights, draped in tattered flags and painted red, white and blue.

I'd rolled the beanie down over my face so my nose was nice and warm when I breathed out. Fucken freezing when I breathed in though. I'd burned three holes in it – two for eyes, one for the tattoo. I looked like a Cyclops with a woolly face. Cookie the hood.

I broke off from the path and trudged through the swampy grass towards the riverbank. I told the camera-man I'd stay out of sight and keep watch for him. My legs shook as I followed the slope. There had to be fairies down there but I couldn't detect them. I clutched at the thin whipping branches of bushes and monster weeds that lined the water. The street light above the bridge gleamed off its black, scummy edges. I could wave to the path from there and still not be seen from the bridge.

I crouched opposite the river's standard issue trolley with waving kacks attached. I wrapped my arms round my knees and waited, breathing in rot and the nearby sewage pipe. I looked up to see the stars but lost my balance and sank back in the cold mud.

'Fuck's sake.' My fingers pressed into sticky, gritty sludge as I tried to push myself up. My arms shook so much, I couldn't do it.

'Look at the state of you, y'tit.'

I looked round. 'Bonehead?'

Short, bare legs stepped up beside me. 'No, it's me.'

'Who?'

'*Me.*' It was a bloody kid. About ten. He wore a kind of purple tunic that stopped just below his knee.

'Who's fucken me?'

'Setanta.'

'Oh for fuck's sake. I know you're not here. Fuck off.'

He helped me back up to my crouching position but I shrugged him off.

'Would you ever just fuck away off?'

'I only wanna help yuh.'

'What the fuck would you know? You're a kid. Fucken killer kid. Not even real.'

'No but listen, Cookie. Anybody can kill a dog, right? But you can't take on the whole pack.'

I looked at the bridge. There they were, there they were, dogs' heads on people bodies but no burger to spring up for this time. Just fresh flesh to tear apart. Four of them, snarling, snapping, pawing at Bonehead.

I shot to my feet but collapsed into mud again. 'Help me then!' But he was gone. I looked back to the path. No camera-fucken-man either. That'll teach you to improvise. That'll teach you to rely on somebody else. That'll teach you to think you can do it on your own you can't you tit you lose.

One kept watch at the bridge while the other three led Bonehead into the bushes on the opposite bank. I paced them through the shallows, tripping over roots and rocks, water slushing up round my knees wasn't his fault it was me my rats not him.

'Leave him!'

They led him deeper into the darkness and I waded

across, my feet sliding around on the stones and no fucken fairies and that wee shithead goes and leaves me.

'Don't it was me don't I swear to God it was me it was me!'

I pushed on through the freezing water. The riverbed was uneven and I knew it dipped away in places but I forgot and went down and under up cold gasping grasping.

A muffled shot and my friend's squealing, squirming in the weeds, bandaged finger glowing and glasses gone, hands wrapped round his skinny calf.

I trailed myself up the sticky bank. 'Leave him McCullough it wasn't him it was me he wants ...'

But it wasn't McCullough. I didn't know any of them.

Two more shots for my loyal bloody friend.

Two laughing shots for me.

First and foremost, I'd like to thank 1970's disco. Where would we be without the likes of Gloria Gaynor? So offensive to punk but still popular today. Just so damn catchy. *I got all my life to live and I got all my love to give, I will survive, I will survive, hey hey*, over and over and over and over in my head as I lay on the bank. It was the last song I heard in the taxi to Weirtown.

If you learn anything from this story, make it this. Choose the song you would like to die to. Not the song you want played at your funeral. You won't be bloody there, you won't care. But if you're lying dying with Garth Brooks or Celine Dion in your head, you'll really suffer.

And secondly, thanks must go to Satanic Hearses. Thanks, mate. Every time I drifted into unconsciousness I saw myself lying in the morgue with him standing nearby, pulling on his rubber gloves with a loud snap. Even though he wore a surgical mask, I knew he was overjoyed. Then I'd open my eyes.

Thanks must also go to the man out walking his dog. Yes, it was him, poor fucker. As if insomnia wasn't bad enough. Every time he goes out, he finds one. Sometimes two. The dog was a lurcher, wiry thin, softly tanned and friendly as fuck. Just an ordinary dog like.

And finally, thanks to whoever or whatever made it possible for me to sleep for weeks without waking up. I missed the festival on TV. I missed myself kicking Billy Dick up the ass, on selected satellite channels. I missed Billy getting shot in the head for helping police with their enquiries. I missed Christmas. I missed New Year. I missed the snow. I missed Bonehead's funeral.

I would've liked to go but Big Julie helped to carry his coffin and I don't think I could have survived that.

Jay showed me how she could make herself sick without making any noise and I showed her how I stole from other patients' lockers without anybody noticing. She had a private room with flowers and toys and books and she had this TV/CD/DVD thing which I thought was totally class, even though I was disgusted at myself for being so materialistic. I had a room all to myself too, but only because I had to be barrier nursed. I had hepatitis.

I couldn't stand it. Not the disease – I could put up with the disease. Just knowing I had *something* explained all the weird shit with my stomach. And having to give up cider and vodka and Maserati wasn't so bad if I could still smoke my brains out. I was probably going to need a hearing aid at some point too. Most people inherit a couple of quid from their da but oh no, not me. When I explained about the window frames and the girder and the plughole, they decided that was psychosomatic. I only heard the first two syllables, and then I shut up. But my big mouth had already done the damage. I was officially a mad bastard.

What I couldn't stand was being in that room alone. Having nobody to talk to meant sitting through soap after soap after soap because it was the only thing I could think of that would stop me thinking. The car that was used in the attack on Billy Dick was a black Ford Puma, stolen from the multi-storey car park in Chichester Street in November. Police invited anybody with information to call the confidential phoneline. I broke the casing on the TV.

And then there was Prince. Thought was just wasted on him. He'd phoned Dave from Amsterdam. He'd sold his guitar to go to Amster-fucken-dam. I could've forgiven him if he'd gone to the States, but going to Amsterdam proved he was just the same as her after all.

And as for her, taking off had nothing to do with me and my nature/nurture argument. I saw that now. When Boo told her why he needed the tins, she thought she was going to get drawn into an argument with the PPA. And as was her wont, she baled.

It was a bright dry day and I took myself to the wall outside the emergency exit for a smoke. I'd actually made a few friends at the smokers' corner and I made a point of not stealing from their lockers. I was waiting for Jay. The nurses were happy to stand over her while she ate but nobody wanted to chase her round the grounds as she burnt it all off.

She smiled as she approached, shiny with sweat. Her freckly skin was dull and her hair had dried out and gone frizzy at the back. Her head seemed too big for her body, her nose was too long and her teeth looked horsey. But I still wanted to be with her.

'Hiya.' She sat beside me, careful to keep her distance. I understood. 'Got a new wardrobe, I see.'

Boo bought me pyjamas from Marks & Spencer's kid's department and I huffed. He took them back and brought some old grey joggie bottoms and a bag full of Boo T-shirts instead. His staff didn't want them any more. The restaurant was losing business and I think he was losing interest. The murder investigation stalled when Billy Dick decided he couldn't go ahead (sorry) and everybody knew I'd eaten the evidence. Boo was a cannibal by association at least. Would you want to eat in his restaurant?

I flicked my cigarette away and folded my arms. I had to do something to keep from touching her baby bird features. 'Can I get yuh anything?'

She smiled. 'I have everything I need and anyway, you can barely stand, never mind run errands.'

'Whatever you want, I'll get it for yuh. Just say the word.'

'Cookie, stop it.'

'Stop what?'

'This. It isn't right.'

I lit up another Consulate.

'Don't be offended,' she said.

'I'm fucken not, alright?'

'You know, sometimes you look like you could chew off your own leg.'

'That supposed to be funny?'

'Just an observation. So anyway, how's Josie doing?'

'D'y'think radiant is just a nice way of sayin' her baps are humungus?' I laughed and sobbed at the same time. Josie Baps was pregnant.

'You know what?' Jay said. 'When I get out of here, I'm going to make you chump.'

'Champ!' I wailed, giving in to the tears. 'It's fucken called champ!'

She creased over with laughter and I fought to control myself.

'That's him!' a skinny old man barked from the door, spraying the path with hard green phlegm as he plunged into a coughing fit.

'Right,' the nurse said, standing in front of me, arms folded. She had tight, hard lips and her bulk strained to escape her uniform.

'I didn't do nothin'!'

'How can somebody who knows so many big words have such bad grammar?' Boo drifted silently into the doorway.

'He knocked my dube-dubes!' The old man pointed and choked.

I heaved myself onto my crutches and hobbled shaky-slow for the door.

'Cookie!' the nurse shouted. 'What about this man's dube-dubes?'

I stopped in front of the old man. 'Ask the doctor for a lick of his dangleberries.'

He looked at the nurse. 'Can I do that?' He twisted in another cough.

The nurse scuttled after me. 'Cookie, you know you shouldn't be out of your room. Besides that, I'm getting far too many complaints.'

'Just a second,' Boo spoke to the nurse. 'Jay's coming home soon. Maybe Cookie could be nursed at my house? Would that be possible?'

'Fucken sure I'm not goin' to your house.'

'No, it's fine, Mr Boo,' the nurse said. 'We're moving him to the psychiatric ward.'

'Well, cheeri-fucken-o then. I'm away.'

'Where are you going?' Boo asked me.

I drew in a breath but I'd temporarily run out of ammo.

'Stay at my house.' He shrugged as if it was obvious. 'I'll bring you some outdoor clothes and you can stay with me.'

'Outdoor? Out-fucken-door?' I got my second wind. 'Where did you learn English? Millets?'

I put my hand in the pocket of my joggie bottoms and tossed a shower of wine gums over my shoulder as I went back inside, relishing Jay's laughter.

I took a raincoat from the old man's locker, raided another locker for money and phoned for a taxi before he could bring me some out-fucken-door clothes.

'Oh my God, it's Greyfucker's Bobby,' Prince said.

I knew he was standing behind me, even before he spoke. I know his vibes. He rattles like a nervous marionette.

'I've got somethin' for yuh,' I said, without looking round. I sat on the soggy gravel path beside Bonehead's grave, holding my Stiff Little Fingers badge tight in my pocket.

The grave still didn't have a headstone. Most of the flowers had wilted but some were so new they deflected the rain like plastic, including a heart-shaped wreath from somebody called Claire xxxxxxooooooooxxxxxxx Forever. The grave was on a slope in Carnmoney Cemetery and it pissed me off that he appeared to be lying at rest at 35 degrees.

'Somethin' for me?'

I drew in a crutch and he gripped my arm to haul me up. His fine beard had disappeared into gingery stubble and his hair lay flat and unspiked on his forehead. The natural colour had burst through.

You've never seen anybody quite so ginger as my brother. And he loathed it. But it was so phenomenally orange, it took a lifetime to dye, and that didn't even include the time spent on his eyebrows, eyelashes or beard.

Oisín Fitzpatrick. Aka Prince of Orange. Aka Persistent Hogger of Bathroom Sinks.

'It was Billy Dick, wasn't it?' I said.

'Is that *tattooed* on your forehead?' he said. 'An anarchy sign? Tattooed? On your forehead? Are you fucken nuts?'

'Billy Dick's your da, isn't he? That was her stupid postcard, wasn't it?'

He looked down at Bonehead's grave. 'So what's this thing you've got for me?'

'Oh yeah. It's this.' I swung my fist at his sculpted face and we both went down. I cradled my hand, shrinking in pain and nausea, and he rolled around, both hands over his bloody nose.

'Fuck yuh, Cookie! You're *dead*! When you're better!'

'Fuck you, Prince! Fuck you!'

Eventually we sat up. The ground was freezing damp and I couldn't stop shaking.

'You fucked off on me,' I said.

'*You* were doin' my head in.'

'I can't believe you went an' stayed w'her.'

'How could I do that? I didn't even know where she

was.' He dabbed at his bloody nose and leaking eyes. 'I went to look for her.'

'Aye right.'

'An' I found her.'

'Well done. Your quest is complete. Now fuck off.'

'She was on sale in a window.' His pale green eyes were puffy and dark. I read somewhere that travel can be tiring. 'An' I brought her back.'

'What da fuck for?'

'Because she was on sale in a fucken window!' He looked at the blood on his hands. 'Don't suppose you'd have a bitta bog roll on yuh?'

I searched the old man's pockets and found a sharply ironed cotton hankie. His wrinkly old wife had ironed it. I gave it to Prince and he wiped at his face and hands.

'When Boo told her what was in the tins . . .'

'I couldn't give a rat's ass, Prince.'

'When Boo told her what was in the tins, Cookie, she freaked.'

'Yeah yeah, the PPA were goin' to do her in, wank wank wank wank wank.'

He tilted his head at me. 'It was nothin' to do with the PPA. It was what was in the tins. Who was in the tins. And how it . . . he . . . got there. And you eatin' it and what it meant. About her. About her and you. It had nothin' to do with them. She just freaked. She said her guts were on the outside of her skin.'

I could imagine it. Vomiting up my own liver. A huge hard fat jelly lump forcing itself up my throat, splatting out onto my chest. My intestines slung in a heap across my stomach. My muscles breaking open like anatomy drawings. Looking down at myself in horror. Seeing what I was made of. I knew exactly what she meant.

'She's still not OK,' he said.

'I'll tell her about my epiphany.'

'Fuck it, Cookie, don't, I swear to God, just don't.'

'It's OK, mate, seriously. She'll be alright.' I even smiled at him but he rubbed and rubbed at his eyebrows.

'How long were you away for?' I asked.

'Well, what month's this? Is this still January?'

'Dunno.'

'It was probably about ...' He looked up into the rain and tried to calculate. Not his strong point.

'Forget it, Prince, doesn't matter.'

He nodded past me to the cemetery gates. And I looked. Boo stood by the stone gatepost, arms folded, all ninja-ed up.

'He gave me a lift down,' Prince said. 'Says he'll givvus a lift back up.'

'Here, Prince, so am I goin' to be an uncle then?'

'I dunno, mucker. Maybe it's fucken yours.'

'Come on, who d'y'think I am? Superdick? I didn't even make it in.'

He pushed the side of my head and got to his feet. 'Come on. Y'comin' then?'

'In a minute.'

He walked away, his loose puppet feet trailing along the gravel path.

I stared at Bonehead's mound, then I moved closer and pushed my Stiff Little Fingers badge into the soil.